An Excerpt from

Her heart slammed a

the man who stepped through the front door. Dane Reese, the man her sister hoped would help around the café in her absence. Ariel could feel the heat enter her cheeks as her hands curled into fists at her sides. That bastard. Prick. Dom. If he thought he'd walk in and bark out orders, she'd soon disabuse him of the notion. No way she'd knuckle under to some stranger. Especially him. She clenched her teeth and pressed her lips tightly together to keep from saying something she would regret.

Soft summer sunlight shone through the windows and glinted off his sun-streaked blond hair. Despite its short length, she could see the way it curled around his ears and along his nape. His sapphire blue eyes took in the customers and two waitresses in the café, then shifted to rest on Ariel. Their bright color highlighted his darkly tanned skin. His high cheekbones; strong, clean-shaven chin; and sexy smile pushed him past movie-star handsome into thigh-quivering, panty-creaming hot.

Damn it.

As she watched him step toward her, she fought the urge to pick up Jake's half-eaten breakfast and dump it over the smug son of a bitch's head. *If I could reach it.* It only took a glance to notice the twelve- or fourteen-inch difference in their heights. She yanked the black bandanna from her hair and twisted it in her hands. Her knuckles went as white as the skulls and crossbones on the cloth square.

"Ariel Valerian?" He held out his hand. "I'm Dane Reese. Your sister—"

"Get out," she snapped before she stepped away from Jake's table and turned her back on the newcomer.

Loose Id®

ISBN 13: 978-1-60737-727-6
AN INVITATION: ARIEL'S PET
Copyright © July 2010 by Qwillia Rain
Originally released in e-book format in April 2010

Cover Art by April Martinez
Cover Layout by April Martinez

All rights reserved. Except for use of brief quotations in any review or critical article, the reproduction or utilization of this work in whole or in part in any form by any electronic, mechanical or other means, now known or hereafter invented, including xerography, photocopying and recording, or in any information storage or retrieval is forbidden without the prior written permission of Loose Id LLC, PO Box 425960, San Francisco CA 94142-5960. http://www.loose-id.com

DISCLAIMER: Many of the acts described in our BDSM/fetish titles can be dangerous. Please do not try any new sexual practice, whether it be fire, rope, or whip play, without the guidance of an experienced practitioner. Neither Loose Id nor its authors will be responsible for any loss, harm, injury or death resulting from use of the information contained in any of its titles.

This book is an original publication of Loose Id. Each individual story herein was previously published in e-book format only by Loose Id and is a work of fiction. Any similarity to actual persons, events or existing locations is entirely coincidental.

Printed in the U.S.A. by
Lightning Source, Inc.
1246 Heil Quaker Blvd
La Vergne TN 37086
www.lightningsource.com

AN INVITATION: ARIEL'S PET

Chapter One

Day 1

The brunch crowd inside the Valerian's Root café had thinned out for the morning, and only a few customers remained scattered among the booths and tables. Through the order window, Chef Ariel Valerian spotted DeeDee Rhodes chatting with a customer as she refilled the man's coffee cup. Back in the kitchen, Ariel piled a plate with scrambled eggs, bacon, and hash browns. She settled two wedges of golden brown toast on the edge and added a twisted slice of an orange as a garnish.

Plate in hand, she stepped through the double doors between the kitchen and dining area. She nodded at Sadie Lundquist, the café's other waitress, as the woman stood behind the register at the end of the front counter, ringing up a customer's check.

“Here you go, Jake.” She grinned down at the elderly man in dusty overalls—one of the café's regulars—and set the plate on the table in front of him.

His pale gray eyes widened. “Thanks, Ariel.” He scanned the café before he returned his attention to her. “Haven't seen your sister today. Where is Alayna?”

Ariel fought to keep the smile on her face. Jake hadn't been the first customer surprised to see Ariel outside of the kitchen or to mention her older sister. She was sure he wouldn't be the last when Alayna didn't appear in the café to wait tables, ring up sales, or do any of the myriad tasks she normally did. Every time someone asked about her, Ariel bit back the angry words and the temptation to glare at the empty table closest to the counter near the kitchen doors, where Masters Dane and Logan—proprietors of A Master's Gift—sat every day for lunch.

It was all *that* blond bastard's fault. Maybe both of those bastards. For the last six months the men had come in every weekday for lunch. Ariel might spend all her time in the kitchen, but she had seen the way her sister responded to the dark-haired guy, Master Logan. Then, just a few days earlier, the blond one—Master Dane—had left a card for her sister. An invitation to their facility that specialized in BDSM, kinky sex, and Dominant/submissive training, according to the research Ariel had done. Master Dane had tempted Alayna to go off to explore her submissive side. For a month. Thirty damned days. Ariel wondered if the two men would show up today now that they'd convinced Alayna to play at their little dungeon.

Jerks, buttheads, pricks. Why did they have to do this? Ariel was sure there was more to Alayna's invitation to A Master's Gift than her older sister claimed; Ariel hadn't figured it out yet, but she would. After Alayna told her she'd committed to thirty days of training at the facility with no outside contact, Ariel had done her homework on the men. In her mind, it didn't make sense for two well-established businessmen to look for submissives to train. The possibilities had kept her from sleep most of the night. Thoughts of the two men skulking around, ferreting out secrets about her and

Al's finances, plagued her. Or perhaps they wanted to use Al's sudden curiosity about bondage, leather, and whips to blackmail them into selling the café to an interested investor.

The more Ariel tried to reason it out, the more elaborate her imagination became each time it picked the whys and what fors. She just needed to figure out a way to get her sister to come home. Then everything could go back to the way it was supposed to be. Then things would get back to normal.

Her tone cheerful, she shrugged and replied to Jake's query. "Al decided to take a little vacation. She's worked so hard, she figured a few weeks at a bed-and-breakfast would help her relax."

It wasn't much of a lie, but Ariel didn't intend to tell anyone Al had gone off to learn what life as a sexual submissive was all about. Grimm Dawson, a longtime family friend who verged on overprotective, would freak if he knew the particulars of Alayna's time away. She doubted even the Douglases, a sweet septuagenarian couple who'd known her and her sister since they were children, would have understood Alayna's need to experience her inner wild child.

And I'm the idiot who encouraged her to go. Talked up BDSM, submission, and various elements of the lifestyle—not my smartest idea. I was even stupid enough to tease her with the possibility of shake-the-rafters sex with Master Logan. Like a Dom's attention is worth having. She shuddered at the thought of some man bossing her around. *Why didn't I keep my mouth shut? I should have—*

The front door swung open, and Ariel stopped midthought. Her heart slammed against her ribs when she recognized the man who stepped through the front door. Dane Reese, the man her sister hoped would help around the café in her absence. Ariel could feel the heat enter her cheeks as her hands curled into fists at her sides. *That bastard. Prick. Dom.* If he thought he'd walk in and bark out orders, she'd soon disabuse him of the notion. No way she'd knuckle under to some stranger. Especially him. She clenched her teeth and pressed her lips tightly together to keep from saying something she would regret.

Soft summer sunlight shone through the windows and glinted off his sun-streaked blond hair. Despite its short length, she could see the way it curled around his ears and along his nape. His sapphire blue eyes took in the customers and two waitresses in the café, then shifted to rest on Ariel. Their bright color highlighted his darkly tanned skin. His high cheekbones; strong, clean-shaven chin; and sexy smile pushed him past movie-star handsome into thigh-quivering, panty-creaming *hot.*

Damn it.

As she watched him step toward her, she fought the urge to pick up Jake's half-eaten breakfast and dump it over the smug son of a bitch's head. *If I could reach it.* It only took a glance to notice the twelve- or fourteen-inch difference in their heights. She yanked the black bandanna from her hair and twisted it in her hands. Her knuckles went as white as the skulls and crossbones on the cloth square.

"Ariel Valerian?" He held out his hand. "I'm Dane Reese. Your sister—"

"Get out," she snapped before she stepped away from Jake's table and turned her back on the newcomer.

DeeDee's mouth fell open, and her blues eyes went wide as Ariel stalked past her. Beyond DeeDee, Ariel saw Sadie blink in surprise at her reaction to Mr. Reese. Their stunned looks mirrored the expressions on the faces of several of the regular customers. Ariel winced at the attention her out-of-character behavior drew.

A firm hand landed on Ariel's upper arm, halting her in midstep. "I don't think you understand, Miss Valerian. Your sister, Alayna, asked me to come here—"

Ariel spun around and glared up at the man, then fought to ignore the interest his looks stirred deep inside her. "No, you listen to me, Mr. Reese. I know exactly who you are. You may have convinced my sister you're here to help, but you aren't welcome." She pulled her arm free of his loose grasp and pointed at the door, unconcerned with the shocked audience watching the exchange. "Now there's the door. Don't let it slap you in the butt as you leave."

She spun around and stomped into the kitchen. Her fingers shook as she retied the bandanna in place over her hair. Snickers, gasps, and rapidly whispered conversations followed her, but Ariel was still too pissed to pay attention to them. If that bastard thought he could casually stroll into her café after he had convinced her big sister to run off for a month of wild, wicked, freaky sex, she'd make sure to correct his assumptions. "He won't have another chance to—"

"Wrong, Miss Valerian. I'll have plenty of chances to talk to you about your sister's instructions and my presence here for the next month." Dane stood in front of the double doors, arms crossed over his broad chest, legs braced apart as he watched her.

Outrage burned in her chest as she spun around to face him. When he started to move farther into the room, she glared at him and held up her right hand. “Stop right there.” Her command halted him in his tracks. She stomped back toward him and didn't stop until she'd practically plowed into his chest. “This is my kitchen. You aren't allowed—”

“Your sister asked me to help while she's at—”

She reached up and clamped her hand over his mouth, stopping his words and dragging his gaze down so it clashed with hers. The spicy scent of cardamom and rosemary tickled her nose, but she ignored it.

“Don't you dare say it out loud, you bastard,” she hissed, her tone quiet so it couldn't be heard beyond the kitchen doors. The warm brush of his lips against her palm sent tingles through her breasts. *Traitors.* She snatched her hand back and rubbed it against the hem of her white chef's coat. “She's on *vacation.* I don't want anyone to know she went off to your little dungeon playground,” Ariel whispered and crossed her arms over her breasts.

He watched her for a moment, his face without expression. “I was under the impression you wanted your sister to explore her interest in Dominant/submissive relationships. That you were in favor of it.” He followed her lead and kept his tone soft so it didn't carry. Dane lowered his hands to the pockets of his trousers. He offered a tentative smile, probably an attempt to encourage her to fess up to her culpability in her sister's decision to leave.

“And what makes you think I'm not?”

“Your attitude.”

Ariel smirked. "Well, what do you know? You're smarter than your average blond beach bunny."

She passed the largest of the freestanding islands anchored on the sea of white tile in her kitchen. It held a stainless steel counter where she assembled and disassembled dishes and food items on one side and the grill on the other. She rounded it and headed for the long counter beneath the pick-up window where bins, bowls, and containers held the various garnishes and condiments she used. *No damn way I'll let him know how irritated I am with myself that I told Al to go for it.* She looked over her shoulder at him.

Only his narrowed gaze hinted at his possible irritation to her taunt. "If you didn't want her to go, why did you tell her it was okay?" His attention roved around the wide area as he came farther into the room. Like a thief casing a potential mark, he seemed to note the three entrances: double doors from the dining area, back door from the alley behind the building, and a third swinging door with a porthole-type window three-quarters of the way up that led into the hallway and faced the office Alayna used.

"I lied," Ariel admitted and then turned away from him. Through the order window she spotted the two waitresses and Jake as they hovered on the other side of the tiled counter, trying to peek into the kitchen. Her glare was meant to discourage them as she covered the garnishes, spreads, and condiments in the prep station.

"You lied?"

Ariel looked back at him. He sounded almost amused at her confession. That only irritated her more. *What the hell kinda reaction is that?*

“Yeah. Just what kind of sister would I be if I didn't encourage Alayna to explore the BDSM lifestyle if she was curious about it? It would be selfish of me to keep my sister from doing something she wanted simply because I don't agree with her choice of the place she's gone to.”

She wondered what he saw as he glanced around the kitchen. With a rack of pots, pans, and smaller cooking trays to the right of the double doors and another set of shelves to the right of the back door stacked with to-go containers and plastic trays and boxes for the desserts and pastries she sold, the kitchen might seem a bit disorganized. But she knew every inch of the place better than she knew her name.

He seemed to mull over her comment as he walked toward the smaller central island set a foot or so from the grill. “If you kept her from doing something you didn't approve of, at least you'd be honest.” He pulled a stool from beneath the island and sat down. “I'm sure Alayna would have wanted to know the truth. And perhaps you need to learn the truth about the Dominant/submissive lifestyle and BDSM instead of assuming you know what they're really about.”

“You don't know shit about me and my sister, Mr. Reese.” She stomped back toward him. “Don't presume to tell me how to deal with Al. We've gotten along fine without a home wrecker like you screwing with things. As for learning about your kinky sideline, I know all I want to know about it, thank you very much.”

“Home wrecker?” His eyebrows rose on his forehead, but his face remained devoid of expression. “Kinky sideline?”

"Exactly. What else would you call a person who intentionally introduces a separation that attempts to undermine the bond between family members?" Ariel cursed her attraction to the man. To her immense irritation, it sent a swirl of heat from her core to the flesh at the apex of her thighs. The heavy cotton chef's coat she wore at least hid the peaks of her breasts from discovery, but the gleam in his gaze hinted he might be aware of the sensation she fought.

"I get the impression you don't like me very much." The grin on his lips suggested he wasn't bothered by the prospect of her dislike. Or he felt his charm could change her mind.

With the way her body felt, it would be a hell of a battle to keep from betraying her interest. *Why now? Why him?*

But the questions weren't enough to distract her. There was more to his selection of Alayna to be a master's plaything than simply a means to help Al find her inner sub. There had to be some benefit he stood to gain. *And I'll figure it out, eventually, whether he wants me to or not.* Until she got to the truth, she intended to keep as much distance as possible between herself and him. First things first, she needed to get rid of him so Al would come back home where she belonged.

"You're not worth the time it takes to like or dislike someone. All I want is for you to leave and let me run my café without any help." Ariel propped her hands on her hips as she waited for his response.

Dane shook his head. "Sorry, but that isn't what will happen."

She hoped he could see the irritation flare in her eyes. The heat stole into her cheeks and the way she pressed her lips thin should have been clear evidence of her irritation with the man. When she drew a deep breath and then exhaled in a slow, frustrated sigh, his lips quirked at the corners. Like he wanted to grin. *Bastard.*

"How much?" she asked.

"How much what?" The sudden bland disinterest on his face and narrowed eyes were a strong indication her words had hit their mark.

If the man wouldn't leave because she asked him, maybe money would do the trick. After all, he and his buddy, Logan Abram, could be two-bit hustlers trading on her sister's sexual curiosity. Maybe it was the café they were after. No way would she let Dane Reese anywhere near the restaurant's books. Let him think she was pissed about his interference in the running of the cafe; she knew there was more to the situation than he was telling. If all they wanted was to make a buck, perhaps she could cut to the chase.

Determined he understood her offer, Ariel said, "What'll it take to get you to go away? How much money do you want?"

"Nothing, Ariel," he assured her, his voice cool. "I promised your sister I would help out with the paperwork while she was away, and that's what I intend to do."

She stepped close and smiled up at him. "The day I let you touch the books here, surfer boy, is the day I'll get in line with all your other brainless bimbos waiting to be told what to think, tied up, and fucked by a narcissistic control freak."

The smile he returned held as much determination as she'd put into hers. "I keep my promises, Ariel. For the record, hon, if your promise included you tied down to one of the tables out front, I might be inclined to let you cut to the head of the line."

Dane could feel Ariel's stare as she stood, mouth agape, and watched him exit the kitchen. Out in the dining room, the customers had their heads bent together; their whispers buzzed through the café as he walked past them and headed down the hallway to the office. It seemed dealing with Ariel would be an exercise in the old adage about never letting people see you sweat. If he was going to help run the café for the next month, it was important that the two waitresses and as many of the customers as possible witnessed his resistance to Ariel's attempts at intimidation.

Once through the door, he crossed to the desk. A pile of papers was neatly stacked on one corner of the battered desk, right where Alayna had assured him they would be when he'd spoken to her after her arrival at the mansion earlier that morning.

She'd warned him Ariel would be upset about the changes when they discussed how he'd help out at the café, but she hadn't warned him her sister would be such a brat about things. The natural inclination to coax Ariel to heel tugged at his control. He'd have to resist picturing her as a willful submissive in need a firm hand to train her in the ways to meet her master's requests. The temptation to revert to his dominant tendencies would be hard to fight, but to keep the peace, he'd definitely make an effort.

He reached for the stack of papers.

"Keep your hands off those." Ariel was poised in the doorway. Her bright green eyes glared at him. The black bandanna she'd worn was gripped in one hand, exposing the vibrant blue hair that covered her head in a silky cap, matched the dyed eyebrows, and emphasized her soft ivory skin.

There was no doubt Ariel was sexy. Dane appreciated the full curves of a pretty woman; what man wouldn't? Short, yes, but full figured and comfortable in her skin. He could read the satisfaction she took in her appearance in the way she stood, how she walked, even the way she plunged ahead when she confronted him. He cursed the buzz of attraction thrumming through his body. Now was not the time to get turned on by all the features Ariel possessed. Not when those elements fused with the acid tongue and nasty disposition of a termagant. He'd be smart to keep his distance.

Hands braced on the desk, he leaned forward and watched her step into the room. The look on her face and the glare in her eyes warned him she wasn't about to give up. *She's not your sub. Let her vent. She'll get over it soon enough.* “Ariel, let's not argue over this, okay?”

“Oh, there's no argument, Mr. Reese.” Ariel stepped forward and swept up the papers. “I'll take care of the paperwork. I'll take care of the kitchen. And you can toddle on back to your big old mansion down the road. Play master to all the little girls who've paid for the opportunity to be trained by you and your pal Logan Abram.”

Dane drew a deep breath and counted to ten in his head. *There's a reason I volunteered for this. Keep it in mind. Logan needs to face his fears. Alayna wants a man strong enough to command her. They must have time together to figure out they're meant for one another. It's only thirty days. I can handle this kid for thirty days.*

He waited a few more moments before responding. "You doing the books isn't what your sister expected. She and I discussed how to take care of the café while she's away this month. She was very clear that you were better suited to work in the kitchen while I handle the financial aspects of the business."

"Well, Alayna isn't here to cast a vote. You and your business partner made sure of that. So that leaves me in charge, and I vote you leave."

"Not a democracy here, kid."

"I haven't been a kid in ten years, Mr. Reese. And this isn't a democracy. It's a dictatorship. And I'm the head bitch in charge." She stepped close, dropped the papers on the desk, braced her hands inside his, and leaned in. "Now get the fuck out of my café."

There was no doubt she meant every word she said. Dane could see the determination in her eyes, the set of her mouth, even the way she squared her shoulders as she faced him. He reached for the papers on the desktop between them.

Her hand slapped down on top of them to halt him.

Not about to let the situation devolve into a tug-of-war over a bunch of papers, Dane waited. Silent.

"Will you ever figure out I mean what I say?" Ariel asked, her tone waspish, her mouth tight as she held his gaze.

"I'm aware you mean what you're saying. Now."

"Then leave. Go back to your office and make some businessman more money than he ought to have."

"And let you think you've won?" Dane shook his head. "No, Ariel, I think I'll stick around a bit. See how things are run around here." He leaned closer. His voice dropped to a whisper. "Get a feel for the place." He sauntered around the desk and toward the door. "You never know."

"Never know what?" Ariel demanded, her hand still planted on the papers as she turned to watch him.

Dane grinned over his shoulder at her. "Maybe *if* Alayna returns, you'll decide to take some lessons. Then you can see the real difference between kinky game play and a true power exchange."

* * *

Sunset filtered through the curtained windows of the home Ariel shared with her sister, while Ariel sprawled on the sofa and ignored the baseball game on the television. Dane had refused to leave the café until after they'd closed the doors behind the last customer. Through cleanup and counting down the till, he'd stuck around and simply watched her. He'd even hovered at the end of the block and kept an eye on her as she walked home, until she'd shut the front door. A voice niggled in her head. It warned her he was a man of his word, and she'd soon come to regret that.

Things needed to get back to normal. Alayna needed to be home. If she would just come home, things would be okay. Getting rid of *him* meant her sister would come back.

"If it weren't for him, Alayna wouldn't have run off and abandoned the shop. Oh she was good with the song and dance about being curious, but I'm not blind. She's hot for that Logan guy," Ariel muttered as she keyed the A Master's Gift Web site into her laptop. The computer rested on her thighs as she stretched her legs out across the cushions. "I may stay in the kitchen most of the time, but I can see through the pick-up window how much attention she gives Dane's long-haired buddy.

"An invitation, my ass," she grumbled. Dane was the one who had left the invitation. The crumpled business card lay discarded on the coffee table where she'd tossed it after she keyed in the user name and password scrawled on the back for her sister's use.

She ignored the welcome prompt and immediately went to the photo-gallery page. Ariel grimaced at the memories of how she'd egged Alayna on to make the call. "Shoulda kept my mouth shut."

Should have denied her personal interest in BDSM, no matter how hard. Especially after she and Alayna clicked through the various pages on the Web site. Images of lovers, male and female, bound or in submissive poses still sent tingles through her body.

As she clicked through the images, her mind substituted herself in place of the women who knelt before their masters. Ariel squirmed on the cushion, cognizant of the increase in her heartbeat and the way her breath sped up with each new image she viewed. After scanning down through another section, she halted on a series of photos that depicted a woman as she received punishment. One picture showed the woman as a man's bare hand spanked her naked bottom. Another showed him wielding a red leather paddle. A third offered a view of the black leather thongs of a flogger as they reddened the woman's bum.

In each shot, an expression of exultation, of sexual bliss, suffused the woman's face. What made Ariel's blood rush through her veins was the man who handled the tools. There was no mistaking who he was. The golden, sun-streaked curls that dusted the man's nape easily identified him. His broad shoulders were bare and damp with sweat. Each muscle was clearly defined, visible beneath his tanned flesh, and glistening from his exertions.

Heat pooled in her center as she stroked a finger over the laptop's screen, followed the way his wide back tapered down to narrow hips and a tight ass hugged by black leather pants.

With a curse, Ariel slammed the computer closed. "No. Uh-uh, not going there." She drew a deep breath, then a second. For ten years she and her sister had managed Valerian's Root. No way would she let her libido aid an outsider who wanted to push his way into the only home she had left.

"We ran it after Mom and Dad died. We'll keep running it," she whispered to the empty room. "It's all I've got left."

Pain seared her belly, her chest tightened, and she relived the moment ten years earlier when two police officers broke the news about their parents' deaths to her and Alayna. Knowing Alayna wasn't in the house, Ariel felt a heightened the sense of isolation and aloneness—cut adrift from the familiar—wash through her.

Ariel left the laptop on the coffee table, rolled off the sofa, and headed into the kitchen to mix up something for dinner. For herself. Alone. A chill skated up her spine, despite the warmth that lingered from the early-summer evening. Her hands rose and rubbed at the chills that rose along her upper arms.

If she wanted to get the man out of her life—out of both their lives—Ariel was sure she'd be required to resort to a bit more than bluntly telling him to leave the café. It clearly hadn't worked today. He wanted the books, so they were the key.

If I don't let him look at the books, eventually he'll get frustrated enough to go.

"So how do I keep him from the paperwork? Al does it all online. I can't throw away the computer." Ariel paused in the doorway of the kitchen and looked back at the laptop on the sofa. A smile spread over her lips. "Or maybe I can."

* * *

Day 2

Dane was surprised Ariel didn't stop him at the front door the next day. It could be because he'd waited until after the lunch rush started to wind down before he entered the café. Through the pick-up window, he could see her watching him. The grin on her lips gave him pause as he strode down the hallway to the office.

"Round two," Dane muttered.

He didn't doubt she was up to something. Apparently it was too much to ask that she would have taken the time last night to resign herself to his presence this month.

In the office he shrugged out of his suit coat and tossed it over the back of the battered desk chair. One look at the computer and he knew what had prompted the damned grin on Ariel's lips. He rolled back his pale blue silk shirt cuffs and grimaced at the computer in front of him.

“Problem, surfer boy?” Ariel leaned against the office door with her arms crossed over her breasts, a smug grin still on her lips.

“Where are they, Ariel?”

Her bright green eyes opened wide in an attempt to appear guileless. The haughty grin and aura of self-satisfaction spoiled the illusion. “I'm only a cook, remember? I don't know anything about the business. That's why my sister asked you to take care of things, isn't it?”

“Having a bachelor's degree in restaurant management doesn't mean you're just a cook,” Dane pointed out.

Ariel obviously tried to hide her surprise at his knowledge of her degree, but he could see it in her slightly widened eyes. She brushed her hands together as if she dusted off dirt, then turned and walked away. Soft laughter spilled from her lips. Dane cursed and shook his head.

He looked back at the computer where it sat on the corner of the desk. It was a useless paperweight without the power cables, mouse, or keyboard. If he took the time to go to his office to retrieve the necessary components to get the machine running, the last of the lunch customers would be gone. Dane didn't doubt Ariel would lock the doors against him. This early in the game, he wasn't about to divulge the fact that Alayna had given him her key to the café as well as the alarm code. Ariel was sure to react badly if she knew how much her sister trusted him. And a woman with access to very sharp knives and the knowledge of how to use them was not someone a smart man pissed off.

"Day two and she's still a brat," he muttered. He dragged his suit coat from the back of the desk chair and dug his cell phone from the pocket. "Logan better fucking appreciate all I'll have to put up with for him." Dane punched a number in speed dial and waited.

"A and R Consulting, how may I help you?" The tone was crisp, professional. Dane hadn't expected anything less from Logan's assistant. "Jordan, it's Dane. Lock up the office and go down to Randolph's to pick up a few items, then deliver them to me at Valerian's Root."

He ran down the items he wanted and waited for Jordan to confirm before he hung up and returned his phone to the jacket pocket. Dane didn't bother with the desk chair. He considered it more prudent that he be in the dining area of the café to make sure Jordan made it past the blue-haired guard dog. He did tug open the top drawer of the desk to find the sheaf of papers Ariel had snatched away from him the day before. "At least I'll have some work to do while I wait."

Only a few customers filled the seats in the café. A quick glance at his watch confirmed there were still nearly forty-five minutes until the café closed. At the counter, Dane smiled at the petite blonde behind the register. "DeeDee, can I get a cup of coffee, please?"

A blush filled the girl's cheeks as she smiled back. "Sure."

Through the pick-up window over her shoulder, he saw Ariel's head come up and her eyes narrow as she glared at him. Ignoring her, he crossed the dining area and settled into the empty booth nearest the door. He slid onto the vinyl seat and made sure he faced the kitchen so he could keep Ariel in sight.

He could practically hear the curses in her head as her gaze dropped to the pile of invoices and bills he set on the table in front of him. Dane made sure to smile at her as he put on his reading glasses.

A loud *pop* drew her gaze down to an object in front of her. *Probably wishes she'd taken these files away when she disabled the computer. So much fire in her. And yet she's so intent on locking herself away from the world.*

Logan and Dane hadn't made their money by accident. Strategies to identify the right tools to use to measure the strengths and weaknesses of the investors they assisted also worked well to discover what made the Valerian women tick. Dane had done his homework on both sisters long before he had left the invitation for Alayna.

It was no surprise both of them had pulled together to deal with their parents' deaths in a car accident a decade ago. Or that they continued to share the same house, spent six days of the week—sometimes seven—at the café, and shunned a social life beyond a handful of nights at various clubs on Ariel's part. They were stagnant, unable to see themselves as anything but anchors for each other. Unable to trust anyone outside their chosen circle. Until Alayna had made her phone call.

When DeeDee wiggled onto the seat opposite him, his attention was drawn from his thoughts to her. Her blonde hair was pulled up into a sassy ponytail, and the open buttons on her white blouse displayed an ample amount of cleavage. When she leaned forward to place a cup of coffee in front of him, Dane knew the view of a lacy bra and peaked nipples was intentional. He pulled off his glasses and tucked them into his shirt pocket.

"Ariel mentioned Alayna would be gone for a month, but she never mentioned someone might come in to help with the paperwork," DeeDee said.

"I'm sure she didn't. She seems like a very independent lady."

DeeDee giggled and nodded. "She is. She really doesn't like to have other people trying to run the show." Leaning forward, DeeDee set her hand over his wrist. "I've worked for Alayna and Ariel for six years, and I've never seen either one of them take a vacation."

Over her head, Dane saw Ariel glaring from the kitchen. Her gaze seemed focused on DeeDee more than him, but he was careful to keep his smile hidden.

The bubbly twenty-two-year-old waitress played with her hair and grinned at him. "So will you be here all day while Alayna's gone?" She shifted and propped her arms on the table. The new position plumped her breasts and strained the hold of the buttons on her blouse.

There was more than mere flirtation in her eyes. Dane had seen the same look in the faces of people curious about the Dominant/submissive lifestyle. Women and men who'd played sexy games with their partners. And her comfort in displaying her assets to him belied the innocent-girl-next-door look of sweetness associated with her pretty face and blonde hair. He didn't doubt she would accept an invitation to A Master's Gift were one issued.

A quick glance at the pick-up window made him work to subdue a chuckle. Dane could practically read the displeasure on Ariel's face. No doubt she wanted to label her employee a traitor to the cause.

"DeeDee!" Ariel called, interrupting their conversation. "Get the condoms—*condiments*!"

He saw Ariel's green eyes go wide and her face flush at her verbal gaffe. A choked cough from DeeDee and the crash as something hit the tiled kitchen floor mixed with the soft laughter from the few customers in the dining area confirmed he wasn't mistaken about what he'd heard. Ariel spun away from the window and disappeared from sight.

Dane dropped his gaze to DeeDee's pink cheeks.

"I guess I better get back to work." She giggled and slid out of the booth.

He watched her saunter back to the counter, the sway of her hips more than suggestive, but Dane's mind wasn't focused on her. It was focused on watching Ariel pace between the prep station and the large coolers next to the deep sinks. Her head stayed bent, her eyes down.

The urge to direct her to lift her head and look at him whispered through his mind. *Look at me. Show me what you really want. Show me how much you would do to get what you want. Let me see it. Let me see you.* He shook off the compulsion to command her.

She's not my sub, he reminded himself.

* * *

Day 3

Arguments don't work. The cold shoulder doesn't work. And hiding the damned computer cables doesn't work. Ariel refused to think about the humiliation of her foot-in-mouth error the day before. She'd avoided Dane and kept her mouth shut for the rest of the day, until she'd set the alarm and locked the door. The fact he'd practically walked her to her front door shouldn't have made her feel guilty.

"Day three, and three better be the charm," Ariel whispered as she turned the key in the file-cabinet lock. She'd decided to wait until the end of the breakfast rush before she implemented her plan. "Once he's gone, Al will come back." The satisfactory *thunk* as the mechanism slid into place brought a smile to her lips. "Okay, that takes care of the desk, the file cabinets, and the bathroom." The keys to each item jingled on the ring as she attached it to a lanyard and draped it around her neck. She dropped it beneath her chef's coat and shivered at the chill of the metal against her breasts. "If this doesn't give him the message he's not wanted, nothing will."

"Oh, I've gotten the message, Ariel. I've simply ignored it." Dane leaned in the doorway and watched her, his hands tucked into the pockets of his faded jeans. His gaze drifted over her and lingered on her breasts before it progressed past her to the desk. "I see you continue to hold the computer hostage."

She shrugged and stepped toward him. "You're here awful early." A worn and faded canvas messenger bag rested at his feet. *That must be where he put the keyboard, mouse, and cables he got from the kid yesterday.* An image of a flogger and paddle tucked away in the canvas tote flashed unbidden through her mind. Heat stole into her cheeks, and her heartbeat increased.

"I have some orders to confirm, receipts to input, and payroll to prepare. Per your sister's request." He lifted the bag and walked into the room; his arm brushed hers as he passed.

Her gaze dropped to the inked design visible on the inside of his right wrist. She hadn't pegged him as the type to ink his skin, but the design piqued her curiosity. *Not that I'll be asking what that Japanese-like character means anytime soon.* "I can handle all of that once the café is closed this afternoon."

Before he could respond, Sadie's voice called down the hall, "Ari, we got orders!"

"Go play with your pots and pans, kid. While I get some work done." The flicking motion he made with his left hand exposed a second tattoo, another symbol—different from the first—etched into the inside of that wrist.

She fumed at the arrogant tone of his dismissal but didn't wait around. The café came first. She'd deal with the wannabe Dom and her overactive imagination once the breakfast rush slowed. Her curiosity about the meanings of the body art he wore would have to go unsatisfied. *They probably represent "obey" and "submit."*

A smile crept over her lips as she visualized his expression when he tried to open the desk drawers. Or the ones in the file cabinets. By the time she reached the kitchen, she couldn't keep from laughing softly at how irritated Dane was bound to become once he realized she'd outsmarted him. Again.

Dane wondered if the state of denial Logan had bricked himself up in was similar to the situation with Ariel and Alayna. All three of them had cut themselves off from their desires and their connections to the world around them. In Logan's case, he'd dammed up the dominant that resided within, and refused to admit that the past wasn't his fault. For Alayna—and to a lesser extent, for Ariel—she'd shut off the passion inside herself and ignored the sexual creature within that begged for release. With Alayna as the bait, Dane intended to draw his business partner back to the life Logan had denied himself for the last five years. There were dangers to his plan, but the rewards far outweighed them. Rewards for Logan, Alayna—perhaps even Ariel.

If the stubborn trio would only let nature take its course.

Dane plugged the computer into the new surge protector and switched it on. He set glasses he wore for reading and computer work on the desk beside the keyboard. The hum of the hard drive as it booted up was drowned beneath the rumbled conversation and occasional bursts of laughter from the café. He'd noticed the crowd of customers had thinned when he arrived at nine that morning, but he wasn't here to worry about how fast the tables received their meals.

"Let her take care of the kitchen; I'll take care of the bills." He reached for the drawer of the desk where he'd tucked the invoices the night before, and tugged.

It didn't budge. He pulled again. Still nothing. "This is not—" Dane didn't bother to finish the thought. He controlled his frustration, reached for the next drawer, and tugged. No movement. And the same result with the next. And the next. Once he'd gone through the desk, he stepped to the file cabinets. With the same result.

"Locked." He pulled the ring Alayna had given him from his pocket, but the two brass keys that dangled from it were too big to fit the desk or file cabinets. It appeared Ariel could stay one step ahead of him. Anticipate his actions. Counter any advance he made. Part of him tipped his hat to Ariel's ingenuity. Too bad the part of him used to being in charge was simply pissed.

"Damn it." The ridges gouged the palm of his hand before he shoved the keys back into his jeans. "Twenty-seven more days of this shit." He stalked down the hallway.

In a submissive, behaviors such as hers were considered an asset. The Dom in him tugged at the restraints he'd put in place when he made his promise to Alayna. Ariel's actions made his hands itch to take a paddle to her heart-shaped ass. Show her who was master and who was slave. Perhaps now was the time to remind the woman who really was in charge.

Dane didn't bother to knock and give the brat any warning. Instead he shoved through the door into the kitchen that faced the office. "Where are they, Ariel?" he demanded.

He ducked to avoid the tray of hot cinnamon rolls Ariel pulled from the oven.

"Get outta the way, bunny boy."

The rack to his left vibrated as she shoved the hot tray into place and then lifted another baking sheet from the next shelf up. The uncooked pastries replaced the cooked ones in the oven. Ariel slammed the door closed, tossed the towel she'd covered her hands with over her shoulder, and headed for the grill.

"Where are the keys, kid?"

"I don't have time for this." Ariel didn't look at him. The spatula in her right hand flashed across the grill, flipped hash browns, and then stirred eggs before she scooped pancakes up and slid them onto the plate she held in her left hand.

At the prep station, she ladled strawberry compote on top of the pancakes, then covered them with a swirl of whipped cream from a can. The silver bell on the order window chimed under the slap of her fingers. "Order up, Sadie."

She didn't wait to see if Sadie collected the dish. Back in front of the grill, she scooped the eggs and hash browns onto another plate as toast popped up in the toaster near the prep station. She buttered the bread, stacked it, sliced it into neat triangles, and placed them on the edge of the plate. Finally she tucked two orange wedges between the triangles of toast and the hash browns.

The bell went off again. "Last order, DeeDee."

The efficiency of her movements impressed Dane, but not enough to lessen his irritation. “The keys.” He held his hand out to her.

Ariel glanced from his hand to his face. The expression on her face didn't change, but the glint of amusement in her eyes should have warned him. She tugged the towel from her shoulder, dropped it into his hand, and motioned to the chrome sink beside the huge dishwasher against the back wall of the kitchen. “If you really want to help, Dane, go take care of the dishes while DeeDee and Sadie bus the tables.”

One, two, three… Dane counted in an attempt to overcome the temptation to shake her. “That isn't—”

“We're short-handed since you talked my sister into running off to your little dungeon playground.” Ariel waved at the kitchen. “Since it's important I be in here, and necessity requires Sadie and DeeDee be on the tables, that leaves you to clean up.”

He tossed the towel onto the central island. “No, Ariel, that leaves me to take care of the invoices and payroll like Alayna asked me. Now give me the keys.”

She didn't even pretend to be intimidated by his tone. “I told you I'd take care of the paperwork—”

“The. Keys.” A bit of his frustration and annoyance slipped into his voice.

Something in his expression must have warned her he wasn't about to let this little prank of hers slide. She backed away from him and hurried out the double doors into the dining area.

Well, she's smarter than I thought. He blew out an exasperated breath and followed her.

"Running won't help you, kid," he warned. That drew the attention of the few customers who remained from the breakfast rush to Ariel's presence behind the front counter.

If she wants a damned audience, let her have it. One way or another this will be settled today. He was only a few steps behind her as she grabbed a gray plastic tub and carried it to one of the tables waiting to be cleared.

"I'm not running."

"Looks like you are to me." Dane followed her into the center of the dining area. "I thought busing the tables was DeeDee and Sadie's jobs."

He and Ariel ignored the amused and watchful attention of the customers.

"There's work that must get done. If I stand around, it won't get finished." Ariel set the dirty dishes in the tub. When she picked it up, she started to turn toward the front counter but halted when she noticed him poised to intercept her. She spun to her left and hurried toward another dirty table.

"Give them to me." His voice was firm, inflexible.

Her back went stiff, her head came up, and she spun around so fast, Dane ran into the plastic tub.

"You want 'em?"

"Yes."

She slammed the tub into his solar plexus. His breath whooshed out, but so quietly he doubted anyone other than Ariel heard him.

Her eyes narrowed as she watched him regain his breath. "They're all yours. Make sure you rinse them off before you put them in the dishwasher," Ariel told him as she sidled to the opposite side of the table.

Dane set the tub down on the table. He was sure his face reflected his irritation and intention to get what he wanted. When her eyes went wide and the color in her cheeks faded, he knew she would ignore the instincts telling her to run. Instead she would stand her ground and continue to defy him. Even if it meant she put barriers between them. Not that he would allow a table to keep him from his goal. "The keys, Ariel." Again he held out his hand.

Ariel ignored it. "No." She crossed her arms over her chest and glared back at him. Her voice wavered slightly. Another sign she might actually possess a bit of common sense, but her damned bravado wouldn't let Ariel admit defeat. Not yet.

"Your sister warned me that you could be difficult, but she didn't tell me you tended to behave like a two-year-old in a tantrum," Dane reasoned, his voice quiet, calm. Two steps brought him around the table and closer to her. "I made a promise to your sister to take care of the office responsibilities while she's train—"

Ariel's eyes narrowed, and her mouth went tight.

He modified, "On vacation. While she's on vacation." A softness entered her features and signaled her relief at his altered phrasing. Leaning close, he added in a firmer tone, "Nothing you do will stop me. So you have to decide if you intend to cooperate and act like an adult, or fight me."

Ariel rolled her eyes. A smug grin lifted one side of her mouth, an eyebrow cocked higher on her forehead, and the arrogant look in her eyes reflected her choice long before she opened her mouth. "What if I go with *fight*?"

"Then you'll have to deal with the consequences." *Oh the lessons I could teach her. Maybe I should show her how a Dom corrects his sub.* His hands rested on his hips. While he awaited her decision, Dane was careful to keep his expression bland and unresponsive.

"And those consequences would be?"

Was that a flash of curiosity—perhaps even excitement—he spotted in her eyes? "Depends on if you want them to be public or private." Dane could see a hint of unease seep into her bright green gaze. It overshadowed the arousal. The eyebrow lowered back into place, and her lips smoothed into a straight line. Her face looked pale beneath the skull-patterned black bandanna that covered her hair.

Dane didn't bother to look around at the few customers who witnessed the confrontation. Over Ariel's head he could see the waitresses watching them. Neither DeeDee nor Sadie shifted from the tables they stood beside, their faces a mixture of amusement and uncertainty. "Which will it be, Ariel?"

Her expression gave more away than she knew, Dane thought. He sensed she'd fight him, and the challenge intrigued the dominant part of him. But he could also detect a hint of dread. He wasn't sure, however, if it was worry connected to her not knowing what he'd do, or actual fear of him. It made him wonder if a lover in her past had used his fists on her. The blast of fury he felt at the thought surprised him, but he quickly contained it.

She swallowed, stood up straight, and looked him directly in the eye. “Fight.”

“Public or private?” He took a step closer. Her fear was still there, but she controlled it. And the fire of arousal appeared to rekindle in Ariel's eyes. The master within him almost purred with satisfaction.

Ariel didn't flinch or hesitate. “Private.”

Dane nodded. “Private, it is.” He reacted quickly. Reaching forward, he bent enough to set his shoulder in her stomach and flip her over it. She stayed stunned for less than two seconds.

Her fists pounded against his back, and her legs tried to kick, but the arm he wrapped around them hampered any heavy blows. Dane ignored the gasps and stunned looks from the people around them, turned, and headed down the hallway to the office. If she wanted to act like a brat, he'd treat her like one.

Chapter Two

"Put me down, you bastard," Ariel demanded. Her breath impeded by the jostle of her stomach over his muscular shoulder, she wriggled to get free. She could have been a child based on the way he disregarded the blows from her fists.

A firm swat landed on her bottom. "Private, remember, kid?"

When she tried to wiggle a second time, Dane bounced her, pressing the breath from her lungs. The most difficult aspect of her position was listening to the snickers and giggles from the dining room and being unable to turn around and quell them with a look. Then there was the added issue of the scent of spices that filled her head every time her cheek bounced off the muscles of his back. She'd thought the cardamom and rosemary had merely been stray smells from her kitchen, but the tangy scents clung to Dane's clothes.

By the time Dane shoved the office door closed, Ariel had passed irritated and entered into a determined smolder. Any fear she'd had when he confronted her in the café was gone, washed away by the irritation and anger his treatment of her spawned. She refused to acknowledge the hum of sexual interest that buzzed along her nerve endings. Tension vibrated through her. She clenched her teeth to quell the urge to sink them into the contoured muscles beneath his T-shirt, afraid once she latched on, she wouldn't let go until she tasted blood.

He must have sensed her rage, because Dane didn't ease her off his shoulder and onto her feet. No, the prick dropped her. Dropped her!

She stumbled backward, thrown off balance by his manhandling, and landed on her ass. She glared up at him as he watched her. Ariel scrambled to her feet and charged forward. “Get out!” Her hands hammered his chest and bounced off. He caught them in a firm grip.

“You said private. I gave you private.”

She tugged and twisted, trying to break free of his hold, but he wouldn't release her. A head butt was out of the question because of the differences in their heights. When she thrust her knee at his groin, Dane deflected it with his leg seconds before he yanked her forward. Impacting his chest, Ariel struggled to keep her feet even as he pulled her arms behind her and lifted her onto her tiptoes.

“You chose to fight rather than cooperate.” His calm tone was gone, replaced by a firmer, authoritative timbre. Ariel cursed her body's reaction to him. His touch, the press of his chest against her breasts, even the vibration of his voice, stimulated her nipples. Her panties grew wet as her body reacted to the way he controlled her, how he held her pinned to him, her hands captured behind her back. That betrayal pissed her off even more. *Focus, damn it. He's the enemy. I want him to get out of here, not crawl into my bed!*

Teeth bared, she warned him, "Let me go, you son of a bitch, or I'll scream this place down."

Adjusting his hold, Dane kept her hands restrained and freed one of his own. He wrapped it around her throat. His fingers slid over the taut muscles as he stroked down toward the collar of her chef's coat. "No, you won't. This is between you and me now. You don't want to involve anyone else."

Her heart tripled its beats when his touch left her neck and began to ease open the buttons on her jacket. She squirmed and twisted, but a second button slipped free, then a third and a fourth. "So what? Do you molest me now to teach me a lesson? Is that how all your little slaves like to play? Well, not me, damn it. Get your hands off."

His fingers dipped beneath the heavy cotton garment. Ariel flinched from the heat of his touch, disturbed by the shiver of excitement that zinged through her belly. Her nipples hardened and pressed against the sports bra and tank top she wore beneath the jacket. One last attempt to free herself sent Ariel staggering backward, released from his hold.

The lanyard she'd slipped over her head earlier dangled from his fingertips. The arrogant grin lifted his lips. "You can go back to work now."

Ariel didn't suppress the urge to charge. There was no damned way she'd allow him to keep the prize. "Give me those."

"No." He flipped the brass keys into his palm.

She reached and missed as he held the lanyard out of range. Remembering a self-defense maneuver she'd learned from an ex, Ariel tucked a leg between his, hooked it behind his calf, and shoved at his chest.

Off balance, Dane bumped up against the arm of the sofa and fell onto the cushions. He snagged one of her wrists and pulled her with him.

The tussle was brief.

Hands scrabbled for purchase; hips rubbed against hips while they each fought for control of the keys; bodies pressed together, draped over one another.

Arousal seeped past the anger that drove her. Surprise halted her struggle for a moment, long enough to allow Dane to shift into a seated position on the sofa and leave Ariel draped, belly down, over his lap. Determined not to let him keep the keys, she drove her elbow into his hip, narrowly missing his privates.

Dane grunted. A curse slipped from his lips. His hand landed on her bottom with a solid *thwap.*

"Ow!" she screeched and twisted in his hold but was unable to get loose. He pushed her hands aside when she tried to cover her bottom.

Two more swats, one to each cheek, and Dane rolled her off his lap and onto the floor. Sprawled over his sneakered feet, Ariel was unsure how to react. She didn't know if she should be pissed or offended. He hadn't hit her hard, just enough to get his point across. Worse yet, her body sent aberrant signals to her brain. It flashed pictures in her mind of the images from his Web site. Determined to ignore the arousal that smoldered deep inside her, she glared up at him.

Heat darkened his blue eyes as he met her gaze and propped his elbows on his knees. "I'm staying. Nothing you try will make me leave until your big sister waltzes through the front door in twenty-seven days." He leaned over farther and tapped her nose with his left forefinger. "It's time to grow up and act like an adult instead of a temperamental two-year-old, Ariel. You may not like the situation, but you'd better learn to deal with it. This is the only warning you'll get, little girl."

"Where the hell do you get off telling me what I need to do?"

He watched her struggle to button her jacket. "You don't get it, do you?"

"Get what?" She huffed and shoved at the coffee table that pinned her close to his legs.

"How long did you think it would last?" His expression seemed to reflect a combination of disbelief and…pity.

A knot formed in her stomach; it quashed the growing desire. She didn't want to know what he hinted at, but at the same time she couldn't stop herself from asking, "How long, what? Your words don't make sense."

The fingers of his left hand traced her cheek, then eased around to cup her chin. "This little cocoon you and your sister built around yourselves. Your attempt to keep the world out and the two of you in. It had to crack sometime. I happened to be the catalyst."

Ariel swallowed. She fought the shiver that snaked its way up her spine and the smell of him that clouded her mind. He wasn't supposed to be nice. Not after spanking her. Not after the things she'd done to him. "No. That's crazy."

“Alayna chose to leave. I'm here. Nothing crazy about that.”

Ariel slapped his hand away and clambered to her feet. “I hate you.”

He didn't flinch or bother to respond. He rose from the couch and crossed the room to the desk. A glance at his watch and he added, “You might want to go check those rolls you put in the oven.”

Ariel didn't bother to say anything, but the walls rattled from the force of the slammed door as she exited. Her mind swirled with denials and confusion as she pushed into the kitchen.

It wasn't possible there was any truth to his accusations. It was crazy to think she and Alayna had spent ten years in a self-imposed limbo to keep from being hurt. To not let anyone get close.

On autopilot, she opened the oven and reached for the tray of rolls. Pain seared her fingertips. She cursed, pulled them back, and reached for a towel. Hands covered, she removed the tray and set it in the rack below the rolls she'd baked earlier.

I can't think about him now. Not now. Focus on the food. That's all I need to do. Ariel breathed in and out. She ignored the curious stares from DeeDee and Sadie as they called in orders to her. *Later. I'll take care of it later.*

* * *

Day 5

Two days later Dane had accepted the state of armistice that existed between Ariel and him. Nothing happened to keep him from the billing. No pranks. No confrontations. For the most part, Ariel simply avoided him.

He didn't count on it lasting. Ariel was sure to come up with some trick to establish her superior role at the café, but there hadn't been any blatant sabotage of the computer or the paperwork since their last scene in the office.

It didn't mean she was polite or that she welcomed him with open arms. Oh hell no. The snippy comments and lethal glares she directed toward him every time he crossed the threshold of the café spoke eloquently enough of her determination to see the last of him, but she seemed to have resigned herself to his presence for the next twenty-five days.

Her tendency to buzz around him while he worked on the finances or orders reminded him of an annoying mosquito on a muggy summer day. Or more like the way the little cartoon fairy acted toward the villainous pirate in *Peter Pan.* He grinned. When he considered the machinations he'd put in place to force Logan to face his fears, wouldn't it be ironic if Dane had to suffer his own form of sexual torture? His personal, life-size pixie for a pest? Curvy, sexy, and too damned determined to use her pixie dust to fuck *with* him when he'd rather she simply *fuck* him.

It wasn't difficult to imagine. Ariel probably spent hours every night coming up with plots and various ways to irritate him. Dane was determined not to let her get the best of him. As a result of his patience with the brat, he'd spent more time than intended with the records that afternoon. A gurgle of protest sounded from his stomach—a reminder that he'd missed lunch.

"Hey, Dane, can I get you anything before Sadie and I take off?" DeeDee asked as she leaned in the doorway.

The soft swells of her breasts pressed against the white blouse tucked into her black skirt. Dane wasn't oblivious to the fact that the woman's skirt was shorter than the one she'd worn the previous day. The higher hem exposed a pair of sexy, long legs left naked and colored by a light golden tan. He shook his head. "No, don't worry about it. I'll grab a bite on my way home." He watched a pout of disappointment cross her lips. She'd flirted and teased for the last few days. Any other time the girl's interest might have tempted him, but not now. There was no way he'd walk into that trap. "You have a good night, though."

"You too." She wiggled her fingers in a wave, then turned and left with a distinct sway in her hips.

"I take one step in DeeDee's direction, and the pixie will go for blood," Dane muttered and turned his attention back to the papers on the desk.

But his stomach wouldn't listen to reason as it bubbled and growled to be filled. Dane pulled his glasses off, and put them on top of the papers he set aside, before he pushed the chair back and stood up. A pat to his left front pocket confirmed the keys to the desk and file cabinets were still there.

Not sure what he'd be able to find in the kitchen with all the provisions stored away, Dane pushed through the door and stepped inside. Ariel didn't appear to be around, but he was sure she was still somewhere in the building. There was no way the woman would allow him to be alone in the café without her supervision.

From the two brief forays he'd made into the kitchen, Dane had a rough idea where the majority of the foodstuffs were stored. It only took him a few minutes to assemble two sandwiches and put everything back in its place.

Dane added a small bag of chips and a soda before he picked up the plate and turned toward the door.

"The kitchen's closed." Ariel glowered at him from the doorway.

He ignored her taunt and instead asked, "Did you see Sadie and DeeDee out?"

She didn't respond to his query. "I don't like people messing around in my kitchen."

"You don't like people messing around with anything of yours, Ariel." He lifted the plate and showed her the contents. "I only used a few things."

Ariel didn't ask for permission before she reached out and took one of the sandwich halves from his plate. She pulled the top piece of bread off and inventoried the ingredients. "Wheatberry bread, roasted turkey breast," she muttered. "Is this sliced Parmesan?"

"Yes." Dane subdued the inclination to grin at the intent inspection Ariel made of the sandwich. "It's a good thing I made two."

Ariel lifted a red tipped green leaf from the stack. "Lettuce?"

"Red leaf," Dane clarified.

She eyed him as if his choice of greens was a mystery in want of solving. "Why? Why not green-leaf lettuce? Or iceberg? Or even romaine?" she quizzed him.

Dane set his plate down and stepped close. Taking the leaf from her, he held it up to her lips. "Taste."

Her gaze remained on him while he watched her nip a piece of the lettuce from his fingertips and chewed. "Crisp, but I think it requires more," she observed.

"More what?" He looked from the opened sandwich in her hands to her face.

"Flavor. Zest." She carried the sandwich to the counter and looked through several containers. "Yes." The lettuce was discarded, and other greens replaced it.

"Spinach?" he asked skeptically, peeking over her shoulder at the rounded leaves she layered onto the meat and cheese.

"Baby spinach," she corrected, then put a leaf to her lips and took a nibble. "Try." As she looked up at him, Ariel held the leaf near his mouth.

He couldn't read her, but the way she cocked an eyebrow at his delay showed her attitude of triumph. Dane wasn't about to concede to her challenge. He held her gaze, hesitating only for a moment before he leaned down, nipped off a piece of the greenery, and chewed. "Tangy," he admitted.

"The perfect complement to the Parmesan." Her tone held conviction and confidence, despite the fact that she hadn't taken a bite of the sandwich.

Dane nodded, then took the reassembled sandwich from her hands and held it to her lips. “How can you be sure if you haven't tasted it yet?”

It was Ariel's turn to hesitate. Her gaze was steady on him before she opened her mouth. She bit off a chunk, making sure to get a sample from all the ingredients. Her eyes closed. She chewed slowly, as if to evaluate the textures and flavors as they blended on her tongue.

Dane could almost sense the various components of the sandwich by the expressions on her face. The turkey was mellow, smooth on her tongue from the way her lips softened and a smile quirked the corners. The tiny furrow between her eyebrows signaled the subtle bite from the Parmesan as it enhanced the flavor of the turkey. The crisp tang of the spinach blended with the Parmesan. The heat of the spicy sauce he'd found in a bowl and used as a spread for his sandwich filled her cheeks with the slightest flush.

Watching her eat could easily become an exercise in seduction, Dane decided. Her absorption in the tastes that filled her mouth was almost sexual in nature. Her entire focus centered on the texture and zest of the food she consumed. Her body seemed to quiver in anticipation of the next flavor to burst over her tongue. The way her features reflected the emotions aroused by the essence of each ingredient. Her lips parted slightly to pull breath into her mouth, an attempt to enhance the heat and burn of the peppers in the sauce. It made him swallow, desperate to wet his suddenly dry throat. He could feel his body sway close to hers, smell the mingled scents of the sandwich ingredients and a hint of cinnamon and spice as she exhaled.

Her voice was soft, sensual when she finally spoke. "The Parmesan works well—not too mild, not too sharp." She opened her eyes, the green the shade of a deep primal forest. Her expression grew uneasy as she continued to watch him.

Dane knew his eyes were focused on her mouth, the way her tongue slipped out to lick away the bit of seasoned spread caught in the corner of her lips. He could see her breath hitch, her body respond to the sensual expression he was sure suffused his face. It seemed to put her off balance, to distract her enough that she required a moment to collect her thoughts, perhaps to even calm her stirred emotions. She glanced at the bowl she'd left on the counter. "You used my red pepper sauce."

"Is that a crime?" His voice was low, almost husky in the quiet of the kitchen.

She seemed determined to fight any attraction she might begin to feel for him; her body swayed toward him, but she drew a breath and stepped away, putting a small pocket of distance between them.

She watched him slowly raise the sandwich half to his lips and take a bite. His nod and the rumbled hum of appreciation that vibrated through his chest sent a visible shiver through her. Dane was sure she'd deny it, but he sensed the heightened interest within her.

"It's dangerous," she taunted.

Dane doubted she meant her warning to be a double entendre. He looked at the remaining bit of sandwich. "Are you saying there's more in your sauce than roasted red peppers and cayenne?"

"Could be." She almost seemed to challenge him to eat more.

"If that was a hint at food allergies, I don't have any." He popped the last bite into his mouth. After he finished it, he told her, "Your sister warned me about the four accountants she tried to hire a couple of years ago."

Heat climbed into her cheeks. "It was three."

"Ah yes. Alayna said the fourth one refused to eat in the café after he heard the other three experienced 'reactions' to dishes they ate."

She seemed unsure how to interpret his grin. In hindsight, he had to admit that the fact she'd tried to undermine her sister's attempts to hire an accountant after theirs retired seemed to reinforce Alayna's comments about Ariel's aversion to change.

She fidgeted under his persistent stare, and then Ariel shrugged. "The worst that happened was a bad case of hives."

Dane reached for another sandwich half and changed the subject. "Not a bad choice for the spinach."

She reached past him, picked up one of the remaining two sandwich halves, and took a bite. "Pair it with a small salad or mixed fruit."

He rested against the counter behind him and finished the sandwich. "A salad or fruit would be good, but I'd go with chips or maybe celery or carrot sticks. You know, something crunchy to go with the soft." Dane opened the bag of chips and munched on a few.

She finished her sandwich and leaned closer to try to see the label. "That could work. Plain or even salt and vinegar chips."

He turned the bag to show her the type. "Sea salt and cracked black pepper."

Ariel's body went stiff, her chin came up, and her arms folded over her chest. Every particle of her being seemed to vibrate with displeasure. She looked up at him, bright blue eyebrows arched. "Who's the chef around here?"

"You are, I'm—"

"Just because you wormed your way into handling some of my sister's duties, don't get ideas about horning in on my territory," she warned as she fidgeted, shifted her feet, and settled her hands on her hips.

I knew it wouldn't last. Dane resisted the temptation to roll his eyes at her pugnacious attitude. "I'm not. I merely thought sea-salt-and-black-pepper chips would add an extra kick to that sauce you made," he suggested and kept his tone cool and reasonable.

"As long as you remember who's in charge here."

"In the kitchen, yes." He crowded closer to her. There didn't appear to be any rationale behind her animosity. It could be her determination to avoid any kind of change. It could stem from the resentment he knew she carried because he was the one to coax her sister away from the café for a month. No matter what the cause of her anger, he'd be damned if he would back down now.

Her gaze narrowed. "And out of it."

Dane shook his head. "Sorry, doll, but only in the kitchen. I run the rest of this place until your sister gets back." The fire that flared in her eyes probably matched the one in his gaze.

"You are not in charge."

"If you have any complaints, talk to your sister," Dane offered, his arms crossed over his chest. "I have no doubt she'll side with me when it comes to who should run the financial side of your café."

"Why do you think that? Because you've played on her interest in sexual submission?" The flash of varied emotions in her gaze disappeared, replaced by icy disdain. "And I would contact her, but you seem to have forgotten the rule about no communication with the outside."

"Ah, so Alayna did discuss the rules with you."

"Rules?" Ariel scoffed. "Prison sentence is more like it. Thirty days trapped at your mansion with no way to contact anyone."

Dane shook his head, marveled at Ariel's dogged misinterpretation of the facts. "Not trapped or without a way to contact anyone. Alayna chose to accept the rules for her training, as a submissive is expected to do—"

"Without the right to think for herself, without being allowed to—"

"Again you show your ignorance of the D/s life." The deepened pitch of his voice silenced Ariel. "Negotiation is key between a Dominant and a submissive. Nothing happens until both parties agree and expectations, limitations, and safe words are in place. You have this fanciful notion that

Alayna languishes under a whip, bound and helpless beneath the control of some faceless, nameless man." Dane leaned forward, and his tone dropped to a whisper as he held her gaze. "Maybe because that's a particular fantasy of yours? Fostered by a lover who tempted you to push the boundaries you desperately cling to?"

Resolved to make the little shrew see the errors in her thinking, he continued. "There is a difference between BDSM and D/s, Ariel. Dominance and submission do not require bondage and discipline practices. They are an exercise in trust and control. Leather, whips, ropes to tie a partner up—those can be part of the play, but at its core, a D/s relationship is about an equal exchange of power."

Dane was sure Ariel didn't realize her expression was a mixture of disappointment and envy. He knew she would heatedly deny any desire to be in her sister's place, to experience the training Alayna was undergoing, but her gaze and the tone of her voice betrayed her curiosity about it all. Or perhaps his increased interest in controlling her was coloring his analysis. "What has you so angry, Ariel? That your sister asked me for help to navigate a new world? Or that she's doing something for herself for the first time in ten years but didn't include you?"

She blanched at the observation, and Dane cursed his impulsive comment. Retracting it would be useless; he watched the cool mask Ariel consistently adopted around him slip into place. It reflected her refusal to listen to reason. At least from him. This only seemed to exacerbate the fact that his ability to maintain a professional attitude toward

Ariel was a facade. One that crumbled easily when she pushed him.

"You have some sauce on your face." She pointed toward his chin.

He reached up to wipe away the gooey spread, wary of the keen look she gave him. It made him wonder what form of retribution she might concoct.

His suspicions grew when she stepped in close and gripped the tie he'd loosened earlier. "You may have my sister thinking you're needed here, Master Reese"—she tugged his face closer to hers—"but we both know it isn't true."

Taking her time, she smoothed the tip of her tongue along his chin and licked away the smear of sauce before swiping upward to his cheek.

The damp track of her mouth removed any of the spread. "Be careful who you try to push. I'm not Al. And I have no intention of ever calling you my master."

And that's where his problem lay, Dane admitted as he watched Ariel scoop up one of the covered containers on the prep station and carry it to the walk-in cooler. In that moment he realized those were the words he wanted to hear. *My master.* His imagination readily conjured images of Ariel kneeling before him, her bright green eyes ablaze with desire, her naked body dewed with sweat as she trembled at the cusp of orgasm, requiring only his touch, his words, to slip over the edge.

* * *

Long after he'd left the café and returned to the mansion where he and Logan educated clients in the D/s lifestyle, Dane settled onto a seat at the table tucked away in the breakfast nook of the quiet kitchen. Steam rose from the chicken and mashed potatoes with gravy on his plate. Late-night snacks wouldn't solve his problems with Ariel.

"You're up late, Master Dane." The housekeeper who lived at the mansion, Shendah, paused on the threshold of the kitchen. The robe she wore covered her from her neck to the soft, fuzzy slippers on her feet.

"I hope I didn't wake you," he said. Strain showed on her face; her shoulders were stiff with tension. Dane assumed a nightmare from her childhood had wakened the twenty-eight-year-old, not his scavenging for leftovers in the fridge and using the microwave.

"No, sir." She crossed to the stove and set the kettle on to heat.

"Couldn't sleep?"

She didn't admit anything but Dane could see the answer in her tired eyes. "We've missed you these last few days." From the cabinet, she collected a coffee mug and a tin of tea.

Dane laughed softly. "I doubt that, Shen." He ate a few bites of chicken and a scoop of potatoes.

Shendah smiled. "I'm sure if Master Logan were more himself, he would."

"More himself?" He ate slowly, waiting for her explanation.

"I don't wish to carry tales." Shendah prepared her tea and moved to take the chair opposite him.

"Please explain how Logan isn't himself, Shendah." If he made it an order, he would alleviate any unease she might feel about revealing information about his business partner. She'd acted as housekeeper and cook for A Master's Gift for nearly twelve years. Logan and he considered her family, and she often said she felt the same.

"He seems preoccupied with the training of the new submissive, Alayna."

"How so?"

Shendah shrugged. "He's ordered that I keep fresh flowers in her room—something he hasn't done for other guests. Although he occupies Room Four upstairs, the one Alayna was supposed to use, he doesn't sleep in the bed."

That was news. Dane had a suspicion where Logan slept at night, but he wanted to confirm it. "Where is he sleeping?"

"In his bedroom. With Alayna."

"In the bed?" *Damn, maybe my plan is working better than I thought.* His satisfaction was short-lived as Shendah shook her head.

"No, I believe he is sleeping in one of the armchairs beside the bed."

"And you know this how?" He finished the last of his meal and took a sip of the milk he'd poured.

"Indentations in the cushions, the way he rubs at his neck when he thinks others aren't watching, the position of the chair when I go in to clean each day." Shendah shrugged.

"He watches Alayna as if she is a beloved treasure, but when she tries to make conversation, Logan treats her like a pariah."

Dane fought the urge to curse. Keegan McAvoy, one of the mansion's residents and his and Logan's part-time chauffeur, had told him Logan had overridden Dane's directive and moved Alayna into Logan's bedroom when she arrived. It seemed his best friend was proving as stubborn as always. Determined to control his environment without admitting to his attraction to the elder Valerian sister. "And Alayna? Do you think she's aware of his nightly visits?" *Perhaps...*

Shendah shook her head and took a sip of her tea. "Not consciously. She seems aware something is happening, but Logan's actions toward her appear to have her confused."

The smile she gave him next was a familiar one and pulled a groan from Dane. Now it was Shendah's turn to ask questions, and there would be no avoiding answering. "Alayna has asked about how you are doing at the café."

Dane nodded before rising to carry his dishes to the kitchen sink. When she reached out to take them from him, he motioned her back to her seat. "I can take care of these, Shen. I'm not useless."

Before he turned away, he noticed her eyebrows rise and fall in a quick look of surprise. "You sound as if someone has questioned your abilities. Is there trouble with Alayna's sister?"

After he rinsed his plate, Dane braced his hands on the counter and then grimaced. "Nothing I can't handle."

Shendah watched him, her curiosity apparent in her expression, but years of training as a submissive enabled her to control her inquisitiveness. She only asked, "And how do you want to handle her?"

Visions of how Ariel ended their conversation in the kitchen earlier made Dane nod. "She would make an interesting challenge."

"Challenge?"

"Ariel is a woman of strong opinions."

Shendah looked at him, her eyes assessing. "You want her." It wasn't a question.

"If I weren't concerned she'd cut my balls off and feed them to me in a special marinade, I'd lay her out on one of her countertops and fuck her until the only orders she could give were 'harder' and 'faster,'" Dane admitted with a grin.

Shendah's soft laughter filled the quiet room. "You look like you'd actually enjoy it."

Dane smiled. "If you mean the fucking, damn right I would."

Shendah laughed again and shook her head. "No, the castration. You actually sounded as if the idea appeals to you."

Dane dipped his head in acknowledgment of her amusement. "You haven't tasted my pixie's special marinades, Shen. I'd probably be first in line for seconds." Then he changed the subject, despite the thoughts rebounding off one another in his mind. "Do you think you can sleep now?"

She didn't protest the abrupt closure of subject. She swallowed the last of her tea before she rose from her chair and crossed to the sink. “Yes.”

He took the cup from her, careful not to make contact with her hands or fingers, rinsed it, and then settled it onto the rack in the dishwasher.

“Good night, Master Dane.”

“Sleep well, Shendah.”

Dane watched her leave the kitchen before he turned off the light and returned to his place at the table. Clouds scuttled across the moon, and its glow dimmed as it bathed the estate's acreage. As much as he trusted Shendah, he wasn't about to discuss the situation at the café in detail with her. A flash of light drew his gaze toward the neatly trimmed hedge bordering the vast, well-manicured lawn of the backyard. Another, then another, and his lips lifted in a grin. Fireflies. Capricious insects that teased and taunted with their shine.

Like Ariel. Calm and predictable one minute; waspish and snippy, the next. Dane doubted he'd ever figure her out.

And the need to understand what motivated her, what made her tick, continued to grow. Five days of harassment by the little termagant should have had him ready to avoid the café, but something in her very defiance taunted the dominant in him.

Despite her prickly nature and almost rabid determination to hate him, Dane sensed there was a fire within Ariel. Similar to the one smoldering in her sister, Ariel's sensual appreciation, her enjoyment in savoring the flavors in the sandwich he'd made, identified an untapped sexuality waiting to be explored.

The spanking he'd given her a few days ago hadn't fazed her. Proximity only brought her hackles up. It would be interesting to see how she'd respond to a full-on battle. His gaze unfocused, Dane no longer saw the twinkling lights of the fireflies beyond the glass door. Instead his body responded to imagined moments. Ariel held close, the ripe curves of her body against his. Writhing and twisting to be free. At least at the start.

Once he stripped away the white chef's jacket, black slacks, and black shoes, he was sure he'd find naked ivory flesh. Pussy damp with the arousal he was sure he'd caught fleeting whiffs of throughout the day. Her nipples would be tight pink crowns for her full, round breasts.

He shifted in the chair, enraptured by the fantasy as it unfolded in his mind. The thick length of his erection pressed against the faded denim of his jeans. His eyelids drifted down, closed on the image of bearing Ariel to the floor of the café's kitchen, her legs open, hands clutching at him, fingers scoring his back as he thrust inside her. Fucking her hard and deep, just as he'd described to Shendah.

A low rumble that closely resembled a purr rolled from his throat, and he opened his eyes. His hand dropped to his lap and cupped the thick erection throbbing there, while his gaze slowly focused once again on the flickering lights of the insects in the yard.

With a woman as wicked as that, one who understood the sensuality of food and methods to stimulate the senses… If he had a woman like Ariel under his command, Dane wondered if the boredom and ennui that usually crept into all his relationships would be eliminated. To be certain, he'd never know exactly what she was thinking.

And he'd never have to wonder if she was pissed off at him. The sassy pixie would be more than ready to get right in his face to voice her displeasure.

Chapter Three

Day 6

Ariel had come to terms with Dane's presence by the end of the first week. But she still didn't like it. She continued to hope the bastard would go away and her sister would return, but she was certain Alayna would be gone the rest of the month. At least the café would be closed the next day, and she wouldn't have to deal with Dane hovering in the background.

It didn't mean, though, that she would roll over and let Dane do as he chose. Saturday afternoon, Ariel stood toe-to-toe with Dane beside the desk and refused to give an inch. "I don't care how much you *think* you know about our ordering system, Dane. I'm telling you what you should do."

"And I explained that Alayna gave me explicit instructions in regard to the suppliers the café uses," Dane responded coolly.

His lack of heat only irritated Ariel more. "Do you always have to be so damned in control?" she demanded.

Dane shifted his arms so they crossed over his chest. The green polo shirt he wore emphasized the bulge of his biceps and the corded muscles of his abdomen. "A master learns to stay in charge of his emotions to better provide protection and guidance for his submissive."

Ariel gritted her teeth, her belly jumped at the words, and the tingling sensation at her core ratcheted up. The man was dangerous, and hearing his philosophy as it related to his sexual interests only turned her on more; she fought long and hard to keep from betraying that to him. "Gag me, Reese." She rolled her eyes and copied his crossed-arm stance, the papers in her hands crumpled in her grip. "I couldn't care less about your sex life or the lessons you and your business partner are trying to teach my sister. What I'm talking about now is your stubborn, pigheaded refusal to listen to my instructions about whom to order from."

The grin flashed his white teeth and set a twinkle off in his sapphire-colored eyes. "I could say the same about you, Ariel." Leaning down the full foot that separated their heights, he nearly bumped noses with her. "When are you going to figure out that I don't take orders from you? Your sister put me in charge, and I'll take care of things. Just the way she asked me to." He paused, then added, "As for gagging you, I have a sweet little ball gag that would perfectly match your hair if you're interested in trying it out."

The step back she took wasn't a retreat so much as a reestablishment of personal boundaries. At least that was the excuse Ariel tried to give herself. The craving building in her pussy, the increased dampness of her panties, and the painful tightness of her nipples were merely side effects of her frustration at his opposition. And maybe the images of what he'd do to her if she were to take him up on his challenge to try out the ball gag.

She drowned her attraction with an indignant snarl. "Listen, you—"

"Uh, Ari?"

DeeDee's choked-off laughter had both Ariel and Dane turning toward the door.

"Yeah?" Ariel snapped.

"I wanted to let you know that Sadie and I are leaving." The strap of her purse was over her shoulder, and she tipped her head toward the front of the café.

"All the tables taken care of?"

DeeDee nodded. "Yes. We refilled all the condiments and shakers as usual." She jerked a thumb over her shoulder. "Oh, and Grimm is at the back door."

Ariel glanced at her watch. "Is it that late already?" Not waiting for a response, she tossed the papers she'd clenched in her hand onto the desk and headed for the door. After she squeezed past DeeDee, Ariel hurried up the hall, with the younger woman walking fast to keep up.

"Yeah, we didn't want to disturb you guys." DeeDee grinned. "But Grimm was a little antsy, and I figured you'd rather I interrupt than he go off empty-handed."

"Thanks, Dee." Ariel patted her shoulder, passed her, rounded the pastry case, and scooted around the tables with their upended chairs on top. "I'll see you guys Monday." She waved at Sadie where she waited in the main area of the eatery.

Both waitresses said their farewells and made sure the CLOSED sign was in place as they headed out the front door. Torn between locking up and getting to the back door before Grimm left, Ariel hesitated near the cash register at the end of the counter. When she heard Dane following her out of the office, she didn't hesitate to rope him into service. A glance over her shoulder confirmed he was there. She pointed to the front of the café. “Can you make sure we're all locked up?”

She didn't wait for an answer; instead she pushed through the swinging doors that led into the kitchen. She wasn't about to admit she was running *from* Dane instead of hurrying to get to Grimm. At least not out loud. Or to Dane.

Ariel passed the racks with the foil and plastic carryout containers, headed for the back door, and swung it open. “Grimm, you don't have to wait out here.” She told him that every time he came by the shop to collect the leftover bakery items and perishables he gave to the men living at his halfway house and some of the homeless camped outside Ayerstown. In ten years, she'd yet to convince the man to take a seat inside her kitchen, unless she or Alayna was with him.

“Hey, Miss Ariel.” Grimm's deep voice was soft, but it resonated in the dim shadows of the alley.

As he rose from the piled crates beside the door, Ariel grinned at how similar to his voice the big man was. He easily topped Dane's height by two or three inches. The breadth of his shoulders and the size of his muscles would make a world-class bodybuilder appear puny beside him. If his size didn't intimidate others, the deep ebony skin, bald head, and gold hoop in his left ear often sent people scrambling to cross the street.

But not Ariel or her sister. He'd played with them when they were little and he was a teenager. She knew how gentle he really was. Holding the door open, she smiled. "Come on in. Have you had anything to eat yet?"

"You don't have to feed me. I'm doin' just fine." Grimm turned sideways to get through the doorway. He reached over Ariel's head to ease the door shut.

"It's no trouble, Grimm. The usual?" she offered, walking to the central island and pulling bread from one cabinet. While Grimm settled onto one of the high stools she kept tucked near the prep station, Ariel crossed to the double-door, walk-in refrigerator and stepped inside to retrieve sandwich meats and other fixings.

As she returned and stepped past him, Ariel wrapped her arm around Grimm's waist and squeezed. "You been takin' care of yourself?"

Grimm's beefy arm settled around her shoulders and returned her hug.

Dane wasn't about to let Ariel walk away from their argument. It was necessary that he keep reestablishing his control in the office in order to avoid Ariel's resuming her attempts to take over and drive him off.

Dane pushed through the swinging doors and came to a sudden halt inside the kitchen, deciding to proceed carefully. To say the man with his arm around Ariel was scary was an understatement. Even seated, the man towered over Ariel, and from the size of him, Dane doubted he could take the man in a fight should it become necessary. Advancing cautiously, he stepped toward the pair.

"All locked up." Ariel and the man swung around to face him.

Dark sherry brown eyes measured him with every step closer he took, but the other man remained seated. Dane assumed this was the "Grimm" DeeDee had mentioned before she and Sadie left.

"Thanks." Setting down the container she held, Ariel turned back to face him. "Grimm, this is Dane Reese. Dane, Grimm Dawson."

Dane extended his hand and watched the other man's huge fist swallow it. Amusement more than fear brought a grin to Dane's face. "I have to say, other than the grim reaper and some rock-and-roll-band members, I've never heard of someone named Grimm."

White teeth glinted against full lips as the other man returned his grin. "Named for my mama's side of the family, Grimmsby."

"Pleased to make your acquaintance," Dane offered.

Grimm eased his hold on Dane's hand. "Likewise."

Over the other man's shoulder, Dane watched Ariel assemble a thick sandwich, slice it, and put it on a paper plate. She smiled when she set it in front of Grimm. "Go ahead and eat up, Grimm."

She cleaned up the containers and carried them back to the refrigerator. From inside the space, the scrape of plastic over metal, then a soft *oomph* had both men on their feet and moving forward. Dane reached her first and eased the big green plastic tub from Ariel's grip. It wasn't particularly heavy, but the size made it awkward for a person of her diminutive height.

"We've had a few slow days, so there are quite a few leftovers," Ariel pointed out before she motioned Dane to set the case down near Grimm. "There's about half a dozen cinnamon rolls left over from this morning that didn't sell, and some cookies, cupcakes, and pastries from yesterday."

Dane stood aside and marveled at how easily the lies tripped off Ariel's tongue. The leftover items she had listed weren't from this morning or any morning. Not three hours ago he'd seen her mix up the cookies and then bake the cinnamon rolls and cupcakes that had gone into the green tub. When Sadie had mentioned a customer was interested in a roll to go, Ariel had told her they were a special order.

"I do appreciate it, Miss Ariel. And the men do too," Grimm assured her. He finished the last of his sandwich and carried the paper plate to one of the recycling bins.

"I'm happy to help in any way, you know that. How many do you have at the house now?"

"Deacon left last week to go back home, so there's only six right now." Grimm hefted the container and strode toward the door. "I'll be on my way and leave you two to finish what you were working on."

Dane's "thank you" tangled up with Ariel's "oh we weren't doing anything important" and drew Grimm's attention. He stopped and turned to face Ariel and Dane. His expression shifted from concern to confusion and, finally, to amusement.

"We were discussing the supply order," Dane reminded Ariel. He suspected she would try to avoid him, but he wasn't sure how she would accomplish it. Not when she'd been so determined to change his mind about one of the suppliers he'd ordered from.

She waved her hand and shrugged. "I can take care of that later. I think I'll go with Grimm and make sure there's enough for everyone."

Dane could tell by Grimm's surprised look that it was unusual for Ariel to accompany him, but the big man didn't voice a protest.

"We really ought to discuss the order, Ariel," Dane reminded her. He slid his hands into his pockets to keep from reaching for her. Whether to drag her to his side or throttle her, he wasn't sure. Having Ariel dismiss his directions grated. His reaction to her behavior was equally disturbing. He fought to suppress the possessive declaration—*mine*—that rose in his throat. Never in any of his relationships had he felt inclined to stake a claim on a woman and warn off other men. Why did he suddenly feel it was essential he do so with her?

Was it because she was so at ease with Grimm but not with him? Or was it her eagerness to be with the other man that set Dane's teeth on edge?

"I'm perfectly capable of submitting the order myself, Dane. Why don't you head on home, and I'll be back in an hour or so to finish up the order." She turned to Grimm and smiled. "Let me go get my backpack, and I'll be right with you."

Dane didn't bother to say anything as Grimm nodded and exited through the back door. Instead he followed Ariel into the office and blocked her path. "You can't wander off with him, Ariel."

"Excuse me?" She shifted her backpack over her left shoulder and faced him.

"Do you even know where he's going? What he's doing here, besides begging for food?" Dane wasn't surprised at her defensive posture. Hell, the assumptions he'd made would have his back up if someone had said the same to him. If he pressed the issue, it would only create more tension between them, and that was damned tiresome. He wished she would simply see reason and recognize the advice he offered was a means of protecting her. Even he doubted his actions were wholly altruistic. He realized the fact that she wanted to be with the other man was what truly grated on his nerves.

"Who are you to tell me what I will and will not do?" She poked a blunt-tipped finger in his chest, emphasizing her irritation with every word. "I've known Grimm a hell of a lot longer than I've known you."

"We have work to get done here." Perhaps the reminder would get through to her. Not that he'd get much work done if she were around, but at least he would know where she was and that she was safe. Again the niggling voice in the back of his head issued warnings, but Dane disregarded the notion that his interest was directly associated with the attraction building since they'd argued over the sandwich the day before.

"And I told you I will take care of it when I get back." Pushing past him, she headed for the door.

Dane grabbed her wrist and halted her exit. “I don't think you should go with him.”

“You aren't my father or my keeper, Dane. You don't get a vote.” She glared at him.

“Your sister put me in charge—”

“Of the books, not me. I'm a big girl. I don't need you to tell me what to do or whom to go with.” She pulled free and left.

Dane followed her to the door and watched her climb into the red crew-cab pickup parked in the alley between the café and the bookstore in the next row of buildings. The hydraulic hinge prevented him from slamming the door, and the urge to punch a wall sorely tested his training as a dominant. *Damned woman won't listen to reason. She'll do anything to flout my instructions. My authority. Can't even accept that I only want to look out for the welfare of the restaurant.* A snort of disgust echoed in the quiet kitchen. “Yeah, I believe that like I have a great bridge I'd part with in Brooklyn,” Dane growled, admitting he carried more than a bit of resentment over Ariel's unflinching trust in Grimm.

“If she thinks for one minute I'll walk off and leave the café without making sure she's safe…” He strode out of the kitchen and into the office, then booted up the computer. Once he logged on to the Internet, his fingers flew over the keyboard. “Dawson, Grimmsby. Can't be many people with that name.”

The orders were set aside as he gathered information. With each new detail Dane gleaned, his anger built as he identified the man with whom Ariel had driven off. The smart-mouthed little termagant was suspicious and interfered in every transaction he conducted, but she waltzed off without a care with a man like Dawson? Did she have some kind of death wish? Or maybe she considered herself impervious to the same dangers that plagued the rest of the mortals around her.

By the time he had read through the final article he'd found about Grimm, Dane was more than ready to do battle. He'd show his annoying little pixie the error of her ways. The second she returned.

* * *

Ariel unlocked the café door and stepped toward the alarm keypad to punch in the code. With her fingers poised over the numbers, it took a moment for her to realize it hadn't been set. She stepped to the door, opened it, and waved at Grimm to assure him all was fine. She watched her friend drive off and then relocked the door. There were only two reasons the alarm wouldn't have been set. First Dane may have forgotten to set it before he left. Doubtful, since the bastard was such a stickler for rules and schedules. Ariel shook her head and shrugged her backpack onto her left shoulder.

Second option, he was still here. Which would mean the row that had begun to brew when she walked out was about to be finished. The light from the office spilled into the hallway and supported her theory that Dane waited for her.

“I knew I should have gone home,” she grumbled, stepping into the office and grimacing at the sight of Dane seated behind the desk.

"I would have merely gone there."

"I told you I'd get the order done when I got back." She dropped her backpack next to the leather sofa and settled onto one of the cushions.

"Already taken care of," Dane informed her. Leaning back in the chair, he watched her.

"Okay"—she reached over and grabbed her pack—"I'll head on—"

"Stay." He barked out the command and rose from the chair.

Ariel ignored it as she let loose her pack and rose to square off with him. "I'm not a pet—"

He overrode her protest. "You should explain to me why you felt it necessary to ignore my advice to go off with Grimm."

"I don't have to explain anything to you."

"The hell you don't. He's a convicted felon, Ariel." Dane stepped closer, his tone quiet and resolute. "Did you know that? Did you know he did seven years for assault?"

"Been doing a little Web surfing, Dane?" She propped her hands on her hips and stuck her chin out at him. "Did you bother to find out why he committed the assault? Did you bother to find out that while in prison, he completed a bachelor's degree in psychology and master's in drug-addiction counseling?"

"And that he runs a halfway house on the other side of town," Dane finished for her.

"I was perfectly safe."

"But it wasn't necessary for you to be there at all, Ariel. I could tell by his reaction that you don't go with him to deliver the food."

Ariel shrugged. "So I felt like going. Like I told you earlier, you aren't my father or my keeper—"

"And I told you I am. I promised your sister I'd keep an eye out for you."

Ariel glared up at him; her finger jabbed his chest to stress each point. "No, you promised my sister to help out with the finances here, not to babysit me."

"Since it's your cooking ability that draws the customers in, I'm living up to my duties by telling you not to go off with men like that again."

"You don't own me. And you don't tell me what to do." Again Ariel emphasized her response with repeated pokes against his chest.

Dane's hand rose and gripped hers to stop the prodding. He tugged her forward. "You better watch it, little girl." His voice was low, almost cold. His face revealed no expression.

Ariel discounted it. "Oh really," she mocked.

"Umm hmmm. That mouth of yours is writing checks that you can't make good on."

The heat of his gaze warned her, but Ariel ignored it. Bound and determined to make him submit, to knuckle under and assume his rightful place beneath her, she met his glare with one of her own. "And you think you can try to collect?" She tried to tug her right hand free, but his grip was too strong. The first twinge of unease slithered along her spine.

His free hand cupped her chin, making it impossible to turn away. Warmth emanated from his fingertips and palm, but it didn't dispel the chill that crept through her. Ariel refused to cringe, to give in to the urge to put as much distance between her and Dane as the office would allow.

"Most definitely," he assured her.

Ariel started to snap a scathing response, but the sound was lost in the confines of his mouth. His lips captured hers, rubbed and pressed against them as his tongue delved inside to stroke over hers. The hand holding one of hers resettled so her captured hand pressed between her back and his hand. He pulled her snugly to his sinewy frame, while the fingers gripping her chin eased away and speared through the short blue strands of her hair.

The scent of his body infused every breath she dragged in through her nose. The slide and plunge of his tongue coaxed a response from her body that sent silent curses through her brain. The tips of her breasts throbbed, nipples drawn tight and sensitive to the scrape of the silk-and-lace cups holding them.

The fire in her pussy increased to an intense yearning; it spilled her arousal and soaked her panties. As if he sensed her desire, Dane slid his thick, muscled thigh between hers, stroking and caressing her center. Her free hand reached up to grip his shoulder and pulled him closer so she could soothe the ache in her breasts with the force of his firm chest against hers.

He felt so good. Her body rocked upward into his. The heat emanating from him seeped deep into her core. Her hand moved from his shoulder to the soft curls over his ear, threading through them to keep his mouth sealed to hers. The smell of cardamom and rosemary filled her senses. It twisted the longing tight and heightened her arousal. Her head spun with the sensations, feelings she'd never dealt with, even in the few brief encounters when she'd made love with her college boyfriend. Her heart thundered in her chest; her tongue tangled and played with Dane's, each of them attempting to stake their claim to who was in charge.

Desperate for breath but unwilling to release him, Ariel shifted and strained to get closer. As if he sensed her surrender, Dane pulled away. He tugged her fingers from his hair. In quick, efficient motions, he settled her onto the couch and stepped away from her. No emotion showed on his face. Where Ariel's body shuddered to maintain a modicum of restraint, Dane looked as if he'd just stepped out of his office to greet a client. He straightened his slightly mussed curls with a flick of his hand, removing the only evidence of their kiss.

"Don't test me again, Ariel. You may end up with more than you bargained for," Dane warned her and then stepped out of the office.

As she gasped for breath and tried to regain some semblance of control, Ariel listened to his soft footfalls as he stalked through the café and out the front door. Body trembling from unquenched lust, it took three attempts for Ariel to make it to her feet and sling her backpack over her shoulder.

She refused to think of his parting words; she wandered through the office, shut off the lights, and then exited the room. One hand braced against the wall or on a table to keep her from toppling onto her face, Ariel crossed the café slowly, reached the alarm panel, and set the alarm before she made her way out the door and secured the lock.

Several deep breaths later, she stumbled down the street to her house, up the porch steps, and inside. In the dark entry of her home, Ariel let her bag slip to the floor. Eyes closed, she leaned against the wall. Nothing she'd felt before had prepared her for the sensations pulsing through her body.

With a slow, careful swallow, she opened her eyes. It couldn't be much past eight in the evening, she determined. She could easily identify the shapes of the different pieces of furniture. Distraction would only last so long, Ariel admitted. She pushed away from the wall and staggered down the hall to her bedroom.

Facing the fact that Dane had been the one to stop the kiss would come, but not right now. Right now she had to focus on how to wrestle her body back under control and keep it there while in Dane's presence for the next three weeks. If she was aching and desperate for a good fuck after six days of dealing with him under her feet and stirring up things at the café, she was bound to be nearly certifiable by the time he left.

Her stomach dropped at the sudden thought of his leaving, but she forced the discomfort aside. She hated him around; that was all. It was her café. Her kitchen. His attempts to push her around, to take over where he wasn't wanted, were the sole reason her body behaved so irrationally.

Once he left, it would all go back to normal, Ariel tried to assure herself. *Only have to make it through twenty-four more days.* Any fallout associated with her body, she'd deal with later.

Much later.

Chapter Four

Day 7

A long night tossing in her bed left Ariel cranky and out of sorts. With the café closed on Sundays, she decided to come in the next morning to check on the orders Dane had said he made the night before. There was also the matter of the “special item” she'd somehow managed to leave in the office the previous afternoon. Unlocking the door and switching off the alarm, Ariel grimaced at the thought of Dane coming across the adult toy she'd purchased the day before from the shop two blocks over from the eatery. Before he'd come in, and after the café had slowed in the morning, she'd run an errand and swung by the bank to get change for the register.

The store had been on her way—a spur-of-the-moment excursion that had caused images and ideas to tumble and turn in her mind. Her bottom tingled at the memory of the wall of floggers, paddles, and leather whips she'd passed to get to the vibrators on display. She'd gone through her backpack several times last night looking for the item she'd purchased. Nothing.

She glanced around the office, but she didn't see the paper bag. She looked around the base of the sofa, then dropped to her knees to see if it had somehow been kicked under the sofa or one of the end tables when she and Dane—Ariel shied away from the thoughts associated with the reason she was on the hunt for her new toy.

She bypassed the desk and headed for the file cabinets and the table along the wall behind the desk. It was possible it had fallen out after she'd set her pack down and fished out the change she'd brought from the bank. The fact that she'd required her new toy last night when she returned home only made her grumble louder. The vibrator she kept in the drawer beside her bed was okay, but the device she'd picked up the day before was much more suitable to meet the cravings Ariel had experienced since Dane's arrival.

"Not that he has anything whatsoever to do with…*that*." She spotted the brown paper bag tucked between the two file cabinets. She reached for it, dragged it out, and opened the bag. Peering inside, she grinned.

The blue color of the toy had reminded her of Dane's eyes, and she'd judged the size to be close to his proportions. She couldn't suppress the giggle that rose to her lips, when she imagined the expression on Dane's face if he were to find this little gem stashed in the office. The giggle grew to a laugh. "I should tuck it into one of the drawers simply to see what he does," she told the empty room.

Heat flared between her hips, then drizzled lower. Images floated through her mind at the thought of Dane finding the toy. The suggestion he'd made about the ball gag would be mild in comparison to what he might say about the bright blue vibrator. The ache from the previous evening returned and wiped the smile from Ariel's lips. Her breathing increased, and the beat of her heart sped up at the wicked thought of Dane using the toy on her.

Would he use it to tease? Perhaps he'd make soft, gentle strokes over her mound before he slid it inside. Or maybe he'd start slow but pick up the pace, thrusting faster and harder until she couldn't stop her climax.

In her hand, the paper bag rattled. The weight of the lubricant and batteries pulled at her fingers; her mind taunted her with the temptation to see how well the toy could satisfy.

Taking a deep breath, she proceeded to the sofa, dropped onto the cushion, and leaned against the backrest. The scent of cardamom and rosemary whispered in the air around her, making her moan and squeeze her eyes shut.

Her head sank deeper into the back of the sofa, which only intensified the smell. She rolled her head to the side and realized the scent wasn't part of her imagination; it came from the black leather car coat Dane had worn into the café the previous afternoon.

Bag and vibrator abandoned in her lap, she dragged the coat from behind her and buried her face in it. Her nipples strained at her bra; her panties grew wet from the response of her body. Need coiled in her abdomen and pulsed in the emptiness of her pussy.

"God, this is insane," she growled. But she didn't hesitate to set his coat aside and rip open the toy's packaging. "It's crazy," she told herself and stumbled into the bathroom to rinse the vibrator beneath the tap.

She gazed into the mirror and noted the flush in her cheeks, the dazed look in her eyes, but it didn't deter her. The hunger was too intense, too encompassing. If she didn't deal with it now, she doubted she'd be able to concentrate on any of the cooking or supply orders she'd hoped to process today.

She smoothed a towel over the blue tube, set the vibrator and towel aside, and stripped out of her clothes. She left them in a neatly folded pile on the sink and returned to the office.

She gave in to the urge to slide the coat over her naked body. The cool silk lining caressed her skin; her nipples crinkled tighter. She hugged the jacket close and absorbed Dane's essence from the garment. Her shaking fingers shoved buttons through holes, surrounding herself with the fantasy of Dane's heat enfolding her.

The jacket's sleeves hung over the tips of her fingers, and the hem nearly reached her knees. The difference in their heights only made her grin. Fingers fumbling, she ripped open the battery packaging, inserted some into the vibrator, and set the rest aside. She unsealed the lubricant. The *pop* of the cap was loud in the room. She kept the coat between her bottom and the sofa cushion as she sat down. Her hand shook as she drizzled the clear gel onto the blue toy. After placing the bottle on the coffee table beside the batteries, she smoothed the lubricant over the thick blue shaft.

She drew a deep breath. "Oh God, am I really going to do this?" she asked, although the answer resounded in her head and through her body. *Fuck yes*! Head resting on the seat cushion, she swallowed and eased the vibrator between her thighs. The feel of the slick tip on her mound made her jump.

She reached down with her other hand to hold herself open. Her fingers growing wet with her juices, Ariel worked slowly. She eased the vibrator deeper with a gasp. Her body pulsed around the rubber and plastic wand. Whimpers and moans slid past her lips, but she wasn't aware of what she might be saying, if anything. Her sole focus was the wonderful fullness inside her.

Her heart pounded in her chest. The breath rasped in and out of her lungs as she arched upward. Her fingers twisted the base, and the motor engaged. Against her eyelids, she could see him leaning over her, his broad shoulders glistening with sweat. His cocky grin taunted her. The heavy thrust of his cock filling her for the first time. “Oh God. Fuck. Dane, please!” She gasped and cried. She began to work the wand in and out, striving to satisfy the fire curled in her womb as the ache gripped the tight nipples on her breast and the coil of arousal twisted in her gut.

Her free hand drifted upward, stroked over the supple leather of Dane's car coat, preserving the fantasy that it was his thick cock working in and out of her pussy. Upward her hand climbed, slipping buttons free, baring her belly and breasts, and smoothing over both. Eyes squeezed tightly shut, Ariel tried to convince her body it was Dane's calloused fingertips sliding over her skin and his thick, hot fingers plucking at her nipples. She increased the thrust of the vibrator inside her channel. “Yes, oh yes, Dane. There, please,” she babbled. Her voice echoed in the silent room.

Only she and the blue toy fucking her knew who she wanted cradled against her hips, pounding at her slit, filling her. How her body ached to have him ride her, his possession of her relentless, his stamp of ownership blatantly obvious, even if she trembled at the thought of bearing it. No damned way would she confess to the sexual urges Dane stirred in her. At least not to his face. And not without a fight.

* * *

If he weren't aware of why Ariel continued to play her little game of "I'm the boss," Dane would have taken her over his knee a few more times since he'd started to work at the café. It didn't help that Jordan had taken up the slack for both Logan's work and now some of Dane's. "He's definitely earned some time off," Dane muttered as he parked in front of Valerian's Root and climbed out of his car. "In the last week the man has gone from assistant to full-time jack-of-all-work. It's a damned good thing we can count on him."

Dane wasn't worried Jordan would suddenly abscond with their clients' money or confidential information; both Logan and he had attended high school with Jordan's parents. In fact, Samuel Bishop was the first man to request Logan's aid in discovering the strength in a D/s relationship.

"I'm more concerned Logan'll have to bail me out for assault," Dane griped as he unlocked the café's front door and crossed to the alarm. The warning ring failed to go off. Twisting the lock closed, he wondered if Ariel simply had forgotten to set the alarm the night before. Despite his irritation, he realized he should have stayed—whether Ariel wanted him there or not; it was his responsibility to see she made it home okay. Ayerstown might seem like a sleepy suburb when compared to some of the larger cities like Plaxton and Richland an hour's drive away, but it still experienced crime. And no man would leave his woman—or any woman—unprotected to walk home in the evening.

If he disregarded the tough facade Ariel projected, she was still nearly a foot shorter than him and could easily be overpowered. "Don't jump to insane conclusions all because she forgot to set the alarm," Dane argued in a whisper. "Considering the steam rolling off of her when I left last night, I wouldn't be surprised if she forgot to lock the doors."

Which didn't bode well for the leather jacket he'd left behind in his haste the evening before. The car coat was one of his favorites, and he'd been over halfway home when he remembered it was draped over the back of the sofa in Alayna's office.

"I wouldn't put it past her to stuff the pockets with some of the contents of the composting bin." An organic farm that supplied a great deal of Ariel's fresh fruits and vegetables used chemical-free compost for fertilization and offered discounts to companies that provided food waste materials. Ariel was nothing if not efficient in collecting leftover raw and cooked foods to send to the farm.

Retribution would be required if Ariel had stooped to such a petty revenge. Dane grinned as he visualized the punishment he'd mete out. Clamps for her plump little nipples, leather cuffs for her ankles and wrists, and a long, sweaty session on the St. Andrew's cross in Room Seven at the mansion. One lash for every pithy word she'd uttered in the last four days since he had spanked her. His jeans pulled tight over his growing erection at the thought of how pink and warm her ass would be when he finished with the flogger.

With his mind bounding between what vicious revenge she might take out on his coat and how badly he'd like to teach her to enjoy surrendering to him, it took a moment for the sounds coming from the office to register. Once they did, Dane paused in the hall. Were he in the mansion, where it was possible to run across random sexual encounters, the noises filtering out into the hall would have made sense. But the throaty moans and the *creak* of leather against leather baffled Dane.

He closed his eyes and visualized the office as he'd left it the day before.

The desk took up the majority of the space. It faced the door and butted up against the wall on the right with the battered chair tucked under it and two four-drawer filing cabinets in the corner. A narrow table was snug against the filing cabinets and held the requisite all-in-one copier/fax/printer, postage machine, and a coffeepot. Built-in bookshelves covered the rest of the back wall, while a beat-up leather sofa and solid oak coffee and end tables occupied what remained of the floor space. A ladder-back chair faced the desk and a flat-screen television was mounted on the wall to the left of the door. Other than the possibility of someone watching adult movies, Dane couldn't believe what he was hearing.

If Logan had slipped in on Alayna in the office, Dane could imagine a little hot-and-heavy petting going on, but

Dane had seen them at the estate a half an hour ago, sound asleep in Logan's bedroom—Alayna in the bed and Logan in a chair nearby. Hell, the sun had barely crested the horizon when he'd pulled his car into a parking space along the street in front of the café.

He kept his footsteps quiet on the hallway's tiled floor, reached the open door, and looked in. Ariel occupied the sofa, with his leather jacket wrapped around her. One hand caressed her body, while the other rocked against her sex. Squeezing his eyes shut, he smothered the surprised curse that tried to escape his lips. He so didn't need this on top of all the shit he had to deal with at home, but he opened his eyes, wanting to look again.

God, she looked good. He had wondered if the ivory skin of her face covered her entire body. Now he knew it did. It was arousing to see how smooth it was, especially in contrast to the black of his coat, the only clothing covering her as she sprawled across the cushions of the sofa. The wet slide and low hum of a vibrator competed with her raspy breaths. The length of his coat hid the juncture of her thighs, but the soft, full mounds of her breasts were visible. One tiny hand—the nails short, but neatly trimmed and clean—palpated a pink-tipped globe before she gripped the taut peak and tugged on it.

"Yes, oh yes, Dane. There, please."

His erection throbbed in response to the sound of her throaty voice calling his name, and satisfaction spread through his chest. Both his hands gripped the door frame until his knuckles showed white, but he forced himself to watch her. The commands and soft pleas for release that whispered through the room could barely be heard as she rocked the vibrator in and out of her wet cunt. Fast, then slow—she didn't seem to know which rhythm worked best. Her hips arched, and her head pressed deep into the cushion, but he could tell climax eluded her.

Your clit, he wanted to tell her. *Forget the fucking nipple and play with your clit, Ariel.* But she couldn't hear his thoughts, and he wasn't about to shatter the scene by speaking aloud. Frustration throbbed through her voice. Dane wondered if the ancient piece of furniture would withstand the press of her bare feet against its arm. She must have spent an extended period of time trying to reach climax, because her body glistened with sweat. Her thighs were coated with her juices, which had probably stained the lining of his coat, but her body fought her efforts. Finally, with her limbs shaking with exhaustion and not climax, she stiffened, then dropped onto the cushions and was still.

"Damn it, damn it, damn it." Her voice was a scratchy croak; her disappointment was evident as she pulled the vibrator from her body, switched it off, and then let it slip to the floor. She curled onto her side, facing the back of the sofa, pulled her knees to her chest, and tugged the coat tighter around her. "Shit. Fucking useless."

Dane eased his hold on the doorway. His gaze stayed locked on Ariel's body as her muttered curses dwindled to soft snores.

Maybe Alayna wasn't the only Valerian who required assistance. Despite her rigid refusal to bend, Ariel had the capacity for explosive sexual power. He had read the intensity in her every motion. In the same way he recognized the submissive in her older sister, Dane knew Ariel carried a depth of passion as yet untapped. Whether as a submissive or a dominatrix, he was still unsure, but he was intrigued about finding a way to unleash that part of her.

Careful to make no noise, Dane moved to stand over the sofa, looking down at her sweat-dampened face, her cheeks still flushed with arousal. A tiny shiver trembled through her, and she curled even more tightly toward the back of the sofa. From the other end of the couch, he pulled a soft blanket and cautiously eased it over her, taking care not to wake her.

The toe of his sneaker bumped something as he started to turn away. Crouching, he grinned at the blue vibrator he picked up. A paper bag, an open package of batteries, and a small bottle of lube rested near the corner of the sofa. He left the other items on the table, carried the toy into the bathroom, and quietly cleaned it before tucking it into his jacket pocket. After returning to the office, he watched Ariel cuddle the edge of the blanket beneath her chin.

It wouldn't work to isolate Ariel at the estate for a month. The food she created reflected her passion, her intensity; every emotion affected Ariel at the moment of culinary conception. Attempts to get her to channel that focus into arousing her body would be a challenge. Once out of the office, he made his way down the hall and then set the alarm against intruders. With the locks on the café's doors secured, he headed for his car. Dane's mind spun with ideas—images of Ariel's body arched beneath him, her wet pussy snug around his cock, her bright green eyes dazed and slumberous with satisfaction as he pulled climax after climax from her body.

"Taming her?" he wondered aloud, then shook his head. "Training, not taming—that's what she needs," Dane determined. He pulled away from the curb and headed for one of the fast-food restaurants around the block. A plan was in order. He smiled. "A very special plan. Something to get her hackles up and make her lose her temper enough to agree before she realizes what she's done."

He wouldn't return to Valerian's Root today. It was necessary that he take time to plot, but tomorrow… "Oh yes, tomorrow." His smile grew wider as he patted the toy weighing down his pocket.

* * *

Day 8

The next day Dane watched Ariel as she wiped down the counter. The force she used to rub the rag over the creamy tiles produced a *squeak*. She'd ordered him about all day; it had kept him from completing the paperwork he'd begun in the office earlier, and entertained the customers crowding the tables. He'd already counted down the till and written up the deposit. He waited for her to finish a few cleaning duties before they left to drop off the money at the bank. It wouldn't make much of a difference to his plans.

"You really don't have to stick around," she told him.

Before he could answer, the glass on the front entrance rattled under the pounding knuckles of a man who hovered outside. The sun had begun to set and cast a bright light through the clear panels, making the polished wood floors gleam. Dane slid off the stool and crossed to the door.

"Where's Ariel?" the man demanded as he attempted to push his way inside.

"The café is closed. Perhaps you can come back—"

"Hey, Ariel!" he shouted past Dane. The bag the guy held in his left hand rattled—bottles clinked together. The scent of liquor wafted closer as he stepped forward.

"Jimmy?"

Dane looked over his shoulder at Ariel's exclamation. That allowed the man to push past Dane into the café.

"Babe, I heard your sister was out of town—"

Dane closed and locked the door and then took his time as his gaze followed Jimmy to the counter. Dane leaned against the wall and assessed the newcomer. The baggy khaki Bermuda shorts, short-sleeved, oversize T-shirt, and brown hiking boots revealed intricate tattooed designs on both arms and legs. The various colored images depicted mythological and fantastical creatures.

"So? Why are you here? I told you it was over." Ariel slapped the counter with the rag.

"I thought you might like some company with your sister gone." Jimmy grinned and hefted the bag, oblivious to her irritation. "We could call some of my buds and have a little party."

"At my house?" Ariel strode around the counter, shaking her head. "No way." She gripped his shoulder and turned him toward the front entrance. "Why would I let you and those slobs you call friends into my home? I showed you the exit six months ago."

"Come on, baby. You didn't mean it. You've gotta be lonely—"

"Don't 'baby' me." She shoved at his back, ushered him across the room, grumbling the entire time. "If I were feeling lonely, I sure as hell wouldn't call you. Damn it, Jimmy, if I'd wanted you when we were dating, I'd've slept with you then."

Jimmy stumbled forward under her urging and put up little resistance. His expression changed as he spotted Dane against the wall next to the door. "Are you bangin' the suit?"

Dane shifted away from the wall. His arms dropped from where he'd crossed them over his chest. Up until that moment, the incident had only been an amusing glimpse into Ariel's behavior toward another man. Now, if he read Jimmy's expression correctly, the little scene could escalate into something unpleasant.

"It's none of your damned business, Jimmy." Ariel shoved him closer to the door.

Jimmy swung around and planted his feet. Standing in profile, Dane could see the scowl twisting the younger man's features as he glared down at Ariel. "I'd like to know if someone else is getting a taste of what you wouldn't give me."

"Like I would tell you? Get real." Ariel propped her fists on her generous hips. "I didn't want you six months ago, and I still don't want you. Accept it and go away."

Jimmy's voice became a whine. "But, Ariel—"

Ariel covered her eyes with one hand and drew in a deep breath. Wiping her hand down her face, she pointed toward the door with one hand and pushed at his shoulder with the other. "Just accept it's over, Jimmy, and go. I don't want to party. I don't want to talk. I. Don't. Want. You."

The tension in Dane's body eased. The slump of Jimmy's shoulders and the sullen pout on his face as he turned toward the door were all the indication necessary for Dane to know Jimmy would pose no threat, intoxicated as he was, to himself or Ariel.

"You're an icy bitch, Ariel," Jimmy muttered as he headed toward the door Dane held open for him.

"Yeah. And you're a spineless prick," Ariel shot back as she turned away and walked back to the rag she'd left on the counter.

There was a moment when Dane wasn't sure if he'd have to assist Jimmy in exiting or if the man would leave on his own. It passed, and with more grumbled curses in the vein of sour grapes, Jimmy strode out of the café and headed toward a green sedan parked on the street out front.

After twisting the lock on the door, Dane ambled back to the stool he'd occupied before Jimmy showed up. Perhaps now would be a good time to lay the groundwork for the idea he'd mulled over since he walked in on her in the office the previous morning.

"So that's your ex?"

Ariel didn't respond but sent him a fulminating look. Dane didn't let his grin slip free; instead he continued to seek more clues about the vixen before him.

"You broke it off?"

"Yes."

"He seems like a...colorful character," Dane prompted.

"You mean the tats?" Ariel paused and met his gaze.

"Yes. He doesn't seem like the kind of person you'd be drawn to."

"Are you wondering how I met him?" Ariel grinned. She propped her forearms on the counter and leaned toward him.

The sight of her breasts momentarily drew his attention. It was hard for him not to look, but he pulled his gaze from the sweet, creamy cleavage exposed by her teal tank top. "Yes, I have to wonder. I've never seen him patronizing the café."

Ariel bobbed her eyebrows. The grin on her full lips grew wide and wicked. "He's a tattoo artist. I met him when I was leaving the Ink Well."

"The tattoo parlor on Hillcrest?" His mind spun with the image of some kind of art decorating a patch of her ivory flesh. His body responded to the fantasy of investigating every inch of her skin to find the inked design. And perhaps commanding her to permanently etch his brand onto her body.

"Yup. Grieg does some great work."

Dane nodded and shifted his position on the seat to ease the ache in his groin. "I've seen some of his art. In fact, he did some graphic-design work for the consulting business Logan and I own." He didn't mention the kanji characters marking the insides of both his wrists. He'd wait to see if she asked about them; he knew she had seen them the third day he'd come into the café. "Were you there looking into getting a tattoo?"

"No, Grieg was finishing up the work on mine when Jimmy showed up."

Dane trailed his gaze from her face to her waist, where the counter cut off his view. "You have ink? Where?"

She winked at him and grinned. "I'll never tell." Her gaze dropped to his exposed wrists. "Grieg did yours?"

"Yes. So Jimmy works for Grieg?" He wouldn't push to find out what her tattoo was. Not yet. The *where* he was sure to learn soon…

Ariel nodded and pushed away from the counter. "He seemed pretty cool when I first met him, but it got boring after a while."

"What got boring?"

"All he was interested in was getting drunk and sex. Usually at the same time." Ariel chuckled. "Not my idea of fun."

"Have all your boyfriends been like Jimmy?"

She carefully folded the rag and set it on the tiled counter. Ariel tilted her head to the side as if trying to identify some verbal trap awaiting her. "What do you mean 'like Jimmy'?"

"I mean men who let you make all the decisions and direct what will or won't happen? Who don't argue with you about the direction of the relationship?" He didn't have to hear her response to know the answer was yes. The way her body stiffened and her shoulders went back told him what he suspected was true.

"So I'm not a doormat to every man who comes along." She sounded almost defensive. "Do you have a problem with strong women?"

"No, I feel every person—man or woman—has the right to stand up for themselves. In a relationship, those involved should be full partners, with neither one assuming full control."

Ariel tossed the cloth into the bin of towels to go in the laundry. "That sounds pretty strange coming from you."

Dane shrugged and folded his arms on the counter. "Why? Do you think because I'm a man I expect the women I'm involved with to do whatever I say?"

"Well, yeah." Ariel propped her forearms on the counter and leaned toward him again. "I mean, you are a dominant, and you train other men to be dominants as well."

"Yes, I'm a dominant, but it doesn't mean I don't respect a person's right to refuse a request, Ariel." He motioned toward her. "You seem to be under the impression that you have what it takes to be a Domme, considering how easily you control the men in your life."

She pushed away from the counter and glared at him. "Now wait a minute. I never said I was a Domme."

"But you never let anyone take charge."

"Alayna—"

"Is the financial manager of Valerian's Root. She freely admits you're the culinary genius, and she doesn't begrudge you that distinction," Dane assured her.

"I know that, but you're making it seem—"

"I'm only telling you what I've observed." He waited for her to take the bait. Since he'd learned in the last week how prickly she was about being in charge, Dane decided it wasn't likely she'd pass up the challenge he was contemplating.

"And you think, based on what little you've seen, that I'm a Domme?"

There's the first nibble. Don't try to set the hook yet. Dane shook his head. "No, I said you're under the impression you've got what it takes to be a Domme."

"You don't think I have the ability?"

Almost there. He shrugged. "It's possible, with the right amount of training and the right submissive, you could pull it off—"

"But you don't think I can, huh?"

Another nibble, this time a little harder. The light of battle brightened her eyes, the flush on her cheeks identified her increased irritation, and the jut of her stiff nipples against the teal tank top betrayed how aroused she was at his challenge. *Patience. Let her get closer.* Dane shrugged again. "I'm only giving you my opinion."

"And it's bullshit," Ariel snapped. She rounded the counter and stepped in front of him. "If I wanted to become a dominatrix, I could do it like that." She snapped her fingers near his face and glared at him.

"With the boys you've selected as lovers, that's not in question." Dane nodded. *Come on, Tinker Bell. Get pissed.*

"Boys? You think I can't take on a man?"

A little more. "Some men, perhaps—"

"But not a *real* man? You mean like you?" Her disparaging tone seemed to imply her doubt in his masculinity.

"I mean you seem to think you'll find more satisfaction in giving directions than in taking them." Dane kept his body as still as possible, predator to her prey, not stirring, waiting for the trap she approached to spring so he could pounce.

If there was one thing he had grown to appreciate, it was the varied facial expressions that betrayed her moods and reactions. The rolling of her eyes at his words only reinforced his belief that she would step into the cage he was constructing without even being aware of the danger.

After watching her attempts to pleasure herself the day before, Dane had imagined innumerable scenarios that would allow him to push her beyond the constricted boundaries she kept on her sexuality. From what he knew about her and her sister's past, it didn't surprise him that Ariel—though more outwardly flamboyant than her sister—carried the same tight control on her body as Alayna did. Yesterday's performance confirmed the suspicion he had that Ariel dealt with the same difficulty to climax as her sister. A few more steps and he'd have her in a situation that would give him the answers to the questions that swirled in his mind.

"Excuse me?" She stepped closer. "Would you mind repeating that?"

"I said you seem to think you'll find more satisfaction in giving directions rather than taking them." Dane shifted. Even with him seated, the top of Ariel's head barely reached his chin.

"Damn straight I do." She smirked up at him. "When it comes to orgasms, I know what to do and when to do it, and I'm not afraid to make sure my men know that."

Another tug on the bait. "Ah"—Dane nodded—"but have you ever let someone else take the lead?"

She shook her head. "No, why should I, when I do just fine on my own?"

Liar. "I understand if you're afraid—"

Arms crossed over her breasts, she spluttered, "Afraid?"

"It's nothing to be ashamed of, Ariel." He injected what he hoped was the right note of condescension in his voice. "I've dealt with any number of clients whose fears have—"

"I'm not afraid. Why should I be?" She waved off his explanation.

"You don't think a man can bring you to climax if he's the one in control." Dane eased closer to the edge of his seat, careful not to startle Ariel into withdrawal.

"If I'm anything, it's skeptical of some guy who thinks he knows my body better than I do."

"Are you sure you're not the least bit scared—"

"No. There isn't a man I'd be afraid to face to prove who's better at my sexual satisfaction."

"Even me?"

"Especially you." Ariel snorted. "In fact, you'd make an excellent pet once I got you broken in right."

Snap. Hook set; fish on! "Prove it." Dane watched the confidence flare in her eyes and then submerge beneath disbelief as she seemed to realize what she'd set herself up for. Before she could wheedle her way out of the challenge, he grinned.

Her tongue peeked out to moisten her lips. "How?"

Dane stayed seated, despite the urge to rise to his feet. Any attempt to tower over her would only irritate her; he'd learned that much in the last week. "There are three weeks left before your sister returns from the mansion."

"I know."

"I suggest we run a little experiment to see who's better at satisfying you sexually."

Her throat flexed as she swallowed, but her gaze stayed focused on him. "Sounds interesting."

Dane couldn't stop the grin her response brought to his lips. She was determined to hide the panic he could read in her eyes. The rapid pulse visible in the skin at the base of her throat was also a dead giveaway. "You seem so convinced your directions bring you the greatest satisfaction, but I think you might find more fulfillment in being directed."

"What do you have in mind? Both of us taking turns?"

"In a manner of speaking." He motioned toward the kitchen. "I freely admit your superiority in the kitchen. And I think you would have to admit my skills with the paperwork and financial organization are exceptional."

Suspicion darkened her green eyes. "To a certain extent, yes, I admit you know what you're doing in the office."

"Then I submit we agree to allow each other control in our respective arenas," Dane offered.

"Are you suggesting we carry out your experiment here? In Valerian's Root?"

Dane nodded. "I'm the boss in the office—"

"And I'm the boss in the kitchen?"

"Exactly."

She seemed to mull over the suggestion. Looking around at the darkened café, Ariel motioned to the empty tables. "And here, in the main dining area, who's the boss out here?"

"No one. This would be neutral territory. Ground available for open discussion and requests from either party to test one another with a specific task or action." He'd been careful to consider all possibilities. "And right of refusal is allowed in this area only."

She stiffened and took a half step back. "Are you saying refusal isn't allowed anywhere else?"

"That's correct. Right of refusal is not permitted in the kitchen or office, unless what is being asked is likely to cause physical harm to someone."

"But no sex, right?" Ariel clarified.

Dane shook his head. "Oh there'll be sex, Ariel. How else are we to determine which makes your orgasms more intense?" Rising from the chair, he crowded her up against the counter, making sure the thick length of his aroused cock pressed into her soft belly. "It's essential we discover if manual stimulation, the use of toys, or a hard cock riding you creates the best results."

"But—" Her expression was a mixture of arousal and confusion. Reactions conflicted with yearning in her bright green gaze. Color flooded her cheeks. Her fingers clutched the counter behind her as if she didn't trust herself to touch him or fought to hold herself away from temptation.

Dane chose to intentionally misunderstand her protest. "Oh yes, let's not forget this sweet, round ass." He slid one hand down to cup her bottom. "We'll find the right plug to get you stretched out, and then we'll see how you respond to anal play."

As close as he was to her, he felt the shudder ripple through her body. He doubted she even realized her hips pushed upward, rubbing against him. It took all his control not to rock forward and press his dick closer. There'd be time enough over the next three weeks to discover how hot, wet, and tight her pussy would feel around him, but right now he merely needed her to agree to his rules.

"I didn't mean—" Ariel's hands released the lip of the counter to press at his chest. "Okay, uhmm…" Her fingers splayed over his upper chest and began to stroke instead of push, stirring the heat and excitement building inside him.

"Okay?" He leaned closer, bending his knees slightly to meet her gaze directly, but more importantly to realign his body with hers. In no way would he give up on the advantage he currently held with her body aroused by his close proximity. "You agree?"

Her expression was a mixture of reluctance and awakened desire, but she nodded. "Yes. I-I agree."

Fighting the protests of his body, Dane stepped back. "Good. Now shall we go?"

"Go? Go where?"

Dane held up the bank deposit bag. "The bank. I want to get this dropped off before I head home. There's a Red Sox game on, and I don't want to miss it."

"But—I—What about—"

Dane suppressed the urge to laugh. Her confusion only made the challenge more interesting. "But what?"

Ariel drew a deep breath and shook her head. "Never mind."

Ah this is going to be fun. Dane led Ariel out the door, his smile of satisfaction carefully hidden from her.

Chapter Five

Day 9

Dane hadn't even made it into the office before she ambushed him the next day. Ariel blocked the hallway, fists perched on her hips. One foot tapped the floor as if measuring off the time before she struck. "You completely ignored my order."

Conversation and eating stopped as the few customers in the dining room turned their attention toward Dane and the blue-haired harpy he faced.

Her neatly buttoned chef's coat hid the impressive bosom that had featured prominently in his dreams the night before.

A soft snicker of amusement came from the register, where Sadie collected payment from a customer.

This on top of the shit Logan was pulling at the mansion made Dane wonder for a moment how much he wanted Ariel. But the slow hardening of his body functioned as a visceral reminder of what had prompted his plan in the first place. His tone cool, he told her, "I haven't set foot in your kitchen in days, Ariel, so there've been no orders for me to ignore."

"I'm not talking sex here, Dane."

A choked cough sounded from the booth near the door.

"We haven't had sex yet—" he said.

The glare Ariel sent DeeDee quickly smothered the waitress's giggle. "And we won't." Her tone was firm, but Dane detected a hint of indecisiveness in it.

A few others around the room echoed Sadie's snort of disbelief. Ariel's glance around the dining room and at the customers seemed almost fearful. Her feet shifted, and her arms crossed over her chest. Color rose in her cheeks the longer the people around them watched her.

Dane didn't bother arguing with her; instead he mentally tucked away the clues Ariel's behavior revealed to him. Could his pixie be shy? Her reaction to the customers' attention hinted at a discomfort he hadn't seen from her before. His cock shifted, reinforcing how attracted he was to this woman. Despite her prickly nature, bossy mouth, and refusal to free her submissive nature to his control, the daily challenge of dealing with Ariel provided stimulation he'd rarely encountered outside the mansion's walls. Pushing back the edges of his suit jacket, he tucked his hands into his pockets. "If we aren't talking sex, then what order did I ignore?"

"The chocolate."

The hum of conversation picked up around them once again as the diners returned to their lunches.

He shook his head. "I ordered the chocolate four days ago. The supplier said it would be here today or tomorrow."

"It showed up."

"If it showed up, then what's the problem? I got what you asked for."

"Bullshit. I told you specifically to get couverture," she snapped, her voice audible over the quiet hum of conversations and the *clink* of silverware against china.

Heads turned and several sets of eyebrows rose on surprised faces. If she didn't acknowledge the curious faces around them, neither would he.

"I ordered—"

Ariel stepped closer. Her right hand rose to poke at his chest. "You ordered *baking* chocolate," she accused in a disgusted tone.

The jabs from her finger didn't bother him as he tried to understand what the problem with the chocolate was. "So? Chocolate is chocolate." Dane continued to ignore their audience.

The heat in her cheeks no longer seemed to come from any embarrassment at creating a public spectacle. The flash of fire in her gaze, the way her lips compressed into a tight, thin line, and even the way the knuckles whitened on the clenched hand she wasn't poking him with communicated her increased irritation. It appeared her anger overrode her discomfort at being on display. "Oh, and which culinary institute did you graduate from? How many hours have you spent in a kitchen? Do you even know the difference between couverture, baking chocolate, and cocoa?"

"Like I said, chocolate is chocolate." His expression must have reflected his disinterest in her lecture, because her fervent explanation halted. The digit she'd poked into his chest along with the rest of the fingers wrapped around his burgundy silk tie and yanked his face closer to hers.

Snickers and some barks of strangled laughter erupted behind him.

"Lesson time, *Master* Reese." Without releasing her hold on his tie, she strode around the counter, through the swinging doors, and into the kitchen, pulling him along by the improvised hundred-and-twenty-dollar silk leash. A few chairs scraped across the polished wood floors, but the doors stayed closed behind him. Dane assumed DeeDee and Sadie would keep the curious customers at bay.

He followed, more interested in the fire and passion Ariel displayed over a supply order than any damage she might inflict on his designer accessory. They bypassed the prep station, grill, and industrial double ovens.

The section of the kitchen she dragged him to was new territory. Situated in a far corner, it was out of sight of any observer who might look through the doors or over the order window. A slab of gray-veined white marble topped the central island. A smaller double oven gleamed with the same brushed-nickel doors as the double-sided freezer along one wall. A stove top with two burners on one side and a flat griddle on the other made him suspect this was where she created the decadent cheesecakes and delicious desserts that filled the small glass display case near the register.

"And what do you think you can teach me, *Chef* Valerian?" Hips resting against counter, he smoothed the wrinkles from his tie as she pulled open cabinets and collected two tins and a box.

He looked too damned smug grinning back at her. Even a confrontation before a room full of strangers didn't faze him. It didn't take a genius to figure out he was dangerous for her. The temptation to sniff whenever he got close, to inhale the subtle blend of spices that clung to him, had Ariel constantly on alert to keep from acting like a bitch in heat. If he even suspected how turned on she got when she was within a few feet of him, there would be no stopping his natural inclination to dominate. Worse, she doubted she'd mind if she let him take control. Damn that fucking agreement she'd made. After twenty-four hours, her body still had yet to settle down since he'd conned her into their little challenge.

Worrisome thoughts aside, she put the box and tins on the counter next to him, every second fighting the urge to rub up against his solid frame. She could feel the burn of his blue eyes on her neck as she sprinkled cocoa from the first tin onto the marble surface. From the box, she shaved off a curl from one of the brown-black squares and set it on the cool stone. From the second tin, she broke off a small chunk of the tempered chocolate and set it beside the other types of chocolate. The everyday sounds of activity and chatter from the dining room created a soft background noise.

“Lesson number one, Dane: don't order the wrong products.”

He didn't bother to respond, but the amusement in his gaze seemed to mock her determination for him to understand.

Fine, she decided. If he wanted a demonstration, he'd get one. Holding his gaze, she sucked her right index finger into her mouth and wet it from the tip to the second knuckle with her tongue. She pulled it out and rolled it through the cocoa powder on the counter, coating her skin thoroughly before she stepped close and lifted it in front of Dane's lips. "Open up," she ordered.

Still watching her, he separated his lips and allowed her to stick her finger inside his mouth. Her intention merely to wipe her finger over his tongue to let him taste the cocoa was quickly derailed when he closed his lips around her finger and suckled the tip. The warm clasp of his fingers surrounded her wrist as he held her hand still and prevented her from pulling away. The rasp of his tongue over and around the captured digit stole her breath. Warmth pooled in her center, going south to stir the pleasure spot between her thighs before spreading upward into her breasts so the tips grew firm; her throbbing nipples pressed against the silk cups of her bra. Around her hip, she could feel the heat of his other hand as he tugged her closer to him. The firm jut of his cock pressed into her belly.

Ariel forced down the desire that surged through her body, and pulled free. The pad of her finger scraped against the edge of his bottom teeth, and she tried to ignore the caress of his fingers over the palm of her hand as he released her wrist. She didn't step back. The fact he was as aroused as she could work to her advantage.

"Mmmm. Cocoa, right?" Dane whispered.

"Yes."

Ignoring the tremor in her fingers, she picked up the curl of dark baking chocolate. She didn't have to say a word as she lifted it to his mouth. He opened, and she popped the morsel inside, then waited.

The grimace he made wasn't unexpected. Not many people liked the flavor of unsweetened chocolate.

"Yuck." He choked and swallowed several times as he tried to get rid of the taste.

"Unsweetened baking chocolate."

"I get the unsweetened part." Dane turned to eye the last bit of sweet on the counter before he reached over and picked it up.

"Eat it," she told him as she stepped out of his hold and crossed her arms over her breasts.

Cautiously he lifted it to his nose and sniffed before he put it in his mouth. A hum of appreciation rumbled through his chest as his lips lifted in a grin. "Mmm, milk chocolate."

Ariel shook her head. "No, that's couverture."

"It's good, but if you add a little more sugar to the recipe, the baking chocolate should be fine," he offered.

Ariel saw red. "Do you know anything about the science of cooking?"

Dane shrugged, his expression unconcerned. "No, but what's the difference between the types of chocolate I ordered? Albeit the unsweetened stuff would take some—"

"God, you are such a guy!" Ariel stepped forward, shoved aside his jacket, and made short work of his belt before she unfastened and unzipped his pants. "Since you obviously aren't thinking with your big head, perhaps you'll understand this more."

She didn't stop to think as she released the heated length of his cock from his underwear. The feel of it in her hands sent her heartbeat tripping. Determined not to show weakness and to get her point across, she stroked the thick column of flesh, marveling at the soft texture of the skin, the golden brown color that matched the tanned skin on his arms, hands, and face, and the fact that her fingers didn't touch when they wrapped around it.

"What the hell are you—"

She ignored Dane's protest and the grip of his hands on her shoulders. On her knees, she wet her lips and then took the plum-shaped head inside her mouth.

"Oh Christ." Dane's groan was so low, it was barely audible in the quiet kitchen.

Ariel's focus shifted. The salty-sweet taste of him intrigued her. She took her time, slipped her hand down the throbbing stalk, and swirled her tongue over the rounded crown. The grasp of his hands shifted from her shoulders to her head as she took more of him into her mouth. Pulling back, she looked up at him and reveled in the stunned expression on his face.

"Hands out of my hair, Reese." She reached her free hand up to push his away.

Slowly he settled his grip onto the counter at his hips. All the while he kept his gaze on her. The wary look in his eyes imbued her with a sense of power. That she satisfied her curiosity and would sate the arousal building in her body at the same time she taught him a lesson only made the event that much sweeter. Ariel lowered her head back to his cock and lapped at the pearly bead of cum welling in the slit. The flavor was interesting, not like the taste of the boyfriend she'd practiced on years ago. Dane's clean, musky scent filled her nostrils as she swallowed as much of his length as possible. She made sure to keep the grip of her fingers firm over the part she couldn't take; each stroke up and back matched the pull of her mouth as she suckled.

The fingers of her free hand wiggled into the confines of his silk boxers to cuddle the heated sac of his balls. Above her, Dane groaned and cursed in tandem to the pull and release of her fingers and mouth. The tension in his body increased as she pressed her tongue against and around his flesh, laving and tasting the tiny pulsing veins and sensitive crest. Drops of saliva escaped her lips to roll down the length of his cock; each aided in lubrication as her hand stroked along his skin.

Her body ached for release: the tips of her nipples scraped against the bra cups covering them, her panties were wet, and she was on the edge of climax from the rub of the seam of her jeans along her sensitive clit. She had to stop, but knowing that was easier than actually doing it, Ariel realized as she sensed Dane's climax drawing near.

The lesson, she reminded herself. He must learn the lesson. Her body protested as she released his dick with a loud *pop* and pushed herself to her feet. Stepping away, she met his confused gaze, wiped her mouth, and drew a deep breath. “There's your lesson, Dane.”

He shook his head; his chest heaved as he fought to keep upright. The knuckles on his hands were white with the strength of his grip on the counter. “What?”

Ariel fought the urge to grin. Dane might try to act like nothing had happened, but the slight break in his voice and his ragged breathing when he uttered the single word assured her she'd made an impression. "Chocolate is like a blowjob. Couverture would swallow. With unsweetened baking chocolate, you've gotta finish the job yourself. Now get the fuck out of my kitchen." She gathered the box and tins from the counter and moved on unsteady legs to the cabinet to put them away.

The blood pounding in her ears drowned out all but the slightest sound of a zipper along its track and Dane's soft curses as he strode out of the kitchen. One deep breath followed another, and she looked over her shoulder toward the sound of the door to the hall swinging shut, then sank to the floor. "I am so fucked." If he ever figured out the hold he had on her, she'd never survive.

A shudder snaked through her body. Ariel couldn't help the chuckle that rolled out of her chest. "But what a way to go," she admitted and dropped her head back against the cabinets. "What a wonderfully wet way to go."

* * *

It had been years since Dane had felt the necessity to jack off, but he refused to do it, even as he grimaced while lowering himself into the desk chair. Her little lesson had shown him a few things about his sexy nemesis. First, she wasn't afraid to make the first move. He winced as a caster bumped over an uneven lump in the carpet, the jarring particularly intense in the hard flesh pressed against the zipper of his slacks.

Second, her mouth was good at more than offering up snippy comments and cutting remarks. He shifted in his seat at the remembered suction and heat she'd applied to his flesh. She would be a tough one to handle, but he'd seen the yearning blazing in her eyes before she'd turned away. He hadn't been the only one left unsatisfied by Ariel's impromptu chocolate experiment.

Perhaps that was the way to best her. Dane considered how stubborn she was about the slightest alteration. Alayna had warned him Ariel didn't accept change well. A result of the sudden loss of their parents when Ariel was on the cusp of becoming an independent woman, he assumed.

Her misperceptions about his approach to Dominant/submissive relationships would take some correcting, which Dane doubted Ariel would be open to hearing. If it didn't suit her interpretation, she didn't seem inclined to amend her opinion. *Stubborn as a mule*, his granddaddy would say. But then again, Dane smiled at the task before him; he'd never found as much pleasure in dealing with training a sub as when he was faced with one who refused to recognize that part of themselves.

But there was another problem he faced, Dane admitted as he booted up the computer and accessed the invoices he'd scanned in earlier in the week. On the desk were two new ones that had arrived with the shipments dropped off earlier today or the previous day. Phone in hand, he punched out the numbers and waited for someone to pick up.

“Dane Reese for John Tobler, please,” he responded when the cheerful voice on the other end asked his name and to whom he wished to speak.

“One moment, sir.” The soft music floated through the handset as he ticked off the items on the shipping invoice and compared them to the electronic invoice he'd been e-mailed when the order was made.

“John Tobler.” The jovial tone didn't stem the irritation Dane felt as he identified the altered information on the documents in front of him.

“John, Dane Reese from Valerian's Root.” He kept his voice cool, professional. No need to give anything away. Yet.

“Mr. Reese, how can I help you? The shipment arrived on time, I hope?”

“It did, but there seems to be an error on your end.” Dane leaned back in his chair, hoping to ease the choke hold his trousers had on his cock.

“Error?”

Dane could swear he heard a warble of unease in Tobler's voice. Maybe Dane would have to take a look at past invoices from the company. For right now, though, with his cock stiff as a post and no relief in sight, he'd focus on fixing the situation that prompted Ariel's little lesson. “Yes, it seems unsweetened baking chocolate was substituted for the couverture I ordered.”

“That's hard to—”

“I have the invoices in front of me, John. I specifically requested couverture when I ordered the various chocolates for Miss Valerian's kitchen. Now you and I both know there is a distinct difference between couverture and baking chocolate.” Dane let a hint of disgust filter into his tone.

It resulted in the response he had expected from Tobler. "I do apologize, Mr. Reese. It must have been an error—"

"An error? I've looked at the invoices, John. You charged me for couverture and substituted baking chocolate instead." Setting the papers down on the desk, Dane carefully leaned forward and grimaced at the protest his hard dick made to the shift in position. He wondered how tongue-tied the other man would get if Dane pushed his suspicions that this wasn't the first time an error had occurred, but he'd hold off. For now. "What I want to know is when can I expect the issue to be corrected?"

John gabbled, hemmed, and hawed for several seconds as Dane clicked through an assortment of invoices. A file in one section held several documents from Tobler's company. Perhaps Alayna had noticed issues as well.

"I have a deadline, John. Miss Valerian has several dishes she's scheduled for specific days, and that couverture is essential."

"I can see about shipping it out immediately, but we'd have to charge—"

Dane's gaze narrowed as he opened the file and the invoices inside. Comments and notes were typed or handwritten on the scanned pages. "I don't think so, John. It wasn't our error that caused this particular issue, and I won't have the Valerian's Root charged for the incompetence of your staff."

"I'm sure it was a simple mistake, but the cost of expressing out the items to you must be paid—"

The chuckle that came out of Dane's mouth had nothing to do with amusement. The man on the other end of the phone seemed to realize that as he fell silent. “Let me put it in a language you can better understand. Don't fuck with me. Don't fuck with the Valerian sisters. I don't know where the error occurred, but your company will fix it. Understood?”

“You don't need to use that sort of language, Mr. Reese. I have admitted a mistake was made. More than likely one of our newer employees didn't read the order correctly. I'll see if we can get the couverture to you by the beginning of next week.”

“Not good enough. I'll expect it by the day after tomorrow.”

“I am sorry, but that won't be—”

“Don't apologize, and don't make excuses. When I order something, that's what I expect, not some piddling-ass lie about a mix-up or new workers,” Dane snarled. “I will expect the couverture to be delivered the day after tomorrow. If it isn't here, John, I'll be contacting your manager to find out why I don't have it. Do I make myself clear?”

A heavy pause sounded on the other end of the line. “Perfectly, Mr. Reese. Your order will be delivered by Thursday, per your request.”

“Thank you, Mr. Tobler. Have a good day.”

“And you, sir.”

The fact that Tobler's tone was in direct opposition to his words wasn't lost on Dane as he cradled the phone. His hard-on had eased enough that it no longer tented his trousers, and Dane could sit more comfortably in his chair.

Admittedly he didn't like being a whipping boy for someone else's fuckup. But when he considered the method of punishment inflicted—Dane grinned, and his hand dropped to stroke over the lessening firmness of his cock—it had been well worth it. He gazed out the office door toward the door that led into the kitchen. Through the round glass window near the top, he spotted Ariel prowling around her domain.

"Battle one to you, my pixie. Let's see who wins this war."

Chapter Six

Day 11

Ariel looked up and down the hall before she pushed open the office door and peeked inside. Feeling like a burglar in her own shop, she listened for noise from the private bathroom before she crept inside. If she had known how sneaky the bastard would get, she'd never have gone down on him in the kitchen. There wasn't an hour that went by that she didn't kick herself for agreeing to his damned contest. The fact his rules about the office meant she had tiptoed in early and stayed later than usual over the last two days to keep from being there at the same time he was only made her frustration worse. She wasn't about to admit to him, let alone herself, the number of times she'd fantasized about Dane taking control since the incident in the kitchen.

Her heart dropped to her stomach at the quiet *click* of the door latch.

“Are you forgetting something?” Dane's request halted Ariel as she turned from the file cabinet.

Until the challenge, she'd never considered how often she wandered into the office on a daily basis. But after their agreement, getting anywhere near the door was like touching a hot skillet without an oven mitt.

"Not that I'm aware of." She bluffed, not quite meeting his gaze.

"Our agreement?" He strolled toward her, his hands tucked into his pockets.

"I came to get my bag." She hefted the black backpack from where she'd left it beside the file cabinet.

"The deal still stands. You enter the office, you have to follow my orders." He reached up to loosen the tie around his neck.

"Does the same hold true for Sadie and DeeDee?" She propped a hand on her hip and cocked an eyebrow. "Are you trying to build your own harem?" She endeavored to stir some feeling of resentment inside her, but her body wasn't cooperating. Damn it. His cool blue gaze and quiet tone only nourished the fire smoldering inside her.

"Sadie and DeeDee aren't part of this, Ariel." He glanced at his watch. "Besides, they've been gone nearly three hours. If you hadn't kept stalling in the kitchen, we could have left after them."

"Hey, you're free to leave anytime." She shrugged and shook her head with a grin. "I'm a big girl. I don't require your help to lock up. I've done it a million times without you around."

His gaze skated over her body, pausing occasionally before it continued on. "My sticking around has nothing to do with the business and everything to do with you."

"If you'd face the fact that I'm not interested, you wouldn't have to waste your time. In fact, Dane, we could end your little challenge right here. I'm perfectly content to stick with the status quo," Ariel assured him as she shifted her feet and scraped her hand through her spiked blue hair.

"It's your satisfaction I want to see to." Dane's tone matched the sincerity in his gaze.

"And I told you I'm capable of taking care of that as well."

"That remains to be seen. For now, though"—Dane stepped forward and removed the backpack from her hand—"why don't we start with the basics?"

Ariel was determined not to let him know how he affected her. Her ovaries were doing backflips in their effort to produce enough estrogen to counteract the levels of testosterone emanating from his every pore. If her body were any more ready for him, she'd be a puddle. She wondered what it would feel like to have that fat cock of his inside her. Letting him in on the secret of her interest wasn't something she intended to do. "And what do you consider the basics, Mr. Reese?"

He grinned, set her backpack on the floor, and held his hand out to her. "Nothing as objectionable as you seem to think, Miss Valerian," he teased.

The residual fear she refused to admit to and tried to hide made her hesitate. Ariel was surprised at the change of expression on Dane's face and the look in his eyes as he stepped closer. Even his touch reassured her when he cupped her chin. Looking away from him wasn't an option.

"I won't hurt you, sprite. I swear." His fingers stroked through her short hair, his touch more soothing than arousing. "Trust me."

No matter how much she might have wanted to, Ariel couldn't dredge up a biting response. She shouldn't be surprised at his concern; she'd seen it after he'd spanked her. He seemed so intent on alleviating any uncertainty she might have, it only made her curse how appealing he was becoming to her. If this was how he worked with the women he trained to be submissives, it was a miracle half the state's female population didn't make a mass exodus to Ayerstown. Instead of speaking, she took his hand when he held it out to her, and nodded.

A curl of satisfaction slid through her when he smiled.

Why should I feel so relieved that I've pleased him? That he finds what I've done praiseworthy shouldn't be a priority to me. Ariel might deny the excitement filling her at his taking command, but she couldn't ignore the rush of her blood through her veins. Heat stirred in her core; a tingle sizzled in her feminine folds; the ache deepened in her breasts. Her body was responding to his control, and it wasn't anger or resentment or fear washing through her. It was pleasure. Hot, wet arousal only he seemed capable of creating.

"Take off everything from your waist down."

"Excuse me?"

"Shoes, socks. Take them off. Then get rid of your pants and panties," he informed her as he swung the ladder-back chair from in front of the desk to beside it.

"What about my shirt? My bra?" She tugged the tail of her T-shirt from her black slacks, flipped open the button, and then slid the zipper down.

"We'll wait on that," he finished, then tugged his loosened tie from under his collar and unbuttoned the cuffs of his dress shirt. Rolling the sleeves back, Dane exposed the sleek, tanned skin over the muscles in his forearms.

As she toed off her sneakers, Ariel could feel the heat climbing in her cheeks. Careful to keep her balance, she stripped off her socks, rolled them in a ball, and tucked them into one of her discarded shoes. The cool look he gave her told her nothing of what was going through his mind. She tried to pull the same cloak of calm around herself. *Hell, this is like a visit to the gynecologist. As if he's seen and done this a hundred times a week and it's nothing new.*

Stripping away her panties along with her trousers, Ariel took a moment to fold the garments. She wondered what he'd think of her bare pussy. Would he find it intriguing or merely strange? She'd tried the Brazilian waxing a few years earlier and liked it, but no one had ever seen it other than herself, her doctor, and the cosmetologist who did the work. Her heart thumped again at the thought of Dane being the first man to view her bare flesh.

When she would have set her clothes on the floor near her shoes, Dane surprised her by taking them from her hands and setting them on the desk. He motioned for her to take a seat in the chair and waited until she sat down before he rolled the executive chair from behind the desk into the space directly in front of her and took a seat.

"No, shift forward," he instructed. His hands reached out to cradle the outside of her thighs. He eased her forward on the chair until her bottom was right at the edge of the cushion.

"I'm going to fall off," she complained. Her hands dropped to grip the sides of the chair seat behind her hips.

"Okay. Stay right there." He smiled at her, his hands trailing slowly up and down her thighs. His thumbs slid from the inside to the outside of her knees; the warm, work-roughened pads smoothed over her kneecaps, then stroked the soft, sensitive flesh behind her knees. "Now open." He tugged lightly on her legs, spreading them out, exposing her body to his gaze.

He could see the flush of embarrassment turn her cheeks pink even as the soft flesh of her pussy glistened with a hint of moisture. Her bare mound didn't surprise him. As sensual as Ariel was in her culinary creations, it only made sense that she extended her sensory enjoyment to her body. Beyond flavor, the sense of touch seemed her most expressive feature. He'd seen her use it often with the waitresses through hugs and pats on the shoulder or back. With the regular customers and the little kids who occasionally came in with their parents. Even Grimm was treated to hugs and teasing touches from Ariel.

Though he'd resented the man at first, Dane had grown used to Grimm's hulking presence in the café. The ex-con, as dangerous as he appeared on paper, was in no way someone to fear. As long as people intended no harm to those Grimm considered under his protection, he seemed to treat everyone with quiet deference and respect. It hadn't taken long to gain a small measure of trust from the man, but only after Dane had confirmed that there was no interest beyond friendship between Ariel and the ex-convict.

Turning his attention back to the woman in front of him, Dane nodded. "Very nice, Ariel. Nothing to interfere with the lesson I have for you. Although I have to say, I wondered if you might dye your pussy curls to match your hair." Beneath his fingertips, he could feel the muscles in her thighs tense and tremble as he repositioned his touch upward.

Her responding laughter choked off as she protested the first part of his comment. "Lesson?" Her voice sounded strangled. She coughed to clear it, then repeated, "A lesson? What kind of lesson?"

He could feel her resistance to keep her legs open, so Dane eased his chair forward and set his knees against the insides of hers, preventing her from closing her legs. "Merely a little reminder about anatomy." He smiled at her, holding her gaze as the fingertips of his left hand dipped down to coast softly over her damp flesh.

She tried to lever herself up to see where his fingers traveled. Dane shook his head and used his right hand to push her back into her previous reclining position. Despite her lush frame, his hand looked huge, spanning the distance between the curve of her shoulder and the bend where throat met collarbone. "No, I don't want you to look at this. I want you to feel it first." His fingers danced upward to stroke over her brow and urge her eyes to shut. "Close your eyes. Arousal is about the sensations. Sight can be one of them, but in self-stimulation, touch is the dominant sense. Remember, the skin is the largest sensory organ in your body. The heat or cold of a room can affect how you respond." He kept his tone smooth, gentle, even. Nothing should interfere in her discovery of herself.

"One of the biggest hurdles we face at A Master's Gift is a submissive's inability to be aware of herself or himself. You can follow the instructions of your master, but your body is capable of betraying you, either through premature climax or refusal to climax." The fingers between her labia swirled lazily through the tiny pool of liquid arousal her body had produced.

"If I can't see what you're doing, how can I learn how to do it myself?" Ariel protested. Her breath stopped, and a tiny squeak escaped her lips and her eyes popped open as he moved his right hand down to join his left.

"You feel, Ariel. Seeing can distract you. It can mislead you or create a visual barrier to your arousal." He held her gaze for several seconds. "Close your eyes."

"But—"

"Close them." He waited. His fingers remained motionless, despite the minute shifting she did. The mutinous expression on her face brought a grin to his own, which he quickly hid. It also created visions of a tiny, winged pixie stomping her foot in a fit of pique. He held back his amusement until her eyelids drifted shut. "Keep them closed, Tink."

One eyelid rose, exposing a glaring green eye. "Tink? Who's Tink?"

"You. Now close your eyes and keep them closed." He waited, wondering if she'd demand an explanation. It was there in her gaze, the curiosity and suspicion, but she controlled the yen to ask more about the name he'd given her.

"Oh, that begs the question 'or else what?'" Her eye stayed open a moment longer, then clamped quickly shut. "Never mind," she grumped.

Again he had to choke back the urge to laugh. She would definitely be a handful, Dane decided before he dropped his gaze to the moist flesh beneath his fingertips. Damn, she was pretty. Watching her masturbate the other day had been arousing, but with her right here in front of him, his cock was hard and hungry to feel her body around it.

"Lesson one, Ariel, is to know where to touch as well as how."

"I think I know where, Dane. It is my body."

"Oh really?" Dane used his right hand to hold her pussy open to his attentions while the left collected droplets of her juice. The instant his finger touched the opening to her body, she tensed. "Hmmm, interesting."

"Wha-what?" she croaked, then cleared her throat.

"Nothing. Yet." *You need to get used to being touched by hands other than your own. How long has it been since your last lover?* Dane knew better than to voice his questions. He would wait for a time when Ariel would be more receptive and less oppositional. Smoothing the fluid over her exposed sex, Dane proceeded with his instructions. "I want to see if you really are as familiar with your body's anatomy as you say you are."

She obviously didn't believe this was necessary based on the soft snort she gave. He knew better, and soon she would too. “You have two set of labia.”

Ariel nodded. “Yes, an outer and inner.”

Her body trembled beneath the slide of his fingers. “Paying attention to these can increase your arousal.”

Her hum of agreement could have been mistaken for one of enjoyment. It quickly turned into a groan of protest as he pulled his fingers away. Then a purr as he eased his touch higher. “You also have nerve-rich protrusions.”

A gurgle of laughter spilled from her lips before she repeated, “Protrusions?”

Dane allowed himself to grin at her amusement. “Yes. Both can generate sensations, but only one can increase the strength of both arousal and climax.” His fingers coasted over one of the bits of tissue. “This is your?”

“Urethra.” She muttered the answer and fidgeted slightly in the seat as he circled it with a fingertip before he took his attentions farther north.

His finger caressed the tiny covering of skin near the top of her mound. “And under here?” he prompted.

The slight pressure and heat of his fingertip had a shudder rippling through her body. The heated walls of her vagina pulsed, spilling more evidence of her arousal onto the chair seat. He watched the fine hairs on her body rise and the gooseflesh surface as he stroked over the flesh while he awaited her answer.

“My”—she coughed and cleared her throat—“my clitoris.”

Against the white of her bra and T-shirt, he could see the hard peaks of her nipples. As much as he would have liked to pull one of the berry red beads into his mouth, Dane returned his attention to the lesson he was giving. Ariel must understand how to please herself. Her failure to climax days earlier had disturbed him more than he'd like to admit. Hours he should have spent formulating ways to introduce her to submission were spent instead on analyzing how she'd caressed herself and how that related to her lack of release.

Keeping his gaze on her face, he tapped the sensitive bit of skin before he drew away from her. The protest slid past her lips, probably due to an involuntary response to his heavier attention. "Show me how you pleasure yourself."

Her eyes opened wide, and the heat of embarrassment increased in her cheeks. He could see the denial build in her expression, but he shook his head. "Show me." His tone was implacable.

This was going to be worse than she had expected. Challenge gleamed in his eyes and assured her there was no getting out of the situation. Not unless she was willing to concede. *No damned way will I let him win by default. I can handle anything he tries to throw at me.*

Again he ordered, "Show me how you get yourself off."

His knees pressed along hers; his hands were on her thighs, thumbs absently stroking the flesh above her knees. Other than the intent heat of his stare, they could have been discussing the menu for the next day, he sat so relaxed in the chair.

Determined to show him his assistance wasn't necessary for her to achieve climax, Ariel repositioned her right hand from the chair seat to the heated flesh of her pussy. She ignored the niggling reminder that despite the innumerable times she'd masturbated, reaching orgasm had been a rare thing. Two fingers did a cursory slide along her nether lips before she found the wet opening and pressed in.

"Stop." Dane's lips flattened out. His gaze wandered from the hand on her mound to her face.

"You said—"

"Much as you want to be in charge, Ariel, your body craves more," Dane informed her.

The heat of his hand covered the back of hers. He eased her fingers from inside her vagina and stroked her damp fingertips higher. Keeping his hand cupped over hers, he guided her in spreading the natural lubrication her body produced to the plump lips of her pussy.

"Stimulation builds on stimulation." He held her gaze as he smoothed her fingers along her outer labia before sliding inward. "When you know what pleases your body, then you can control the reaction of your body."

Ariel barely registered the words as she followed the pressure on her fingertips and applied it to her delicate flesh. The heat in her belly began to expand, and the look in his eyes mesmerized her.

"Close your eyes and feel." Dane's voice was soft, the whisper of his breath across her face nearly as stirring as the movements he directed along her sensitive flesh.

Her eyelids were too heavy to keep open. Letting them drift shut, she gasped at the increased sensation building in her core. The heat of his hand drifted away as she stroked over her flesh, exploring the frilled edge of her inner lips. The rapid flutter of the tissue echoed the way her empty sheath quivered and pulsed in tandem to the attentions from her fingertips.

"Find your clit." His directive was quiet but resolute.

She transferred her touch upward, her damp fingertips rubbing and pressing against the apex of her mound. Her breasts ached, her nipples taut, but when she lifted her other hand up to cradle the fullness in her palm, Dane's fingers captured her wrist and returned her hand back to the seat behind her hip.

"No touching without permission, Tink."

Her groan mingled with the moans slipping from her lips as the coil of arousal tightened in her core. Her hips rocked against the strokes of her fingertips as climax bubbled closer to the surface. The muscles in her vagina flexed and pulled, desperate for something to grip, but the most intense sensations were focused on the tiny knot of flesh she'd coaxed from beneath the hood of skin.

"That's it, baby. Show me how good it feels."

His voice egged her on, encouraged her to go faster, apply firmer pressure, but there was something missing still. An emptiness that begged him to fill it, and she voiced her yearning to him. "Please."

"Please, what?"

She could hear in his voice that he knew what she wanted—craved. "I want more, please."

He was closer—she could feel the heat of his body along the front of hers—but he wasn't close enough to touch. The desire twisted, grew tighter; her fingers sped up, pressing harder against the nubbin of nerves. "Please." Tears clogged her throat. The sensations bombarding her were different from any she'd experienced in the past. This was nothing like the tepid trembling and heated rush she'd felt before. It thrilled and frightened her at the same time, making her hand pause, hesitate.

"Keep going, Ariel," Dane ordered.

"I-I ca-can't." She shook her head.

Warm fingers covered hers, pinching the aching knot of her clit, shooting fire through her body. Another warm palm cupped the back of her head, his fingers tangled in the short blue spikes of her hair. Dane's breath stilled hers. "Open your eyes."

Fear billowed in her chest. The longing to please him blended with the painful need to climax, while another part of her screamed at her to turn away and run, to get as far away from this man as possible. But her body betrayed her, arching closer.

"Open them up, love. Look at me." His command softened to a purr as he stroked his fingers over hers, squeezed her aching clit, and sent another pulse of pleasure through her center.

She couldn't deny him. He was so close, she could only see the intense blue of his eyes. Like the images she'd seen of Lake Tahoe, the dark blue seemed bottomless, inviting her to dive in and tempt the danger awaiting her. Ariel swallowed, waited.

"I have you, Ariel. You're safe."

How he could be crouched over her, his body close but not touching her, registered only vaguely in the back of her mind, but his words stilled the panicked pounding of her heart. The guiding hand over hers slipped away and drew a whimper from her lips that the recalcitrant part of her sneered at.

His lips brushed over hers. "Time now, Tink."

"Wha-what?" She tried to draw a breath to still the wild snarls in her head. It only made matters worse; inhaling the heated scent of his body and the smell of her arousal jacked her hunger into overdrive.

"Come. Show me how good it feels to have that beautiful climax roll through you."

Her internal rebel cursed, but the orgasm that welled up from her core, spread down her legs and up her belly, silenced the minx temporarily. As shudders and quakes rolled through her, Ariel never lost contact with Dane's gaze. The hand cupping her head and the one he'd slipped around her waist ensured she didn't fall, but the rest of her body jerked and twitched as wave after wave of pleasure broke over her before sweeping her further into the ocean of confusion surrounding her.

It wasn't supposed to be like this, her rebel complained. He wasn't supposed to be able to do this. Tamping down the fear beginning to well up inside her, Ariel forced herself to focus, to return to reality and ignore the blissful lassitude trying to steal over her. No fucking way would she lose this challenge, she determined, drawing one deep breath after another.

He watched her, his body close, its heat wrapping around her like a safe blanket. The flush in his cheeks, the darkened color of his eyes attested to his arousal. Ariel let her gaze drift down. The press of his hard-on against his trousers was visible, but he wouldn't give in to the desire. Not like she had. Rebellion flared in her breast. *If he can ignore the feeling, so can I.* She may have lost this battle, but the war raged on. No way was she letting him win. Her intent must have communicated itself to him, because Dane eased his hold on her body. He made sure she was securely ensconced on the chair before he returned to his seat.

The springs squeaked beneath his weight, but the rollers were silent as he slid back and put distance between them.

"Okay?" he asked. His gaze seemed to measure if she had recovered enough to dress.

"I'm"—she cleared her throat and tried again—"I'm fine. Are we through here?"

He held her pants and underwear out to her with a nod. "Yes, Ariel. Lesson's over."

She shoved the chair away, scrambled toward the bathroom, and slammed the door. The *click* of the lock engaging filled the quiet room. She kept her attention away from the mirror as she dampened a washcloth and hastily bathed her wet thighs and fingers. The smell of her climax surrounded her. Ariel cringed inside at the knowledge that her scent hovered in the air of the office. Dane was probably drawing it in. Savoring it like a trophy, a testament to his power over her. Her clit pulsed, betraying her determination to deny the feelings the man stirred within her.

"I'm my own woman. I don't need a man to tell me how to please myself. My body," she whispered the reminder to her reflection. But the glint in her eyes knew she lied. Or at least was unwilling to see the truth that was right in front of her.

She wanted what Dane could give her, but she'd stay silent if it was the last thing she ever did.

Chapter Seven

Day 13

The café was closed when Dane pulled his car to the curb and shut the engine off. The sun hadn't crested the horizon yet. He fought back a jaw-cracking yawn before he climbed out of the car. Even at five in the morning on a Saturday, there were people heading into the various businesses and shops, delivery trucks making their rounds, and the general hubbub of a city waking. He didn't expect anyone to be in the café since it wasn't supposed to open for another three hours. Considering the way Ariel had avoided him in the day and a half since he'd guided her to climax, he doubted she'd be coming in early. The alarm let out a soft *beep* as he pushed the door open and stepped inside.

"Leave the lights off, Dane." Her voice was pitched so that it made it as far as the door but didn't go beyond to the early foot traffic on the sidewalk behind him.

Intrigued, he followed her instructions, stepped inside, and then shut and locked the door. "You're in early."

"Had a special errand I wanted to finish up."

He could barely make out her form on the other side of the café in the dim light. Ariel didn't leave her seat at the counter. She kept her elbows propped on the tiled surface behind her, the heels of her hiking boots hooked over the lower rung of the stool, and her eyes focused on him.

His body kicked into overdrive, and the snug fit of his faded jeans grew tighter. The scuffed and worn boots on his feet made little noise as he crossed the room. He shed his leather jacket, revealing the black T-shirt beneath, and draped it over his right forearm.

She eased off the bar stool and sauntered toward him.

Dane tossed his jacket into the nearest booth. "Errand?" *And would it happen to involve a bed with both of us naked?*

"Yes. A very important one."

"Really?"

Ariel tried to hide her smile, but he could see it lurking in her eyes. She seemed so proud to be able to turn the tables on him. He wasn't about to let her know it wouldn't be for long. Lessons for a submissive were definitely in her future. Let her enjoy the sense of accomplishment and power. If the thought of pushing his buttons brought her pleasure, he'd show her the true pleasure to be found in following his directions.

He shifted with her as she carefully circled him, her gaze stroking over the faded creases in the denim where the cloth cupped his manhood before dropping to the firm muscles in his thighs covered by the heavy cotton. He could feel the stiff peaks of his nipples poking at the ebony material stretched across his broad chest.

"Oh my, yes." She finally stopped in front of him and grinned.

"And what errand has you here at four in the morning when the café won't open until eight today?" Dane didn't cross his arms or try to conceal the reaction of his body to hers.

Ariel let her eyes drift to the growing bulge behind his zipper and then brought them back to his deep blue gaze. "I thought I'd see if you were willing to put your money where your mouth is." She stepped closer, her fingers stroking his erection, then roaming upward to tease one of his nipples beneath his T-shirt. "Or perhaps more accurately, put your body on the line, Master Reese."

He pretended to mull over her response before answering. "How so, Ariel?"

Ariel used her free hand to motion to the room around them. "Neutral territory, Dane. You can say no and run away to work on your little lists and spreadsheets. Or you can say yes and let me direct you in a little exercise I've been thinking about." Stepping back, she settled her hands on her hips and cocked her head to the right as she looked up at him. "Which is it gonna be?"

"Going to try to play mistress?" He grinned and wasn't surprised at the narrowing of her eyes that signaled her irritation.

She looked so sure of herself, but he could see the frustration his nonchalance stirred in her.

Ariel leaned close and whispered in his ear, "Not play, my pet. Be."

Dane was surprised at the zing of heat that curled around his balls at her declaration. The throb of his erection kept time with the vibrating triangle of flesh at the base of her throat. He'd spent years learning his craft as a dominant—hours, days, weeks, honing his skills and educating himself to accurately read every nuance of a sub's body, voice, and expression. But the determination and challenge in Ariel's gaze heated his body faster than any past lover with the most expert of touches had ever done.

"Show me," Dane encouraged her. He'd taken the role of bottom before. It was a position necessary for him to experience in order to understand more precisely the ramifications of a dominant's behavior on the sub he or she was leading. The role had never held the appeal it suddenly did when he envisioned Ariel in charge of the reins.

His agreement must have surprised her, because her green eyes went wide for a moment before she straightened her shoulders and stood taller. Or as tall as her diminutive height would allow.

"Get a chair down and take it to the counter. Place it on the floor in front of the seat I was in when you entered."

Dane pulled a seat from the top of one of the tables and carried it to the spot Ariel indicated. The rising sun cast a pale glow through the shut blinds on the front windows and door. It glistened off the polished wood floor and shimmered in the glass picture frames decorating the pale walls. He waited beside the chair for her next instruction, noting the increased pulse throbbing at the side of her neck, the jut of her aroused nipples against the pink tank top she wore, and the careful way she stepped as she crossed back to the counter and turned to face him.

"I think a little lesson in anatomy is required." She cleared her throat, then crossed one arm over her chest and lifted her other hand to stroke her fingers along her chin.

"Whose anatomy?" Dane asked, although he was sure from the glint in her eyes and the wicked grin lifting her lips what her answer would be.

"Why yours, of course, my pet. If you're to pleasure me, then it's important to ensure you have an astute comprehension of how your body works."

He couldn't suppress the chuckle at her formal pronouncement. He'd known she'd look for retribution after his lesson the night before last. He just hadn't expected it would be as entertaining as this.

Her humor must have been stimulated, because she let slip a short burst of laughter before regaining composure. "Now you should show me what kind of toys we have to play with."

"Toys?"

She sidled close and held his gaze as her hand drifted from her chin to cup his thickening erection through the denim enclosing it. "Oh yes. This bit of fun is sure to be worth all sorts of amusements."

He settled his hand over hers and pressed her closer. "I wouldn't call it a 'bit,' Tink."

Her fingers squeezed and stroked the shape developing inside his pants. "Hmmm."

His cock reacted to the throaty purr and pushed into her touch.

"Definitely right. This isn't a 'bit.' More like a stalk." She caressed him one last time before stepping back and crossing her arms over her chest. "Show me my toy, pet. Take everything off."

Dane admired her bravado. He could see the excitement stirring her pulse and flushing her cheeks, but none of her body movements betrayed her thoughts.

Taking his time, he slipped the boots and socks off his feet. With the jeans he was more careful, slowly sliding the buttons on the fly free since he'd chosen to go without his usual boxer-briefs that morning. The moment the last button was loosened, his dick popped free.

The pink in her cheeks deepened, and her tongue peeked out to moisten her lips. Dane shed his jeans and stripped off his T-shirt, then folded the garments and set them on the floor beside his boots.

"Oh my, and a very impressive stalk I must say," Ariel whispered.

Dane could feel heat creep across his cheekbones at her declaration. It had been a long time since he'd been uncomfortable with comments about the size his cock, and it surprised him that her admiration of his endowment discomfited him.

Hoping to reestablish some control, Dane smirked. "I haven't had any complaints so far."

"I'm sure you haven't." Ariel didn't seem to realize she'd spoken aloud until Dane laughed.

He watched her shake off her surprise and regain composure. "Ah, but do you know the parts that make up the whole?"

"Do you?" he returned, his inclination to direct overriding his promise to follow instructions.

Ariel didn't seem to identify his insubordination, or she chose to ignore it. "Shaft, glans, scrotum, urethra, meatus, and frenulum."

Dane smiled. "Very good."

"Now, now." Ariel clicked her tongue and shook a finger at him. Her sexy frown and disapproving look reminded him of a teacher correcting a recalcitrant student. Images of her with spectacles, a ruler, and a frumpy dress sent his cock curving upward, closer to his belly. *Her sexy, bossy teacher being taught a lesson by my bad-boy student would be a very interesting role-play.*

Dane brought his attention back to her as Ariel stepped closer and wrapped the fingers of her right hand around his erection. "Tell me which part I'm touching, pet," she commanded.

"Shaft."

Her fingers stroked up and down, the pressure of her grip shifting from soft to firm. She took her time before sliding her hand lower and cupping the sac between his legs. "And now?"

"Scrotum." He kept still, awaiting her next onslaught. The way her fingers flexed around his balls drew pearls of precum from the tip of his dick. Controlling his climax wouldn't be a problem. He'd worked for years on managing his body; his sultry sprite would find it difficult to undermine that training, no matter how his body clamored for her touch.

She worked her fingers through the rough thatch of hair surrounding the base of his shaft before she slid her fingers along the underside of his cock until her thumb smeared the fluids bubbling from the tip over the sensitive head. "No foreskin, I see."

"No." *Shit, she knows all the right spots.* Dane evened the pace of his breath as he fought the urge to tremble under her touch. Tiny as her hands were, each smooth finger unerringly found every special pleasure point along his shaft.

"This seems to be a very delicate spot," Ariel observed. Her fingers caressed the flared edge before slipping along the seam where head met shaft. "What's its name?"

He drew a deep breath to still the moan building in his chest at each teasing flick of her fingertips. "It can be called the head, but the technical term is glans penis."

"And this?" Her forefinger slid over the very tip, caught another drop of precum before she tapped against the opening.

"Urethra, and the urethral opening is also called the meatus." He swallowed another groan as he watched her lift her finger to her mouth and lick away the moisture coating the tip.

"Did I pass?" Dane asked and fought the urge to strip away the stretchy cotton covering her breasts and suck the hard little peaks until his woman squirmed and begged for climax.

"Hmmm, I think we missed a spot," Ariel declared as her fingers returned to grip his cock, settling in the sensitive notch under the head. She squeezed.

Dane hissed and clenched his fists.

"This spot, what's it called, pet?"

"Frenulum." The word barely made it through his gritted teeth. The pleasure was intense; it took everything he had to keep from reacting to it. He could feel his balls pull close to his body, his climax building, ready to explode. *Not yet. Breathe. Think. Control.* He repeated the commands to himself, easing back from the edge she'd drawn him to and calming his arousal.

"All of these parts can be so sensitive. You never know what will push you past your control. If you're going to learn to please me, it's important you know how to please yourself, don't you think?" Ariel asked, her green eyes almost guileless as she gazed down at him.

Dane turned his laugh into a choked cough. "Most definitely, Tink. I should know how to please myself."

"Show me, then." She ambled away and climbed onto the bar stool to face him. "Sit down and pleasure yourself for me."

Ariel fought the temptation to pant. She hadn't expected to become this turned on at the thought of leading Dane in masturbating himself. *Was he this excited when he directed me? Is this the rush a real Domme receives when she guides her submissive*? Her panties were wet with her juices, her breasts ached for his mouth to suckle them, and her pussy throbbed, desperate to be filled. When she'd gone down on him in the kitchen she'd concentrated on the lesson, not how big he was. Her fingers didn't touch when she wrapped them around his shaft. Only when his aroused penis narrowed near the tip was her thumb able to brush the edge of her middle finger. She'd definitely miscalculated his size when she'd bought her vibrator while imagining how big he might be. And it wasn't only his girth, but the length as well.

Pushing away the images of how much he'd fill her when she finally got to fuck him, Ariel concentrated on the way Dane settled into the chair facing her. He slouched low, his shoulders propped against the laddered back of the chair and his butt on the front edge of the seat. Long legs held him in place, his bare feet braced on the polished wood near the base of her stool. His thighs were open, showing off the tanned skin that boasted his tendency to sunbathe in the nude. No tan lines marred the muscled skin of his thighs and belly, and the thick fingers wrapping around his cock were the same brown as the shaft they caressed.

"Stop." She voiced her order in a husky tone. Ariel left her seat and stepped between his splayed thighs.

Dane watched her, waiting, his blue eyes analyzing her, seeming to search out any sign of weakness she might betray.

"Give me your hand." She held her right hand out, palm up.

He put his left onto it. Turning his hand over, she leaned down, her gaze holding his and put her mouth around his forefinger. Savoring the mingled flavors of salt and spices, she wrapped her tongue over and around his finger before releasing it. The next finger was afforded the same treatment.

And the next. One at a time, until all four and his thumb glistened. She licked the palm, then spit into it to provide lubrication before she returned his hand to his erection and then stepped away.

Her body trembled with the yen to touch him. To slide her fingers over his as he stroked his hand up and down his shaft, the shine of her saliva coating the flesh, reminding her of the taste she'd been teased with nearly a week earlier.

Remembering the steady flow of words he'd whispered while guiding her through her exploration and climax thirty-six hours or so earlier, Ariel went to the side of his chair and crouched down. She watched his hand working his body before slowly drifting her gaze along his taut abs, muscled chest, and broad shoulders. The scent of aroused male, cardamom, and rosemary teased her nostrils. She inhaled one slow, deep breath and then another, pulling the aroma into her lungs, tasting it against the back of her throat.

"Every touch should build the craving." She shifted her attention from his chest to his face. The brilliance of his blue eyes seared her. The muscles of her vagina pulsed with desire. Her breasts ached to be stroked, cuddled, caressed, and her breath shortened for a heartbeat, then two.

Unable to stop herself, Ariel smoothed her hand across his chest, tracing the clear lines of demarcation between pectoral and abdominal muscles.

The firm slopes of his chest, topped with the nut brown peaked nipples, drew her fingertips. The crinkled buds felt firmer than hers, the texture of the skin surrounding them only slightly more coarse than the skin covering her breasts. The speed and flex of his hand on his shaft slowed as she played with his nipples. Ariel tugged a brown button between her fingertips, then leaned forward to nip the second with her teeth. “No stopping, pet.”

Her hand proceeded downward from his nipple to cover the hand he had wrapped around his cock. Beneath her fingertips, she could feel the tension and flex of his muscles and fingers as he worked his hand slow, then fast along his heated length. Precum dribbled over his glans. Ariel guided his hand up until the slick fluid coated his palm and fingers.

“Is it the friction from a fast jerking you like?” Ariel asked as she used her hand around him in quick, sharp yanks.

Dane hissed. His back arched, pushing his shoulders into the chair back. His hips came off the seat, and his feet pressed into the floor to keep himself in place. Her arousal spiraled tighter in her belly at the sight of his pleasure and knowing she drew it from him.

The tendons on his neck stood out as he fought to control his breathing before he eased back onto the chair and opened his eyes to capture her gaze. “Sometimes.” His voice was gruff. “But I also like a slow, firm ride.” He wrapped his fingers around hers and pulled them all the way to the tip of his cock. Rolling her palm over the head, he drew her hand back down the shaft, flexing and squeezing until the coarse pubic hair scratched its heel.

Ariel slipped her hand from beneath his and rose to stand over him. “Depends on your mood, huh?” she asked and then stepped behind the chair. She trailed the backs of her fingers over his brow, along his cheeks, and down onto his throat. “How long do you take to come?”

“As long it takes.”

The smile canting the left corner of his mouth teased, but the glow in his eyes held a vow Ariel was afraid to examine. "Is it fast or slow?" She leaned closer and closed her eyes. Her lips smoothed over his brow and down toward his cheek. "Long or short?"

"Whatever my partner requires." His lips caressed her cheek; the scrape of his early-morning beard stimulated her senses as she breathed in the smell of his building arousal.

Levering herself over him, Ariel slid her hands down his chest and onto his belly, her fingertips tingled at the heat of his skin and the way his muscles jumped beneath her touch. She opened her heavy eyelids and met his gaze. "Then give it to me, pet. Long and slow. Give it to me now."

The body beneath her hands tensed. The sound of flesh on flesh increased immediately before the first splash of cum wet the back of her hand where it rested on his belly. Long, slow pulses arched his body toward her; each time it brought his lips to hers for a whisper of a kiss. Time lost its meaning. The rumble of tires along pavement outside, feet along the sidewalk, even a shouted greeting between two men, were merely background noises as the last vibration thrummed through his body into hers.

Their breathing slowed in unison, and the tension eased between them. Ariel stepped away from the chair and staggered to the counter, her mind whirling with the sensations and emotions tumbling inside her, her body off-kilter. A towel rested on the tiles, a half-forgotten bit of preparation she'd made for a scene that had gone way beyond expectation.

It wasn't supposed to become as intimate as it had. Her hands trembled as she reached for the towel. Ariel held her breath. Dane hadn't seemed this affected after he'd brought her to climax. Why couldn't she separate herself from the emotions, the arousal mounting inside her? *Keep it cool. Stay focused. You want him gone; this will speed his departure.* Her pep talk was almost forgotten when she faced Dane, the towel in her hands.

Heat burned in his gaze. He hadn't bothered changing his slouched position in the chair. He sat sprawled in it, one hand on his thigh, the other on the edge of the seat. Even in its relaxed state, his penis was an impressive sight to Ariel.

She forced herself to look away from it as she wiped her hands with the cloth. *If he can do it, so can I. There's no reason to get emotional, clingy. It's just sex.* Despite her efforts to dismiss the feelings, Ariel doubted she'd be successful. There was too much there, but she'd be careful to keep Dane from discovering her secret.

After returning to his side, she wiped the backs of his hands and then smoothed the cloth over the creamy coating on his stomach. "Let's get you cleaned up, pet. We both have some work to finish." She fought to keep her voice steady and avoid the expression in his gaze. *No way am I giving up. No matter how he affects me. Not until he is gone, Alayna is back, and I know my part of the world is safe again.*

* * *

Dane heard the sliding door travel along its track, but he ignored it. The lowball glass of vodka he'd carried out to the porch sat abandoned on the table beside him. His fingers traced the smooth sides of the crystal as he listened to Shendah approach.

"Master Dane?" Shendah's tone was quiet, hesitant.

"Yes, Shendah." He didn't take his gaze from the starlit landscape in front of him.

Her footsteps were quiet on the stone-slab patio. Despite the warmth during the day, the temperature in the surrounding forest dipped at night, even in the summer. "You'll catch a cold if you come out here without shoes," he warned. The fact that his bare feet were propped on the wooden railing went unmentioned.

"You barely touched your dinner. I thought you might be hungry." She set a plate with a sandwich stacked with thick slices of meat and cheese on the table, then nudged the drink out of his loose grip.

When she reached for the glass, Dane stopped her. "No." He made sure not to touch her as he settled his hand over the top of the glass to keep her from taking it. Because of her past, Shendah found unsolicited physical contact difficult to handle. He turned to gaze up at her in the milky light of the stars above and the pale illumination offered by the light over the kitchen stove. Something in his expression, or maybe the look in his eyes, made Shendah gasp and step back.

"Master Dane, has something happened? Are you okay?" A wary, trembling hand alighted on his shoulder.

His left hand lifted the glass to his lips. The measure of vodka slid over his tongue and into his belly with a welcome burn. With his other hand, he reached up and softly patted the one on his shoulder. "I'm fine, Shen."

"Are you sure?" Her fingers squeezed his shoulder.

"Promise."

She waited a moment, eased her hand from beneath his, and then gracefully knelt on the flagstones. "Then why are you out here? Alone and drinking?"

He rolled the empty container between his palms, watching the muted flash of starlight reflect off the surface, his mind shutting doors to paths he'd traveled and opening others he hadn't known existed. "There comes a time in his life when a man has to mourn the life he used to live and face the new one taking shape in front of him."

"And you need to do that by getting drunk?"

He could hear the confusion and disquiet in her voice. In the past Shendah had left behind, drunkenness had never resulted in anything but abuse, so Dane could understand her uneasy feelings. But the reality of how much he wanted Ariel as his woman, his submissive, slapped him in the face once he'd recovered from the climax she'd induced. The realization of how unlikely his success in claiming her was had left him in a less-than-accommodating mood.

"It's either get drunk or shoot myself, sweetheart. And considering the treats I have in store for me if I survive the siege ahead, I'm thinking I'll stick around for a while." He set the empty glass on the table, then splashed another measure of vodka into it before he reached for the sandwich.

"Is she worth it?"

"Worth it?"

Her tone was amused as she nodded. "You despise hangovers, Dane. And vodka always gives you the worst ones. Is this woman worth the hangover you'll have in the morning?"

Trust Shendah to know a woman was at the heart of his dilemma. The smile stretching his lips was involuntary as he imagined the battles and wars ahead of him to convince Ariel of their future.

"Yes. She's worth every second of pain and nausea I'll be dealing with in the morning, Shen. Every second and more."

Chapter Eight

Day 15

Two days later DeeDee pushed open the door of the kitchen and poked her head inside. “Hey, Ari. Alayna's on the phone for you.”

“Is he here?” Ariel rinsed her hands at the sink and dried them on a paper towel as she headed toward the exit.

“No, he said he had to go take care of something at his business.”

Ariel hurried into the office and picked up the handset from the desk. “Al, what's up? I thought you weren't supposed to make any calls? What's wrong?”

“Hey there, baby sister. Miss me?” Alayna teased.

“Damn straight, that wannabe Dom is useless on the register.” *But in the bedroom…* Ariel forced her mind away from the wicked thoughts that had plagued her for nearly a week, keeping her from sleep, and back to her sister's call.

“You were paid on time, right? So that's an upside. And how's Dane making out with ordering your supplies?” Al's voice seemed to hold both curiosity and something else Ariel couldn't quite put her finger on.

Ariel sensed there was more to her sister's call, but she'd play along until Alayna was ready to tell her what. "I'm fine. Money's not everything, and let's not talk about supply orders."

"All right, fine, we won't talk shop. How are you holding up? What's new? How are you and Dane getting along? He hasn't said anything."

Ariel was reluctant to discuss Dane and the situation. Glancing at the ladder-back chair, she fought the urge to blush. "It's going. It's going. I'd rather hear all the details of your training." She laughed at the thought of turning the tables and putting Alayna on the spot. "Is that sexy Logan tying you up or tying you in knots?"

"Oh, I'm in knots, all right." Ariel could hear the frustration in her sister's voice. "But I haven't seen the sexy Logan since I arrived."

Ariel knew the dark-haired man hadn't been in Valerian's Root since Al left for training. It didn't make sense that Alayna hadn't seen him. Considering the way the man had never been able to keep his eyes off her sister, Ariel asked, "Logan isn't around? I thought he owned the place with Dane?"

"He does." Alayna sighed. "But apparently Logan is too busy to bother with the training of subs. Maybe he works with the Doms. I don't know. Rick is great, though."

"Rick?" Ariel shook her head. "Who the fuck is Rick?"

"The fellow Dane set me up to train with. You'd like him, Ari. His sense of humor reminds me of you."

"But he doesn't 'do it' for you." If her sister was as attracted to Logan as Ariel was to Dane, she could understand how substituting another man for the one she really wanted wouldn't quite scratch the itch.

"Not even a little. It's me. I'm sure of it." Al sounded despondent.

"No, Al, there's no way it could be you." Ariel shook her head even though her sister couldn't see it. "You haven't done anything wrong," she assured her.

"You're too sweet."

Sweet? Ariel was sure that wasn't the word Dane would use to describe her. And she'd worked long and hard to make sure of it. And worked him as well. She pushed aside the images of his body stiffening in climax, the ripple of his muscles as he came, and fixed her attention on her sister's call. "I want to know about this training."

"You mean my lack of training," Alayna grumbled.

Ariel frowned, her mind flashing to the careful instructions Dane had given her four nights before. Her body still tingled from the climax she'd reached. Thinking Alayna, who was supposed to be receiving the benefits of A Master's Gift's instruction, wasn't getting what she wanted irritated Ariel. Her comment reflected that. "What? Are they that lame?"

When Alayna didn't laugh, Ariel knew this was more serious than she'd expected. Before she could pry, her sister came clean.

"This is really embarrassing." Alayna paused for a moment, then continued. "Our sessions are a futile endeavor.

Sure, Rick and I have developed a bond, a friendship, but he doesn't do anything to help me tap into my inner sub."

Ariel winced in commiseration for the frustration her sister must be experiencing. "So maybe you need someone who makes you want to submit."

"Ari, I came here because I want it to be Logan…but…since he's more or less MIA, I'm wondering what the hell I'm still doing here. This is a big waste of time. I think I made a mistake coming here. This isn't for me, I guess."

"Are you sure about that? I mean, you seemed so interested in being a submissive." Despite how she'd teased Alayna about her interest in the lifestyle, she never thought her sister would become so disheartened as to give up after two weeks.

"Yes, I did. But who I want doesn't seem to be interested in me."

Ariel muttered, "Sounds like we have the same problem."

"What's that?" Alayna asked.

"Nothing, nothing," Ariel avoided. She grimaced at the slip. Just because her sister was bummed over her situation didn't mean Alayna wasn't still as sharp as she'd been before she left. Ariel reminded herself to be careful not to give too much away.

"What's going on, Ariel?" Alayna's voice was filled with concern.

"If it's Logan you want, can't you request he be the one to train you?"

"Ariel?"

Oh God, not the tone. *She hasn't used that on me since I turned nineteen.* Ariel covered her eyes and fought the urge to groan out loud.

Alayna was still talking. "What is going on with you? And don't try to bullshit me."

She hedged her answer. "I don't like having Dane here. That's all." Ariel worked to keep her voice neutral and tried to turn the conversation back to the reason her sister had called. "Let's keep this focused on you. If you're thinking about quitting, why are you calling me? Why don't you tell them 'I'm out of here' and come home?"

"Well, Rick suggested I talk to someone I trust. I'm thinking of throwing in the towel. And there isn't anyone in the world I trust more than you, baby sister."

"I love you too, Al. But I want you to be sure." And she did, Ariel realized. As much as she'd prefer to have her sister back home, to return to the routine Ariel knew and felt safe with, she wanted Alayna to be happy more. "Is there any chance you'll be happy if you give up now? Or will you regret not taking this chance?" Ariel winced at her challenging tone.

"You know me. Eventually I would regret not seeing this through. I'm so frustrated here." Alayna growled.

"I thought you'd be getting laid like every day."

Alayna laughed. "Not once since I've been here. My first obstacle is to learn how to get myself off, but the information Rick gave me on masturbation techniques isn't helping either.

"Damn, that sucks!" Ariel spat, feeling frustrated for her sister. "They gave you brochures? No hands-on stuff?"

"I'm destined to never come in my life, Ari. Never," Alayna moaned.

"Wait a minute." Ariel leaned back in the chair and shook her head. "Are you saying you're having a hard time getting off?"

"Well, yeah, Ari. I-I…"

Ariel knew, as close as they were, Alayna was having a hard time confessing such a personal thing to her. She heard it in her sister's voice.

In a rush, Alayna explained, "I can't orgasm. That's why I wanted to come here. I was hoping someone might be able to teach me. But it isn't working out well."

"It's okay, Al." She sighed and confessed. "I'm in the same boat." *At least I used to be.*

"Really? Why didn't you say something? Have we never had 'the talk'? How can we discuss everything under the sun but not something as important as this?"

Remembering the stunning climax Dane had led her to in this very office, she wondered if it was the partner and not the technique that could be causing her sister's frustration. As for discussing sexual satisfaction with her sister, Ariel shuddered at the thought. "Eww, that would be like walking in on Mom and Dad when they had sex."

Al groaned. "Nice, Ari. Like I didn't have enough on my mind. Now you present me with that visual."

"I love you, Al, but discussing the birds and the bees with your big sister is not my idea of a good time." She tried to keep it light, but she didn't want to downplay her sister's needs. "Have you talked to Rick about the issue?"

"Rick's aware and, in the beginning, was eager to help me out. But now all we do is talk. I'm supposed to learn about my body and what turns me on before Rick and I can go further."

"It's all in the clit." Ariel winced, then coughed.

"Excuse me?"

"Well, it is, at least according to Dane." Again she winced and knew Al would pounce on that in a second.

"Dane? You've been discussing this with Dane but not me?" Alayna sounded surprised.

"I wouldn't exactly call it discussing—Never mind. Listen, don't give up."

"Oh no you don't. You keep turning this conversation back on me, and I want to know what's going on with you."

"It's nothing, I swear."

Alayna didn't sound convinced. "Are you and Dane—?"

"It's between Dane and me, and we're working it out. Kinda."

"Ari, you're struggling with something. Tell me; I'm here for you."

No way was Ariel giving her any ammunition. "I love you too, sis, but I need to take care of this on my own. I need to figure it out." Again returning the focus to her sister, she added, "I don't want you to give up."

"You're leaving me feeling uncomfortable, Ari. Do you want me to come home? Because I will; you say the word."

She was so not going to be the reason her sister gave up. And she sure as shit wasn't going to let Dane say she had reneged on their bet by having Alayna come home. Winning was her only option, but she wasn't about to push aside her sister's wishes to do so. "I only want you to come home if you think you can't get what you need there."

"If I leave now, I know down the road I'll kick my ass for not seeing this through. But I'm so frustrated. Maybe I should speak with Dane. If I decide to leave, I have to give notice."

"Talk to him." *But keep your hands off* hovered on the tip of Ariel's tongue, making her even more uneasy at the feelings Dane stirred up.

"I will, I promise. I'll let Rick know I need a meeting, and he'll get in touch with Dane."

"Sounds good. I want you to be happy, Al. And satisfied with your decision, and not because I'd love to have you back home and the surf bum out of my hair."

"Thanks. I want you happy too, but you don't sound it right now." Always the big sister, Alayna would try to think of ways to make things easier for Ariel. "Listen, I know I'm not allowed calls here, but take down Rick's cell number. If you need me for anything, you call it, and he'll get the message to me."

"Thanks." Ariel wrote down the number. For the next few minutes she updated Alayna on the different happenings at the café and answered her questions.

"All right, I've got to go, kid," Alayna said when there was nothing else to share. "I love you. Behave. And please,

please, please, try to get along with Dane until I come home. I'll be back before you know it."

"Yeah, yeah, whatever." Getting along with Dane wasn't the problem, but Ariel wasn't about to let her sister know that. "I love you too, Al. And come home when you're ready."

Ariel held the phone in her hand for a moment, her mind trying to process what her sister had said. Alayna's training at A Master's Gift had seemed like the perfect fantasy adventure for her sister to take, even if Ariel regretted talking Alayna into it. Now, though, Ariel worried it was causing more harm than good.

"It's not like I'm an expert when it comes to sex," she muttered as she leaned back in the chair. Glancing around the office, she tried to avoid the images her mind supplied of Dane's directions four nights earlier and the shattering climax she'd experienced.

"Al should be getting that, not me," she grumbled. Heat filled her cheeks as her gaze fell on the sofa.

The experience had eased the frustration that had plagued her since the morning she'd failed to finish with her new toy, but in its place she had another problem—an embarrassing one if a certain Dom tripped over her blue vibrator while working in the office. Rising from the desk, she pushed the coffee table out of the way and dropped to her knees in front of the sofa. "Where is that damned thing?" She shook her head. "I know I dropped it right here."

Leaning over, her ass in the air, her cheek nearly flat on the carpet, she scanned the area underneath the sofa and found nothing. The batteries and bottle of lube were safe in the brown paper bag she'd stashed in the back of one of the desk drawers, but the toy had been missing when she woke on the sofa Sunday.

"Hmmm, I think I've asked this before, but I guess it bears repeating. Looking for something?" Dane's voice teased from behind her.

She hadn't heard him enter. Ariel was sure the way she popped up at the sound of his voice, she must look like a squirrel that had spotted a newly fallen acorn, her eyes wide and mouth open before she was able to compose herself. Scrambling to her feet, she brushed at the knees of her slacks. Dane leaned against the desk, arms crossed over his chest and legs crossed at the ankle.

"No, not really…" Ariel started to reply.

"I'm surprised you came back. Although after the other night, I might start thinking you like having me tell you what to do."

The way he watched her made Ariel curse the fire she knew was in her eyes and the way her back went rigid, both obvious clues that she'd taken his bait. "I could say the same about you after Saturday morning." She tucked her hands in her pockets and eased past the coffee table and closer to the door.

"You might, but then I would have to point out that you're the one who came into the office." He smiled at her.

"Only to use the phone."

"And that makes me curious about why you would break the rules of A Master's Gift and subject your sister to punishment?"

"I—No—I didn't do that." Her eyes went wide again. She thought back to what her sister had told her before leaving for the mansion. Could Al really be punished for calling her? And how did he know that it was her sister she was talking to? Maybe he was simply guessing. It wouldn't be a huge leap for him to think she and Al would talk on the phone if they were apart. He knew how close she and her sister were. The comments he'd made about how long she and Al had avoided separation from one another reflected that understanding.

"You were on the phone with her a few minutes ago, weren't you?"

The look in his eyes stopped her before she could voice the lie about to form on her lips.

"Think seriously before you answer, Ariel."

"Why?" She swallowed, her gaze flickering to the door before returning to him. Neutral territory was her best bet. If she could make it to the door and into the dining area…

"You have one punishment coming for talking to your sister. You lie to me, and you'll earn a second."

"Punishment?" She puffed up with indignation. "I never agreed to—"

"But you did. When you agreed I was the boss in the office, you agreed to follow my instructions no matter what," Dane reminded her.

"But you never said I couldn't talk to my sister." Ariel stepped closer, fists propped on her hips.

"Ah, but that was a rule well understood by both you and Alayna when she agreed to be trained at the mansion."

Dane shrugged. "You break the rule, you deal with the consequences."

"And Alayna? Will she have consequences?"

"Yes."

"From Rick?"

Dane shrugged again. "Rick or…someone else." Striding forward, he smoothed his hand up her arm and curled it around her nape. "Right now you should focus on the punishment I'll be meting out."

Ariel could have cursed her body's reaction. A blossom of heat radiated from the apex of her thighs. Her breasts tingled, and her nipples pressed against the silk cups of her bra. When she most yearned to distance herself from Dane, her body fought hard to draw closer to him.

"So what's it going to be, Master Reese?" She infused as much disdain into her tone as possible and hoped he wouldn't know it for the lie it was. "A spanking? A command to suck you off?" Ariel ached to experience both, but she'd be damned if he ever learned that.

"You really are going to have to learn a bit more about the lifestyle, Tink." The calm and understanding in his blue eyes only increased Ariel's frustration.

The damned man did not lose his cool. Why? Was it the dominant in him that held the reins on his behavior? Wasn't there something she could do to get past his control? She tried to push his buttons again. "Okay, so if I'm so ignorant, give me a little lesson or two on it."

Dane shook his head and stepped away, his hand slid from her collar and transferred to the pocket of his slacks.

"You aren't prepared to listen, Ariel. I can see that. When you're ready, we'll have a long discussion about it."

Pulling a key from his pocket, he rubbed the pad of his thumb along the ridges. "What you need to do now is remove your clothes and go take a seat on the sofa."

"I don't—"

"You don't get to choose, Ariel, remember. That was our deal." He ignored her protest, went to the desk, and leaned down to unlock one of the drawers while she watched him.

"What about Sadie and DeeDee?" Ariel's heart pounded in her breast. Had he found the bag she'd stashed in the desk? Her palms grew wet, and she rubbed them against her thighs. "They could walk in."

Dane shook his head as he pulled a brown paper bag from the drawer before shutting it again. "No. The girls left as I was coming back in."

"The front door?"

"Is locked. As is the rear door." Stepping past her, Dane set the bag on the coffee table. "Take off your clothes, Ariel."

Ariel kept her gaze on Dane as she toed off her sneakers. Her fingers worked the buttons of her chef's coat loose from collar to hem. She pulled it off her shoulders and took a moment to fold it before she passed it to his outstretched hand. Her slacks, panties, bra, and socks followed.

"Now sit down." Dane motioned to the sofa before sliding the buttons at the cuffs of his dress shirt free and rolling them back to the elbow.

Ariel settled onto the cushion, grimacing at the chilled leather touching her bare bottom. She could feel the heat of embarrassment fill her face. The sensation grew worse due to the moisture developing in her pussy and the tight beading of her nipples as he watched her take a seat.

"Last time I showed you how touch can increase arousal and provide climax."

He sounded like a damned instructional video. Ariel smirked and rolled her eyes. "Yes."

"And you learned you can come without having something in your pussy."

He scooted the coffee table closer to the sofa. Taking a seat on the thick oak table, he faced her and smiled. "This time I'm going to show you how a lover, without your direction, can satisfy you."

"Yeah, right." Ariel snorted.

"Open your legs and put your feet on the table."

"Excuse me?" Ariel watched him reach for the bag.

"Feet on the table, legs open, Ariel. One on each side of me." His blue eyes were cool, direct, no amusement whatsoever.

With a huff, Ariel did as instructed. Her gaze focused on the wall beyond his shoulder. Fingers on both hands tapped out a rhythm against the cushions on either side of her hips. "You wanted to be a gynecologist, didn't you?" She dared to meet his gaze and cocked up the brow over her left eye. "I mean, it's the only explanation for your repeated determination to put me in these ridicu—"

The stroke of his fingers over her sensitive flesh stole the rest of her complaint. She arched upward into his touch. The rasp of calloused fingers over her labia and down to the damp opening beneath brought a cry of surprise from Ariel. Or perhaps it was desire—she wasn't sure.

One finger rimmed her vagina. She didn't dare look down, fighting the embarrassment whispering through her at the evidence of her arousal glistening on her pussy and beginning to wet the leather beneath her. The advance of his digits in her swelling folds and the way his fingertips rolled through the natural lubrication her body produced made her twist on the seat. She could feel him gathering the fluid before running his touch upward to coax the hidden knot of nerves from beneath its hood.

Ariel's breasts throbbed, her nipples painfully tight. Her hips surged upward and rocked into his touch. The muscles in her thighs tightened as she shifted to brace her feet more firmly on the slippery oak surface of the coffee table.

Dane's ministrations yielded faster results than hers had during their previous encounter in the office. "Please." Ariel gasped. Her fingers scratched at the cushions for purchase.

Dane's expression remained smooth, unfazed. His free hand shifted to the bag and reached inside. Ariel knew her eyes went wide when he pulled out the blue vibrator she'd been looking for earlier.

"Were you looking for this, sprite?" Dane asked. The twinkle in his blue eyes stirred her interest as much as the touch of his fingers.

The stroke of his hand stole her voice. Barely able to breathe, let alone speak, Ariel only nodded and rocked her hips upward, pressing her clit against the pads of his fingers, wanting the pressure she hoped would assuage the ache.

"No." Dane shook his head. His hand left her crease to pull the bottle of lube from the bag. "You don't direct the play."

Setting the toy in his lap, Dane used his left hand over her lower abdomen. He pressed down, stilled her motions, forcing her to wait. A sound—not quite a growl, yet not a whimper—slipped past her lips as she watched him open the bottle.

He drifted his hand down from her belly to her pussy. Using his fingers, he pushed the swollen folds apart, exposing the pink flesh even more than her spread legs did.

He held the bottle over her clit and drizzled a small stream of the clear fluid onto her before capping the bottle and picking up the vibrator.

The decision to squeeze her eyes shut or keep them open waged a minor battle inside Ariel. Dane's focus was entirely on the wet folds under his fingertips, but she knew he continued to be aware of her every action.

"Don't move, Tink." His gaze met hers and held it for several seconds.

Ariel groaned. She suspected what would come next would push the limits of her control, based on the intensity of his tone. Not like her control existed where this man was concerned. At least none she had discovered so far.

Swallowing heavily, she drew a deep breath and nodded, not trusting her voice to keep from begging for the thick length of his cock. The only consolation she had was the brief glimpse she'd got of the ridge of flesh pressed against the placket of his trousers when he'd settled onto the table.

Thoughts spun away as the low hum of the vibrator began and the blue wand settled against her clit in a whisper of a caress.

Ah fuck. I'm not gonna make it. Ariel used every muscle in her body to keep from pushing up against the toy Dane plied along her swollen folds. She could hear the rush of her blood through her veins. The leather protested the scrape of her fingernails over it, and only Dane's weight kept the low table in front of her in place. *Oh God, let it end. Quit teasing and push it in, damn it.*

She was sure he could see the strain to hold back on her face. The compulsion she fought to keep from speaking or budging from her position. The way her teeth gnawed on her lips. How her fingers clawed against the sofa cushions on either side of her hips. Heat suffused her face. All of it identified the determined effort she made not to take over and direct him in bringing her to climax. But knowing he saw it did nothing to ease how she felt or stop the sensations that coursed through her body.

"You're doing so well, Tink," he soothed as he stroked the vibrator between her labia, making sure to keep the very tip pressed over the hard nubbin of her clitoris with each slide up or down.

Ariel bit her lip to still the moan rising in her throat. She wanted to twist and move her hips, to rub against the stimulation he created.

"So good, but it's going to get harder now," he warned her.

Her vision blurred; her breath grew labored as her arousal increased with each roll of the toy along her flesh.

"Remember, no moving," he ordered.

Dane rubbed the tip of the vibrator slowly around the edge of her vagina. The smell of her cream was heavy in the room. Even as distracted and turned on as she was, Ariel would swear Dane echoed the groan that escaped her lips as he eased the tube inside the first inch.

So fucking good. He knows so well how to touch me. Ariel couldn't decide where to look next: at his face, his eyes, the hands working the toy with such skill within her body. Her inner muscles fluttered and flexed as he pressed the vibrator deeper. His breathing appeared to match the rapid pace of hers. The realization sent pure joy spreading through her. Even knowing she probably sported a blissfully dazed look didn't upset Ariel. Her body felt too good.

His left hand stroked along the outside of her thigh, tugging her open the tiniest bit more. "You feel it, don't you, baby?"

He held her gaze and watched her nod, although Ariel was unsure of what he said or what he meant.

Pulling the vibrator free before he pushed it in deeper, Dane clarified. "The heat. The need. The burn of climax waiting for the right pressure. The right touch."

Her nod was a bit more vigorous, and she could feel the hold she had on her body start to weaken. The rock of her hips increased the depth of the toy's penetration. Ariel noticed something in Dane's expression, but she was too immersed in the sensations pounding through her to try to analyze it.

"Feels good?" he asked.

"Mmm. God yes. Please, Dane." Her voice was raspy, barely audible as she gasped and shifted again to increase the stimulation of the vibe.

"Who's in charge here, Tink?" He breathed deeply, as if intoxicated by the smell of her growing climax.

"Huh? What?" Her head rolled back and forth on the back of the sofa, her breathing fast.

"Who's in charge here?" he asked again.

This time a flash of awareness surfaced in her mind. The hazy glow surrounding her cleared as her eyes went wide, and her breathing stopped for a heartbeat. Two. Three. It resumed, and her body slowly grew tense. Tears burned in her eyes, produced by a mixture of frustration, anger, and self-disgust at her naïveté. She felt him turn the speed control of the vibrator down and then off as he pulled it free of the muscles gripping it.

A shudder rippled through her body, and her throat constricted as she swallowed before her answer came out in a hoarse croak. "You. You're in charge."

"Very good." His grip was careful, soft, when he eased first one of her feet and then the other from the table and onto the carpet. "You are not allowed to come. Just stay still." He stood up and walked into the bathroom.

Ariel wondered why she didn't grab her clothes and walk out. As she fought the burn of climax, to touch herself as he'd trained her, her mind clawed at her reasons for hesitating. She didn't owe him any explanation or apologies if she decided to finish what he started. Hell, the fact that he only took her so far then stopped should be reason enough to defy his orders.

But that would break the rules of our contest. He's boss in the office; I'm boss in the kitchen. Each of us has to follow the other's direction when in their domain. That was the deal.

Closing her eyes, she took slow, shallow breaths and coaxed her body to slow down, to relax. The fever pitch of desire and the painful curl of arousal still twisted in her belly. She could feel the tears building but refused to let them fall. *I'll be damned if that fucker sees me cry. I can do this. Was this how he felt in the kitchen the other day? Did he ache with the need to come when I went down on him?*

The thoughts spun in her mind and drowned out the sound of the water running in the bathroom. Was his pride bruised by the way she'd commanded him to climax the other morning? Was this his way of teaching her to watch her step, in the same vein as her lesson for him had stemmed from the orgasm he'd given her?

She wasn't even aware he'd returned to the room until a warm, damp cloth eased over her mound to cleanse away the drying lube and sticky fluid of her arousal. She waited for him to finish, her body too alert for her to proceed any faster than a slow crawl, before she asked, "Why?"

He put the washcloth, vibrator, and lube into the paper bag and rolled the top down in a neatly creased fold three times before answering.

"You have to know how far to push your body. You know how to make yourself come, but you should also know how to *not* let yourself come."

Chapter Nine

Brain barely functioning, Ariel allowed Dane to help her into her clothes. She stepped carefully, the throb and ache of her flesh making her grimace. If she trod too quickly, the scrape of her bra over her nipples, the brush of her panties between her legs, even the seam in her pants, brought a gasp to her lips.

Despite the fog Ariel seemed to be in as she waited for Dane to set the alarm and lock up the café, the rebellious part of her brain geared itself for battle. Murmurs of discontent and irritation niggled beneath the haze of frustration and unappeased arousal.

Instead of leaving her to walk the few blocks to her house, Dane shouldered her backpack. He ignored her assurances that she was capable of getting home by herself. “The sun has only just gone down, Dane,” she pointed out, but he didn't bother to respond, only kept walking. He was careful to keep his steps short, as if he were trying to accommodate her slower pace. It was hard for her to get a handle on the emotions boiling through her. Unrequited lust was foremost, but beneath it was a morass of confusion and contradiction. She knew she should be pissed, but she wasn't.

His determination to see her safely home wasn't new. So far he'd followed her and watched until she closed the door behind her almost every night. She knew she should resent it, but again the emotion was absent.

"This was payback for the unfinished blowjob, isn't it?" she asked, her gaze focused on the sidewalk in front of her. Her peripheral vision caught the shake of Dane's head before his words reached her.

"No. This had nothing to do with that, Ariel."

"For Saturday morning?"

"No."

"I don't believe you." Turning her head, she watched his shoulders rise and fall in a negligent shrug.

"You can believe what you want, love, but tonight's lesson had nothing to do with your demonstration about chocolate or your attempt at playing Domme." The take-it-or-leave-it tone seemed to support his words.

"Then why?" Her hand rubbed at the knot in her belly while fighting the urge to shift lower and cup her pulsing mound. "If a dominant is supposed to direct the satisfaction of his sub, like you keep saying he is, then what point is there to taking me so far and leaving me in pain?"

They neared the house and stepped onto the porch as Dane responded. "A Dom is also supposed to show the sub that delayed satisfaction can increase the ability to control his or her body and the response it has to varied stimuli." He took her key from her hand and opened the door.

With the porch light shining on his golden hair, he waited outside the door while Ariel punched in the alarm code and turned to face him. She was inclined to believe him, and he seemed to have a bit more to say as he held on to her backpack while she leaned in the doorway.

"Knowing how to control your body, to control your climax, can enable a sub to delay gratification, sometimes for hours. And since the primary concern of a sub should be the satisfaction and comfort of his or her dominant, delayed satisfaction can increase the pleasure of the master."

Ariel took in the information and compared it to the information she'd gleaned online and from some of the books she'd read. Even when she and Alayna had read the pages of A Master's Gift's Web site, the point hadn't been clear. Until now. Now she could see how controlling her body could be used as a tool to please another. Too bad she hadn't stopped herself from climaxing. Dane had done that. *Like I need more proof of what a failure at sex I am.*

Feeling the tears of frustration and disappointment begin to clog her throat, she held her hand out for her backpack. The frustration was understandable, considering the unfulfilled desires pounding through her body. It was the feeling of disappointment that scared her. Especially considering the disappointment stemmed from her failure to please Dane. And the fact that she even cared about his satisfaction pissed her off.

As he relinquished the pack to her, Ariel tried to smile. She knew it came out more as a grimace, from the concerned look that creased the corners of his eyes. "I guess it's a good thing I'm not aiming to be anyone's sub, huh?"

Dane stepped closer. "Why?"

"Because I'd fucking fail every time." She shook her head. "Trying to keep from coming as a means of bringing someone else off would be impossible. Hell, I can barely bring myself off."

She didn't bother to wait for Dane's response. Anxious to get away, to avoid facing the truth about her shortcomings when it came to sex, Ariel stepped back from the doorway. Though the vixen inside urged her to slam the door in his face, Ariel merely closed it with a quiet *click.*

Dane wasn't sure what he'd expected as a response, but he cursed the lesson he'd given her tonight after seeing the look of self-loathing and defeat filling her face and darkening her eyes.

Shit. You idiot! Having watched her struggle to climax last week, you think revving her up and then leaving her is the best way to show her how to control her body? Dane swore under his breath as he hesitated at the top step. The pain and disappointment on her face tugged at him, but he fought the inclination to comfort her. She wasn't his sub. Hell, she wasn't even training to be his sub. *But you're treating her like she is. And you're hoping she will be.*

"It's a fucking bet," he growled, his shoulder propped against the post supporting the roof of the porch. He thrust his left hand through his hair and forced himself to descend the four shallow steps and start down the path. Shoving his fists into his pockets, he stopped, closed his eyes, and drew a deep breath. He hoped the smell of flower gardens, mown grass, and car exhaust would eradicate the aroma of her arousal that lingered in his nostrils. It didn't.

Closing his eyes didn't help either, since the expression on her face pasted itself to the insides of his eyelids. “Fuck.” When the features in the face altered and took on those of Ariel's sister, Alayna, Dane knew he was screwed.

In the two weeks Alayna had been at the mansion, the disappointed expression in her eyes had only grown deeper. The confidence she'd started with was waning, and every bit of her decline could be put squarely at his business partner's feet. Logan's fears kept him from claiming the woman he wanted, which translated to rejection in Alayna's mind. Could Ariel be thinking the same thing? Believing that refusing her climax was his way of pushing her away. Rejecting her.

“Damn it.” He shook his head and tried to take a few more steps toward the street. “It's a challenge. A bet. Hell, she can't even admit she wants to be a sub. Why the fuck am I worried about this?”

“*It's a good thing I'm not aiming to be anyone's sub, huh? Because I'd fucking fail at it.*” Her words echoed in his head, halted his steps, and sent his fingers scraping through his hair in exasperation.

“She wouldn't fail. That's the problem,” Dane muttered. He looked over his shoulder. No lights had come on.

Again Alayna's disappointed face flashed in his mind, followed by the image of Logan creeping into his suite because he didn't have the fucking balls to take the woman he wanted.

“Goddamn it.” He spun around and strode up the walk. Dane took the four steps in one stride, and his fist hit the door as he snapped, "No way am I fucking this up. I'm not Logan."

When the door remained closed, he pounded harder. "Ariel. Open up."

Arms braced on the door frame, Dane waited, not sure what his next maneuver would be if she refused to answer. He didn't have to wait long for the door to swing open. His belly twisted in self-disgust at the gleam of tears on Ariel's cheeks. Her nose was red, and her eyes were pink and puffy, but the fire was back in them.

He couldn't help but grin when her chin went up and she glared at him. The entire effect disintegrated when she brought a wad of tissue up and blew her nose, loud and long.

Still, her words conveyed her irritation. "What? Did you forget something? Some extra bit of advice geared to rip away what little self-respect I have left?"

"No." He couldn't fight the grin. His woman didn't stay down for long, and he liked that about her. Hell, he loved it.

"Then what? Are you finding this amusing? Think it's funny to get the ice bitch all hot and bothered, then dump her on her ass?" Her fist thumped against his shoulder in a solid punch.

Dane shook his head and stepped inside.

"Hey, asshole, I didn't invite you—" Another firm smack from her balled fist landed in the same spot as the first.

He didn't bother listening to her, ignored a third strike of her fist, and merely pulled the door from her hold and shut it behind him. He didn't pay attention to the surroundings; his focus was on her. Keeping his gaze on her face, he slid his hand up the door from the knob until his fingers bumped into the dead bolt. After twisting it closed, he crowded closer to Ariel.

"Get out. I don't want you—"

"You do." He called her on her lie. "You're wet and aching."

"I'd rather spend the rest of my life in a chastity belt than have you touch me," Ariel snarled. The crumpled tissue missed hitting him by inches, but he ignored it, moving in until he'd backed her into the wall.

"Liar," he whispered. He cupped her face in his hands and tilted her mouth up to his.

"You touch me, and you're pulling back a stump, you prick." There wasn't much heat in her threat. The hands against his waist could hardly be considered a deterrent.

Dane brushed his lips over hers. "We aren't in the kitchen, baby. So I think I'll risk it." He didn't give her another opportunity to refuse. Sealing her lips with his, he plunged his tongue inside and stroked in and out, imitating the advance and retreat he would use with his body.

The hands that had been pressing at his waist stilled. Shifting closer, he pushed the thick ridge of his confined erection against her belly, announcing his intent without words.

Ariel cuddled closer, fingers clutching, then releasing the fabric of his shirt before making the effort to pull it free of his waistband.

Lust overrode finesse as he gripped the front of her jacket in both hands and yanked it open; the buttons popped free. Shoving it off her shoulders, his fingers traveled down to release the hook and button securing her waistband before jerking the zipper down and tugging her pants and panties off her hips and down to her ankles.

Ariel gasped as his mouth left hers to trail over her cheek and along her throat. More hooks released, and her bra stripped away and dropped her plump, full breasts into his waiting hands.

"You know that lemon glaze you use on the lemon pound cake?"

"What?" Her eyes were dazed, unfocused, as she watched his lips coast over first one breast, then the other. His tongue flicked out to roll over one puckered nipple before tugging on it with his teeth.

"The lemon glaze for your pound cake," he repeated, his grin hidden by the attention he gave her beautiful breasts.

"Wha-what about it?"

"I've imagined drizzling it over these sweet tits since the first day Logan and I ate lunch at the café." Dane relocated his attention to the other nipple, enjoying the moans spilling from her lips. "In my mind, when I was finished licking it off your nipples, I wanted to cover your pussy with it and bury my face between your thighs."

He could smell how wet she was; he didn't even have to touch her. The scent filled his nostrils as he eased to his knees and yanked the sneaker and sock from first one foot, then the other. After pulling the puddle of silk and cotton off, Dane settled Ariel's left leg over his right shoulder and opened her cunt to his attentions.

One long swipe of his tongue had both of them groaning. Her taste surpassed any he'd imagined as he delved deeper and used the fingers of one hand to hold her open. Again he stroked his tongue from bottom to top, halted at her clit to nip the sensitive knot, dragging a cry from Ariel. The thigh on his shoulder tensed as she arched into his touch. Her fingers tangled in his hair, her words nearly incoherent as she urged him on.

Ariel ached. The fire she'd been able to ease flared to life, pounded through her body, coiled in her belly, waiting to explode. "Please, I want you inside." She groaned, pushing upward to increase the pressure on her clit. Her fingers tangled in his curls, and her head rolled back and forth against the wall behind her.

"Patience, Tink." His assurance didn't help. The stroke of his tongue teased around the throbbing nubbin his teeth nibbled. Then he sent his attentions south, nipping at the inner frill of tissue before stroking downward to the opening weeping for attention.

He teased and nibbled, ignoring her pleas, the tug of her fingers in his hair, even the squeeze of her leg as it curled over his shoulder and pushed him closer to the spot she longed to have filled.

The first thrust of his tongue into her pussy was a teasing foray. A flick against the opening before he retreated to sip at the moisture wetting her thighs. With the next teasing swipe, she rose onto the ball of her foot, and a keening cry slipped free. The deeper penetration shuddered through her belly into her womb and vibrated up to the aching tips of her breasts.

Dane seemed to have a sixth sense about the pulse and sting of her arousal as it made its way to the sensitive flesh throughout her body. With his tongue thrusting and pumping in and out of her pussy, assailing her senses with a preview of the rhythm his cock would use, Dane tugged the fingers of one of Ariel's hands free from his hair and transferred it to her breast.

Moaning, eyes half-closed with the sensations bombarding her, Ariel met Dane's cobalt gaze over the curve of her belly. His fingers covered hers, directing her in the pressure and timing to squeeze her aching tit before shifting her fingers to the taut nipple and pinching the beaded tip with enough force to turn her knees weak and momentarily stop her breath.

Her second cry echoed in the foyer as the pace stopped along with the wet slide of mouth over pussy. Before she could protest, Dane slid her leg from his shoulder and surged to his feet. His mouth, wet with her juices, covered hers, shared the flavor of her body and his taste as his fingers tangled with hers on the slide of his belt and the fastener of his trousers.

Pulling back, he fumbled with his billfold before shoving pants and underwear out of the way. Ariel tried to separate the buttons from buttonholes on his shirt with her shaky fingers. She fumbled, missed, fumbled again, but she refused to give up. The *rip* of cellophane and the *swish* of latex over flesh barely registered. After successfully baring his throat and the smooth muscles below his collar, Ariel pressed her mouth against the pulsing vein in his neck. The blend of spices she associated with him flooded her senses.

His hands gripped the backs of her thighs, lifting her off her feet, making her clutch his shoulders. The hot tip of his cock teased the entrance to her body. Ariel rocked forward in an attempt to draw him in, but his grip kept her separate. Raising her head, she looked at him. As if he'd only waited for her gaze to meet his, Dane thrust inside, filling her empty depths, forcing tight muscles to give way.

Her thighs wrapped around his waist; her hips pushed down, wanting more; her arms wrapped around his shoulders and pulled his mouth to hers. Finesse was lost; grace and gentleness obscured beneath the hammering need driving them together.

The speed, depth, and power of each thrust grew. The force of his possession slammed her into the wall, dragging cries and moans from her lips. He swallowed each one with his mouth. The thrust and retreat of his tongue mirrored the motion of his thick cock, propelling sensation upon sensation through her core.

The neat arrangement of pictures on the foyer table beside them tumbled to the tile. She registered the sound of a crash from some knickknack or picture frame on the other side of the wall as it hit the floor. Her entire focus remained locked on the sensual battle in which she was engaged. Satisfying the craving that had built between them over the last two weeks consumed her attention.

Desperate for air, the fire of climax licking at her womb, Ariel pulled her mouth free of Dane's. She didn't feel pain as her head bounced off the wall behind her. The flames extending outward from her pussy, down her legs, and into her torso scattered all thought beyond ending the craving for his possession. Unable to silence it, a primal scream ripped from her throat and echoed off the walls as the first orgasm rolled through her. A second welled up immediately behind it.

"Ahh God. Fuck." She was barely aware of the nonsense words that spilled from her lips as she slammed her hips down to meet each powerful stroke. The second release had barely faded when a third began to build. "No. Yes. Harder. Dane, I ca… I can't. Not again."

"Again, Tink. And again." His words were a mixture of command and amusement. Laughter mingled with groans as he changed his pace and the depth of his thrusts. The clutch of his hands on her ass was sure to leave bruises, but Ariel couldn't have cared less.

On the edge of exhaustion, her voice hoarse from her cries, she felt Dane's shoulders tense beneath her hold. His body pressed closer; his cock pushed deeper than it had gone before, sending her head back in surprise as the spiral of another orgasm exploded inside her. The way he locked his hips to her, the tightening of his fingers on her ass, the throb of his cock, and his deep bellow echoing off the walls and in her ears signaled Dane's climax.

Ariel was awash in sensation. Feelings, impressions, emotions overwhelmed her, destroying any reasonable thoughts she might have. Sex wasn't like this. It had never been like this in the past. Her body vibrated with every beat of her heart, trying to match the rhythm of Dane's as he held her close to him.

She felt too languorous to contemplate pulling away. Ariel visualized cuddling in bed with him. Hours spent playing, talking, simply being together rolled against her closed eyelids. Worry, sharp and intrusive, prodded her to run, to separate herself from him, to get away. Ariel pushed it aside. *Don't make me think now. Let me just enjoy him. I'll think about this after he leaves.* She forced herself to ignore the shaft of pain at the thought of his leaving.

His knees felt like gelatin, and his throat was raw from the shout he'd given as the universe exploded behind his eyes. His head dropped to Ariel's shoulder as his legs gave out. Dane had barely enough strength left to get from upright to kneeling without dropping the warm bundle of pleasure in his arms. Eyes closed, he breathed slowly in an attempt to regain his composure. Fucking her had been in the cards, but this? Rough, aggressive, almost an animalistic coupling in the entryway of her home, wasn't how it was supposed to happen.

The suspicions he'd voiced to Shendah about how Ariel would change his life buzzed through his mind. He hadn't even come close to the reality. To the tangle of emotions building inside him. All the rationalizations in the world could never override the plain fact that his actions tonight constituted a claiming. Not fucking. Not making love. But an outright stamp of ownership a man placed on his woman.

The line between his past and future hovered before him. He could retreat, keep what was between Ariel and him simply sex. Or he could face the challenge of showing Ariel she belonged with him and allow the feelings inside him to fully develop.

Alarms bells clanged out a warning in his head. And he ignored them. Mentally stepping across the line, he made his choice.

The smell of her satisfaction, the sticky wetness that clung to their thighs, the sweat from her body staining his shirt, had nothing to do with sex and everything to do with love.

And his instincts to run stayed silent. Damn the luck.

Finding her might have been the easy part. The battle he had to win lay in convincing her that submitting to him was the reason she existed. And there were only two weeks left to do it.

Chapter Ten

Day 16

Dane was waiting for her when she arrived at the shop the next morning. Her body responded to the sight of him—her nipples hardened, belly knotted, and the ache inside her cunt increased. "You would have been better off simply staying at my place instead of driving all the way out to the mansion, then back." She grinned as he checked a yawn and followed her into the café.

"Miss me?" He locked the door as she shut off the alarm.

Ariel snorted, then sighed as he pulled her close and pressed his lips to hers. It didn't take much to coax a response from her. The stroke of his tongue across her lips, a gentle nudge, and his taste filled her mouth, making her body hum with sensation. Pulling back, she croaked, "Maybe."

Incorrigibly smug, Dane chuckled and kept his arm around her waist as they walked toward the office. "Hmmm, we'll have to discuss your habit of understatement of, Miss Valerian."

"You're the one calling me with 'we have to talk' excuses, Mr. Reese," Ariel reminded him.

“And we do,” he assured her as he guided her into the office and pushed the door shut. He set the bag he carried on the desk before he turned to face her.

“About what?”

“I'm going to be busy with some clients at my office this morning, so I won't be in until after the lunch rush.” He kept his attention on her face, but his fingers wandered down her shirt, sliding buttons through holes.

Ariel didn't stop him since her fingers were doing the same to his shirt. “Okay, so you'll be in late. Was that all you wanted to discuss?” She stepped close as he opened the front clasp of her bra. The heat of his bare chest against her aching breasts ratcheted up the fire inside her.

“Not completely.” He upended the bag with his left hand, spilling the contents onto the desk. His right hand caressed her bottom, holding her close, allowing her to feel the aroused length of his cock through his jeans and her pants.

Ariel's fingers stilled on his chest once she saw the bright blue toy and bottle of lubricant resting on the desk.

“Are you familiar with one of these?” Dane asked, lifting the rubber cone up for her to see.

Ariel swallowed. “It's a butt plug, right?” She could feel the heat suffuse her cheeks as she envisioned him using the device on her.

Dane smiled. “Yes. Have you ever used one?”

She stroked over the cool surface of the toy with a trembling fingertip. “No.”

“Have you ever wanted to?”

Dane didn't allow her to look away. Hesitantly she bobbed her head up, then down once. "Yes."

"Have you ever had anal sex with one of your lovers?"

"No."

"You have such a sexy ass, Ariel. Didn't any of them try to tempt you?" Dane stroked his hand over her bottom and squeezed one rounded globe then the other before he traced the crease between them.

"One did. I just—I couldn't—didn't like the idea of it," she stammered. "Not with him."

Lowering the toy out of sight before he set it on the desk, Dane held her gaze and asked, "May I fuck your ass?"

Ariel tried to suppress her laughter, but his words and the sincere expression were too much. Her head dropped to his shoulder, breaking eye contact as she snorted and guffawed over his request.

The rumble of amusement beneath her palms as Dane chuckled kept her from feeling uneasy as he coaxed her head up so he could look at her. "I'm serious, baby," he assured her. "I've dreamed of taking your sweet behind for weeks. It'll be so tight and snug around my cock. Not that your pussy isn't the hottest thing I've ever had."

Her amusement drifted away. Her body ached more than usual at the temptation he offered. "You really want—"

"God yes. I told you when we started our challenge that I wanted to get you stretched and ready to take me." Dane settled a hot, openmouthed kiss on her before he pulled back and continued. "The fact that I'll be your first will only make it sweeter."

"You're crazy." Ariel sighed.

"Let me show you how good it feels," Dane whispered. His hands skated to the front of her waist and released the button and zipper on her slacks.

Ariel didn't resist. Her body hummed with curiosity, and the passion he'd slaked the night before rose inside her. "Okay."

Quickly stripped of her clothes, Ariel followed Dane's directions to step around him, face the desk, and lean on her elbows forward across the surface. When his fingers stroked between the petals of her pussy, she couldn't swallow a gasp.

"Just the idea has you wet, huh?" Dane teased as he smoothed the damp evidence of her arousal from her pussy to the tight pucker of her ass.

Again and again he stroked over her clit, drawing the nubbin out, teasing it before he shifted his touch to her rear entrance. Ariel started to pull away when she felt the cool drizzle of lubricant, but Dane soothed her surprise and took his time working the tip of his finger past the opening. "Shhh, it's okay, love. We'll take as much time as you need," he coaxed, his voice soft, the press of his finger slow and steady.

He repositioned the fingers of his other hand to the knot of nerves peeking from beneath its hood, rubbing over it, building the heat, the ache inside her pussy, coiling the arousal in her belly tighter. She wasn't even aware she'd begun to rock backward, allowing his finger to penetrate deeper, until he praised her in a rough, throaty voice.

"That's it, Ariel. Push against it."

Dane took his time working the first finger in, pulling it out, then pushing it back in again. At the addition of a second finger, Ariel spread her legs and rocked forward and back into the press of his fingers as he stretched her tight muscles. The ridge of his arousal strained his jeans, but he fought the temptation to release it. Preparing her to take his cock was the goal, not a quick fuck on the desk, no matter how much they both wanted it.

He pulled his fingers free, used a tissue to wipe them off, then grabbed the plug and bottle of lube. "Okay, Tink. Don't tense up. Breathe deep and push back."

Ariel nodded.

Both her ass and the plug glistened as he set the tip to her entrance and pressed forward. She shifted backward, gasping as he worked the device past the first ring of muscles.

"You know, this wasn't what I expected—*Oh God*." Ariel gasped. He could see her fingers grip the edge of the desk.

"Didn't expect what, love?" Dane teased. His lips coasted over her bare shoulder as he eased the plug deeper.

It was so easy for him to see the warring desires imprisoning Ariel. It seemed part of her wanted to shift away from the toy filling her ass. The heat of arousal built in her center, while another part of her yearned to press backward, to increase the sting and stretch of unused muscles.

"Didn't expect what?" Dane prompted again as he seated the plug completely and smoothed his hand over her bottom.

He smiled and traced the inked design on her cheek before leaning down to nip the rounded flesh with his teeth.

"When you…were waiting…outside this morning." Ariel gasped as she lowered her forehead to the desk.

Dane was sure Ariel debated rising from her elbows because of the burn; he continued to smooth his hands over her bottom, enjoying the way she arched into his touch. "Were you hoping for a replay of last Saturday?"

Her head came up, and she drew a deep breath before releasing it slowly. She ignored his taunt. "I was under the impression our meeting was for business purposes," Ariel finished as she slowly worked herself into an upright position.

Dane's hands gripped her upper arms, held her still as she began to sway. "It was." His lips nibbled on the curve between her shoulder and throat. "Don't you remember my promise to find the right-sized plug for this sweet ass of yours?" One of his hands dropped to smooth over the bare curves quivering in reaction to the arousing stretch of delicate muscles for the first time.

Ariel leaned back. The desperate longing to take her again surfaced with the warm weight of her lush body against him. But he wouldn't, not here. Not yet. Turning her to face him, Dane took a moment to study her face. Her damp brow and flushed cheeks attested to her arousal; the hard nipples and rapid breathing only reinforced his observation.

Bending, he brushed her lips with his. "When I get you stretched out, Ariel, I'm going to take my time fucking your sweet ass. Then I'll push a nice big plug inside and slide into your pussy. You'll be so tight, we'll both come the first time I get all the way in."

"Now. Do it now," she demanded against his mouth. Her fingers tightened around his upper arms as she deepened the kiss, tangled her tongue with his, and pressed her body tight to him.

Careful to go slowly, Dane settled her onto the desk. A cut-off cry escaped her lips as the plug pressed in at a different angle. "I would like nothing more than to spend the whole morning taking you on every flat surface and against every wall in this diner, baby, but I have to leave." He glanced at his watch and cursed. "I should have left ten minutes ago."

"Please." Ariel held him tight.

Dane shook his head. "Much as I want to, I can't. Not enough time, hon. I have papers piled up at the office. Both here in town and at the mansion. I want more than a few minutes with you." Stepping back, he ached to do exactly as she asked. The passion in her face, the desire he knew tormented her, pulled his balls tight into his body, ready to explode. Not willing to leave her unsatisfied, he dropped to his knees and pressed her thighs apart. "Lean back, Ariel."

He didn't wait to see if she complied before he buried his face in her wet mound. The flavor of her arousal, the heat of her pussy, drew him in. He suckled the tender button at the apex of her thighs before dropping downward to lap the cream from her plump lips. From there he returned to her taut clit; his fingers slipped inside her sheath to stroke the pulsing walls.

Beneath his touch, Ariel arched, her climax suspended until she whispered, "May I come?"

Dane didn't deny the sensation spilling through his body at the plea. Pleasure coursed through him when she voiced the request. She deserved a reward for asking permission, for holding back her satisfaction until he deemed her ready. He replaced his lips with his thumb, rose to lean over her; his free hand cupped her cheek. Trapping her gaze with his, he smiled. "Yes, Ariel, show me how I please you. Come."

He silenced her cry with his lips, but the shudders trembling through her body vibrated against his, pushing his need to the edge. Years of practice and force of will helped keep him from climaxing with her, but Dane didn't deny how close it was.

Once she calmed, he carried her to the sofa. He left her only long enough to gather and dampen a washrag in the bathroom. Bathing the residue of her passion from her thighs, he finished the instructions he planned to give her. "Keep the plug in until just before you open for breakfast. I don't want you too sore."

He watched her eyes droop and pulled the blanket from the end of the couch. "Rest. I'll call you in an hour." He pressed a kiss to her brow and set the cordless telephone on the coffee table.

By the time he switched off the lights, she was asleep. Leaving the office door closed behind him, he set the alarm against intruders, left the store, and locked the door. It was a damned good thing there was a shower and change of clothes in his office, Dane decided as he jogged across the street to where he'd left his car in the parking spaces in front of his building before heading to Valerian's Root to catch Ariel as she opened up.

Once he ran out to the mansion for another change of clothes, Dane would try to catch Rick and check with him to make sure his plan to drag Logan out of his self-imposed emotional exile was working, then he'd come back to the café. If things were running smoothly, he wouldn't have to leave Ariel's bed before he wanted to in the evening. First things first, though. A cold shower was required, then a strong cup of coffee.

* * *

The café was packed with customers when Dane walked in a little after eleven. DeeDee and Sadie worked the tables as quickly as they could, but from their harried expressions, he knew the larger-than-normal crowd had them a little frazzled.

All the booths along the walls, the eight round tables in the center of the wood floor, and the counter overflowed with people. Many of the customers wore uniforms streaked with the red clay from the softball fields, reminding Dane about the softball tournament Ayerstown was hosting that weekend.

Play had begun last night and would last until late Sunday afternoon. Word about the café must have circulated among the teams, because it appeared nearly half the visiting players had decided to see if the rumors were true.

Dane didn't doubt they'd be impressed. Ariel knew her food.

"Sadie, order up, table four!" Ariel called out as she slid a plate onto the brushed-chrome shelf of the order window.

Sadie stood beside a booth scribbling the orders from a family of four. She nodded but didn't respond to Ariel's call.

Dane patted the waitress's shoulder. "I'll get it for you." He shed his coat, pulled the tie from his collar, stuffed it into a pocket, and strode to the counter and the orders in the window.

He folded his coat and tucked it into the shelf beneath the register, then washed his hands at the sink beneath the counter and dried them with a paper towel. After he grabbed the plates for the table, he headed back to the main dining area and passed the food out to the waiting diners.

For the next hour, as the girls worked the booths and tables, Dane took care of the orders at the counter. Refilling glasses with soda, coffee, or iced tea, he chatted with the customers.

The first time Ariel spotted him through the order window, her eyes went wide and a pleased grin lifted her lips. It was quickly erased as she ordered, "Keep your hands off the till, Reese. We don't have time to fix your mistakes today."

Most of the regulars chuckled at the reprimand. Dane ignored them. "I'll leave the register to Sadie. You keep playing with your pots and pans."

Near one in the afternoon, the crowd thinned to a few regulars, which allowed DeeDee and Sadie to relax a bit, while Dane helped bus the tables and carry the heavy trays of dishes to the kitchen.

"I thought you weren't going to be back until later," Ariel said as she wiped down the central island.

"Jordan had the paperwork taken care of; all he required was my signature. And the clients scheduled for this afternoon canceled for personal reasons, and rescheduled for next week."

Ariel dried her hands and strolled up next to him as he rinsed and stacked plates, cups, and silverware into the washer. "Does this mean you'll be sticking around for the rest of the afternoon?"

Dane held back his temptation to grin at the hopeful look in her bright green eyes. The stiff nipples pressed against her shirt betrayed her arousal. "You know I would like nothing better than to christen the couch in the office by spreading you out and taking you hard and fast, Tink." He kept his voice low and enjoyed the flush that mounted her cheeks and the way her body swayed closer to him.

He leaned down, brushed his lips over hers, and made his excuses. "But I can't. I have to get back to the mansion by three. I have to talk to someone."

"Order in!" Sadie's voice held a distinct chuckle.

Turning, Dane and Ariel could see both waitresses and a few of the customers stretched up to watch them. Ariel rolled her eyes and stomped to the spindle for the order.

"If you have to be there by three, you better get going," she told him, trying to sound matter-of-fact, but the tone of disappointment was easy for him to detect.

"I'll try to be back by closing time."

She shrugged and pulled the ingredients for the order.

Dane finished the dishes, dried his hands, and crossed the room to stand behind Ariel. Close to her ear, he whispered, “If you're a good girl, I'll bring a few more toys to play with when I come back.” His hands settled on her hips and tucked her close so the ridge of his erection stroked her lower back.

“Quit giving me directions in my kitchen.” The command was voiced around a moan as she pressed back, rubbing her bottom against him, teasing him.

Dane relinquished his hold and headed toward the double doors leading into the main area of the café. “Tonight.”

Ariel rolled her eyes at him. “If you're lucky.” But her smile implied promises her lips wouldn't say.

* * *

Day 17

Twenty-four hours later Dane slammed into Logan's office; irritation and annoyance fueled his anger. When he'd spoken to Rick the day before, Dane had suspected Logan was interfering in Alayna's training. Rick's concern for Alayna had focused on her increased sense of failure and self-doubt. Based on the conversation Dane had just had with Alayna, Rick wasn't far from the mark. Squaring off with his business partner had better provide some results, or Dane would force a few on his own.

Logan looked only mildly surprised as he turned from the broad windows overlooking the back acreage. "Something I can help you with?"

"Alayna wants to leave," Dane informed him.

"Why?"

His expression didn't betray his disquiet, but having known Logan as long as he had, Dane was able to read the emotions in his friend's eyes. "Because she isn't getting what was promised to her."

"She has two weeks to go." Logan's protest was gruff. He moved to his desk.

Dane shrugged. "You're aware of the release clause written into the contract. Her expectations have yet to be met. She wants out, and I'm inclined to let her."

Logan didn't respond.

"I've heard you've made it difficult for Rick to give one-hundred percent to her training." He pushed his friend a little more to see some reaction.

Logan refused to acknowledge the accusation.

"You do realize that by threatening Rick, you've essentially reneged on our contractual obligation to Alayna, right?"

Logan dismissed the comment with a grunt and a wave of his hand.

"Damn it, Logan, I know she's the one that has your balls in a twist." Dane glared at him.

"What the hell are you talking about?" Logan snapped.

"It's more than obvious. You didn't participate in her intake interview—"

"That was your doing," Logan snarled and pointed a finger at Dane. "You blindsided me by bringing Alayna here and not saying a fucking word to me."

"Because she's your match, you ass. And for months you've refused to act on your attraction to her."

"You don't know fuck all."

Dane ground his teeth to keep from yelling. "I'm smarter than you're giving me credit for. You're involved in her training, but not hands-on. Or rather, you've seen to it that Rick can't assist her. You insist Alayna sleeps in your personal suite, in your bed. The first week you were content with sitting and watching her sleep. But then that wasn't enough. Now you're crawling in beside her after she's fallen asleep."

"You knew?" Logan's face paled with shock and surprise.

"Of course I fucking knew. I know everything that goes on around here."

"How?" Logan demanded.

"Shendah smells you in the room when she makes it up. Your cologne is all over the sheets. Stop dicking around, Logan. Take the fucking bull by the horns and go after what you want—"

"Fuck you," Logan growled.

The memories were there on Logan's face for Dane to read. He'd been there when Logan had met his last sub, Tasha, eight years ago. He'd watched the rise and fall of the relationship and the guilt that consumed Logan after Tasha died. Her death hadn't been Logan's fault, but his dedication and commitment as a dominant didn't allow him to dismiss an obligation to protect Tasha, even though Logan had dissolved the relationship because she had begun demanding dangerous play that he refused to carry out.

Tasha's risk taking hadn't been Logan's responsibility, but the man was determined in his belief that he should have been able to dissuade Tasha from her interest in autoerotic asphyxiation. It pissed Dane off that Logan was allowing that guilt to manipulate him so many years later.

"Get off the cross, man. Tasha made her choice. You need to make yours."

"I have," Logan snapped.

"No"—Dane crossed his arms over his chest—"you've been hiding and avoiding making a real choice for five years. So you're going to spend the rest of your life jacking off? Never touch another woman because she couldn't push you to give up your personal ethics? That's fucking lame, Logan."

The stubborn set of Logan's jaw confirmed Dane's suspicions that his friend would fight tooth and nail to stay away from the woman he wanted.

"Christ, Logan, you want Alayna. But what I don't understand is if you want her so bad, why don't you claim her, mark her, collar her—something? Why keep her at arm's length?"

"It's not that simple," Logan said as he dropped into the chair behind his desk.

"Seems pretty fucking simple to me. You're attracted to her, and not just for the purposes of taking her as a sub, and damn, she is a natural sub, my friend. She needs that tapped. But there's more to it than that, any fool can see. Hell, if you aren't interested in marking her, maybe I'll add her to my harem."

A vicious growl erupted from Logan's throat. "You don't have a harem."

Dane shook his head and chuckled. "Maybe I should start one. Hell, the older sister is probably easier to control than the younger one." *Come on, pal. Show me how you really feel.*

"Back off, Dane."

"You know what, buddy? Sometimes a Dom meets his match in a sub, and that's nothing to be ashamed of. Alayna rocks your control, challenges you. So embrace it. Learn from it. Strengthen your control where your woman is concerned. Alayna isn't Tasha."

"I know that," Logan snarled. "Why can't you just leave it be?"

Maybe he should leave it alone, Dane thought. He threw up his hands in exasperation. "You're right. You know what? Fuck it. Throw away what you could have with Alayna while you wallow in your self-pity and guilt over something that was out of your control. Leave her to me. Yup, that's what I'm going to do for you, my friend," Dane said, turning toward the door. "I'll take over Alayna's training. Personally. Then your control will remain intact, and you'll have nothing to worry about."

Dane closed the door with the same solid *thud* he'd used to open it. He must have made an impression, because something heavy slammed into the door behind him.

Chapter Eleven

Dane's grip on the steering wheel turned his knuckles white. He was furious with Logan's intractable determination to bury himself away from life. "Alayna is Logan's match, and the stubborn bastard refuses to see it," he growled as he slowed the car and downshifted to pull out of the long drive and onto the road leading to the highway.

"I'll be damned if I'm going to let him, though," he assured himself. The plans were in place. A twinge of guilt assailed him at the lie he'd told Alayna about allowing her to leave. "No way will I let her leave. Not in twenty-four hours. Not in thirty days. She stays until Logan gets his head out of his ass and sees what he's giving up."

Part of him knew the barriers were falling for his friend. The expression on Logan's face when Dane had told him Alayna had requested to leave was evidence enough for Dane that Logan's resolution to avoid his woman was disintegrating. If the bastard didn't get the hint after Rick followed Dane's commands and arranged for Logan to confront his fears and Alayna to experience her true master, Dane would be the first one to help Alayna pack. But Dane doubted Logan would ignore a sweet treat like Alayna naked and bound for his pleasure. At least not after the last few days Logan had spent sharing her bed. Once Logan started touching Alayna, Dane doubted either one would be able to deny their attraction.

"After tomorrow, if he can still walk, I have no doubt Alayna will be staying." The heat of frustration eased as Dane merged into the afternoon traffic and headed toward Ayerstown.

The same confidence that drove him to know what was best for his friend was warning him that the outcome between him and Ariel could be different.

His pixie was proving to be determined to ignore the bond forming between them. "Alayna told me she didn't like change; maybe I should have listened." He shook his head at the burn of disappointment seeping into his chest.

The promised playtime with Ariel hadn't materialized the day before. After his and Rick's discussion and spending time with the books, he'd made it back to the café long after Ariel had closed up and gone home. At least she hadn't turned him away when he knocked on her door, which was encouraging.

But she still held herself back from him. He could feel the resistance she put up to block any emotional connections he attempted to create. It was more than frustrating to him.

The clock on the dashboard read 3:15. By the time he made it to Valerian's Root, the last customers would be leaving. He could use the time it took for DeeDee and Sadie to clean up to finish the deposit and organize the supply orders.

The bag of toys he'd promised Ariel the day before was still in his car, awaiting use. If she was ever going to recognize his position as her master, it would have to be soon. She needed to understand, as he had come to know, that what was between them was more than a game of sexual role-play. That change was coming, and she should prepare for it.

When he eased into a parking space in front of the café, Dane had mapped out every step of his plan. Once they were alone, it would be Ariel's turn to choose.

* * *

"Here you go, Mrs. Douglas." Ariel set the box of cupcakes on the table next to the older woman. "Thanks for calling in your order."

"Thank you for making them special, dear." The elderly lady's pale gray eyes twinkled. "It gave me an excuse to get Harold out of the house and away from that television of his."

Mrs. Douglas's husband, Harold, seated across from her, snorted. "She's just sayin' that 'cause I was checkin' out that model program. Dottie doesn't like me ogling other women."

Dottie reached across and smacked one of the hands her husband rested on the table. "None of those girls could ever keep up with you, Harold. You know that."

Ariel chuckled at the way the elderly couple fussed at one another.

Dottie smiled at Ariel and pushed the boxed treats toward Harold. "Harold loves your chocolate cupcakes, sweetie."

"Don't let Dottie fool you, girl. I barely get one whenever we buy your treats." Harold eased out of his seat and pulled his wallet from his pocket as Ariel stacked the plates sitting on the table and picked them up.

Both women watched Harold shuffle to the register. His wife leaned over and whispered conspiratorially to Ariel, "I do keep him from getting too many of your cupcakes. It isn't good for his heart."

Ariel glanced toward the register where Harold teased Sadie into a blush as he paid the check for the late lunch and special-ordered cupcakes. "Is Harold having heart problems?"

Dottie scooted along the seat and reached for her walker, a wicked smile lifting her lips as she waggled her eyebrows. "Oh no. Harold has the constitution of a bull. Healthy as a horse."

Behind her, Ariel could hear DeeDee laughing with the only other late customer as the waitress followed him to put up the CLOSED sign and lock the front door. Ariel put down the plates she held to focus on helping Dottie gain her footing and settle into place between the supports of her walker. "Then how are the cupcakes bad for his heart?"

"Why, it's the chocolate, dear."

"The chocolate?" Ariel was perplexed. She stepped back as Dottie shifted to face the door.

"Yes, dear." Dottie smiled sweetly. "Makes him horny as all get-out, chocolate does. Can't keep him off me. Why, he gets so riled up, he'll go all night. I'm afraid Harold'll get so excited, he'll have a heart attack right in the middle and like to crush the air right outta me."

Ariel fought to keep from bursting out laughing. The stroke of a male hand over her bottom followed by a firm squeeze spun Ariel around to face the culprit, half-worried it could be Harold.

She reached for the hand and missed it by millimeters.

"Sorry I'm late." Dane grinned. He offered an innocent look, despite the hearty chuckle from the elderly gentleman approaching them.

"Can't say as I blame you, son." Harold winked at Dane.

Despite the slight shuffle to his walk and the heavy blue veins standing out on the backs of his hands, the twinkle in the older man's brown eyes made him appear decades younger than most people expected. Ariel wasn't surprised by Dane's stunned expression. The Douglases had that effect on a lot of people.

"Sometimes a handsome bottom just begs to be pinched." Harold dropped one hand to fondle his wife's ample cheeks.

"Harold!" The reprimand sounded more amused than angry as Dottie looked over her shoulder at her husband.

"Oh come on, Dot. Can't have the younguns thinking there's no fun after seventy." Leaning toward Dane, Harold chuckled. "Woman hasn't been able to keep her hands off me in fifty years." He patted Dottie's bottom again. "It's like that donkey said in the cartoon the great-grandkids brought over: I like big butts and I cannot lie."

"Hmph." Dottie shook her head, handing her purse and the package of cupcakes to her husband before taking a long look at Dane. Turning to Ariel, she warned, "Keep your eye on this one, young lady."

"Yes, ma'am."

But Mrs. Douglas wasn't finished; as she shuffled forward a step, she nodded. "Yup, he looks to have the same stamina. And I'll bet my cupcakes he loves the back door as much as Harold does."

"Dot, you know you like it that way," Harold admonished. "Leastwise that's what you've been telling me for nigh on fifty years, woman."

"What was that song again, Harold?" Dottie changed the subject without answering.

Harold repeated himself. "I like big butts and I cannot lie."

Ariel could see Dane was at a loss for words as he watched the couple toddle to the door, Dottie's purse hanging from the crook of Harold's left elbow, the box of cupcakes held to his chest in the same hand. Harold mumbled the rap song as he patted his wife's bottom every few steps with his free hand. Dottie didn't mind. In fact, she hummed right along with her husband as DeeDee unlocked the door and held it open for them. Once they'd left, she shut and locked the door after them.

Dane's hand smoothed over Ariel's ass again, then paused to rub his thumb at the top of the crease separating the cheeks. A shiver rushed through her. Leaning close, he whispered against her ear, "I hope we're as hot for each other in fifty years as they are." He didn't wait for her response as he walked down the hall toward the office.

From the register and the door, Sadie and DeeDee chortled with laughter. Whether it was from the display

Dottie and Harold had put on or the stunned expression on her face, Ariel wasn't sure.

Ariel's heart pounded and blood rushed through her veins, thrumming in her ears. Visions of Dane standing beside her, patting her ass, and chuckling over the embarrassment it created in some imaginary grandchild swam through her mind. Anxiety and fear brought the sweat to her palms, and her head began to throb. It was too easy to fall into the little fantasy of being with him a year, five years, a dozen years, from now. *But what happens when he leaves? When he walks away.* Or worse, what if he were taken from her?

Ten years of coping, of living day to day without her parents, hadn't erased the pain of their deaths. A part of her ached to have her father's arms hold her close, to have him tell her how proud he was of her. To have her mother smile at the wild hairdos Ariel wore and the crazy colors she dyed her hair.

She'd had her parents for seventeen years. It wasn't long enough.

Now Dane is teasing me about decades? No. Her stomach knotted at the thought of him leaving at the end of the month when Alayna returned. What kind of basket case would she be if she let him have one year?

She hid her fear beneath a snort of derision. "Yeah, whatever," she muttered loudly enough for DeeDee and Sadie to hear. Keeping her mask in place, Ariel pushed through the doors to the kitchen. "It's a game," she whispered to herself, wandering mechanically through the required steps of cleaning up and shutting down the kitchen.

"He didn't mean what he said. When Al gets back, he'll leave, and things will go back to normal."

Her heart slowed its racing beat. The familiar procedures soothed her nerves. "Nothing to worry about," she mumbled, stacking sealed containers and transferring them to the cooler. "Nothing at all."

* * *

Ariel turned from locking the door behind DeeDee and Sadie to find Dane leaning against the tiled counter next to the register. His expression was remote, cool, but the glint of amusement in his eyes teased her with a promise for more.

"You, Tink, need a spanking."

She rolled her eyes and sashayed toward him, refusing to hide the grin on her lips. "You and what army, surfer boy?"

"I'm sure that ass of yours was no virgin to a paddle or a firm hand before I got hold of it." Dane came away from the counter and met her in the middle of the dining area.

Chairs were stacked neatly on top of the tables. The polished wood floor gleamed in the afternoon sunlight that filtered through the closed blinds over the windows and door.

Ariel shrugged but didn't admit to anything.

"You can't tell me your parents didn't take you over their knee at least once in your childhood?" He stepped closer, crowding into her personal space.

Ariel didn't back down. Her hand lifted to smooth over the tie hanging loosely beneath his collar. The suit jacket he'd worn earlier must have been left in the office. "They did. When I got caught."

"And when was the last time you got caught, sprite?" Dane wrapped his arms around her waist, his hands smoothing over the heart-shaped part of her anatomy under discussion.

"I was eleven. Mom found me poking holes in her diaphragm."

Dane's laughter echoed in the quiet room and vibrated through her chest, stirring the heat simmering low in her belly.

"Why would you do something like that?" He cupped her bottom and tugged her closer.

"I wanted a baby brother, and my parents weren't cooperating." Ariel smiled, remembering how appalled her mother had been that Ariel even knew what it was, let alone how it prevented pregnancy.

"Well, you've been sorely lacking in some discipline, young lady," Dane informed her with a sharp swat to her bottom.

Ariel jumped at the sting, but she gasped at the fire that seared her pussy. "And what makes you say that?" She tried to ease from his hold, but he wouldn't release her.

"Benton Baking and Grill."

She blinked up at him. "Are you talking about the muffin tins I ordered the day before yesterday?"

Dane nodded.

"Give me a break. We've had requests for jumbo muffins—"

"Who's in charge of the office?" Dane asked, holding her gaze without cracking a smile.

"Come on." She groaned. "You can't be serious?"

"Who's in charge of the office, Ariel?"

She crossed her arms and pinched her lips together for a moment before snapping, "You are."

"Did you talk to me about ordering the pans?"

A glare, a huff, then, "Yes, but—"

"Shall I show you what happens when a certain person breaks the rules?"

Ariel knew her eyes were wide. Arousal vibrated through her body. A building thrum worked through her blood into her center, constricting her breath with the varied images skittering through her head. Her heart thumped in her chest so hard, she was sure Dane could hear it. He can't possibly mean—There's no way he'd really—Not again… She swallowed, unsure if the moisture coating her palms was induced by fear or excitement.

There was no denying her panties were becoming uncomfortably damp, but she couldn't really be getting turned on by the thought of Dane spanking her. Could she?

"Shall I?" Dane prompted again.

"I'm not sure," Ariel hedged, too turned on to say no, but too nervous to say yes.

His fingers lifted to smooth over her cheek and jaw. "Neutral territory, remember. We can take it in stages, Tink. Baby steps if you want. Or you can say no."

Ariel cursed the weakness she'd shown him. Swallowing the bit of fear, she stood tall and met his gaze. "Okay, we can take it in stages. But you have to quit calling me Tink."

Dane chuckled and shook his head. "Stages it is, and no, Tink stays."

"Why?"

Dane turned away from her and took his time to push most of the tables in the center of the dining area close to the booths on each wall. "Because that's who you remind me of."

Ariel thought about it for a moment. Her jaw dropped, and she stared at him, sure her disbelief was plain on her face. "Are you saying I remind you of some bitchy little fairy?"

Dane laughed again, striding to the one table he hadn't pushed to the side. Situated closer to the counter than the door, it was centered between the booths on both walls with a clear view of the front of the café and at an angle to the hallway leading to the office. He began to pull off the chairs stacked on top of it. "Not a bitchy little fairy, love."

Ariel snorted and propped her hands on her hips. "Excuse me, but I did see the movie, and that fairy was a bitch. And pushy. And—"

Finished with removing the chairs, Dane stepped in front of her and covered her lips with his hand. "Not a bitch, Tink. Just feisty. She knew what she wanted, and she fought for it. Exactly like you." Leaning down so his forehead rested on hers, Dane continued, "She was also very curvy. Sexy. Sensual."

Ariel swallowed and held his gaze. He slipped his hand away and slowly dragged his fingertips over her lips, down her chin, and along her throat. She wasn't sure what she could say to his comments. "Oh…well, okay. So if you think I'm Tinker Bell, who does that make you? Peter Pan?"

The gleam in his eyes and the wicked grin lifting his lips had the cream inside her melting. "Oh no, Tink. Peter Pan could never have handled his sprite."

Ariel forced her buttery legs to hold her up. *Fuck, this is too much.* "Then who?"

"You know who." His fingers worked the buttons on her chef's coat loose before he shoved it off her shoulders and tossed it onto the counter. He stripped her tank top and bra away and then dropped his fingers to the fastening of her slacks. "Take off your shoes."

Ariel toed off her shoes, fighting the thoughts zinging through her mind.

"Who?" she asked again.

Dane pushed her slacks over her hips, then crouched to pull her panties down as he slid her pants off and helped her step out of them. His warm breath blew across her wet pussy as he answered, "Which character did Tinker Bell torment and tease the most? Who was the only one she harassed without end?"

"You don't mean?" But Ariel could easily picture it. He might not have the pencil-thin mustache, long, black, curly hair, or the metal hook, but he practically exuded the swagger and confidence and pure give-'em-hell attitude of a pirate.

"If you're Tink, that makes me Captain Hook." Dane winked at her as he rose.

"He was the villain," Ariel reminded him.

He shrugged. "One man's villain is another woman's mate."

Ariel could feel her body sway toward him, her breasts tingling, nipples taut, limbs trembling for his touch. The taunt in his words, the hidden message, couldn't be what he actually thought. Trying to regain control, she drew a deep breath and argued. "He was evil."

Dane slipped the tie from his collar and lifted her hands. His lips brushed her knuckles. "No, my pixie, not evil, merely alternatively motivated."

It wasn't until he tugged the knot tight that Ariel realized Dane had used his silk necktie to bind her wrists. "Wait, no. You didn't say—" She tried to twist free of the binding.

Dane gripped her forearms, stilling her struggles. "Shh. Haven't you ever been tied up?"

Ariel shook her head. Her heartbeat calmed as he stroked his hands over hers. "No."

"Trust me?"

The low, soft request caused Ariel to clench her inner muscles, trying to keep the moisture from spilling out. Some escaped onto her thighs, betraying her passion. Even knowing he waited for an answer, she hesitated. No warning sounded in her head. No cautious voice or frisson of unease stirred within her. Her gaze was still connected to his. "Yes."

The smile started in his eyes. Full of pride and satisfaction, it reached his lips and warmed Ariel's soul. A niggling voice of caution finally piped up and was immediately squashed. Later. She'd listen to it afterward, but at this moment, the fact that Dane was proud of her willingness to trust him filled her with a sense of accomplishment she hadn't felt before.

"When you broke the rules, Tink, how did your father punish you?"

The cool question threw Ariel for a moment. She'd assumed the lesson he would teach her would center around sex. Hard, fast sex. Perhaps even a command to suck him off or please him without being allowed to achieve climax herself.

"Come on, tell me. How did your father punish you?" Dane asked again as he led her, using the length of loose tie, toward the table.

"Sometimes a spanking, but mostly he wouldn't let me help in the kitchen."

"Ah. Keeping you from your cooking must have been torture?"

She nodded.

"I promise never to keep you from your pots and pans, Tink, but we'll have to find out what will motivate you to follow my rules."

Her body tingled at the fantasies playing in her head. Dane taking her over his knee again, using his hand, maybe a leather or wooden paddle, or even the sting of thongs applied to her backside, pushed up the heat in her body. *When did pain start being an aphrodisiac to me?*

"Lean over the table," he ordered, holding the end of the tie as he stood beside her.

She did as she was told, barely stifling the gasp when her warm body made contact with the cool wooden surface.

"Arms in front of you."

She held her hands out, watching as he rearranged himself to face her across the table. His hands worked at something underneath. The tie binding her pulled taut, then loosened before he stood up. A quick tug confirmed he had secured her to the table.

Her belly and breasts pressed into the wood beneath her. The muscles in her thighs and calves were stretched, but not too uncomfortable. If she remained like this for long, it might be a different story. Drawing on a bit of bravado, she looked up at him. "Now what, captain?"

He leaned down and braced his forearms beside hers. "Now, my Tink, we see what kind of punishment works best on my naughty pixie."

She stretched her head up and slid her lips over his. "How naughty would you like me to be? I'm sure with the right incentive…"

Dane nipped her bottom lip with his teeth. "I do like when you're naughty, love, but not when you break the rules." He pulled away to better meet her gaze, drew a deep breath, and smiled down at her. "You're wet and ready, but it's important you learn that I'm in charge of the office.

Supply orders, schedules, and purchases must go through me.”

“Now, just you—”

“No.” His tone was implacable. Rising, he stepped around the table until she could barely see him over her shoulder.

The first firm swat landed without warning. The sting along her bottom made Ariel yelp and push up onto her tiptoes. “That hurt!”

Another slap landed against the other cheek. “It's supposed to. And no more than it did the last time I spanked you.”

Four more swats landed, two to each plump cheek, but Ariel didn't cry out again. She clenched her teeth and glared dry-eyed at the closed blinds on the front door.

The pain was bearable. Dane wasn't applying any real force to his slaps. If he thought a few swats on the ass were going to keep her from running the café the way she wanted, he was sorely mistaken.

When he stepped around to face her, her determination must have been clear in her face.

“Not enough?” he asked.

Ariel didn't bother to reply; she glared past him as if he weren't there.

“Discipline is required to reinforce the rules when a sub disobeys,” Dane explained.

“I'm not your damned sub,” Ariel snarled.

“When you enter the office, you are. Whether I'm there or not, you agreed I am master there.”

"It was only a couple of muffin pans."

His fingers gripped her chin and held her face close to his as he pushed into her space. "Which I ordered a week ago when you first mentioned it. They haven't arrived because they're on back order."

Ariel's ire deflated. "Oh."

"Exactly."

"If you had told me all this—"

"Why should I? It isn't required for me to explain the whys. You're the one who has to remember to follow the rules, Tink."

"Okay, fine. Point taken. Are we done?"

Dane sighed and shook his head. "Huff and puff, pixie, but the lesson isn't over until you've learned it."

"What do you mean?" She turned her head to watch him walk away from the table and head down the hall toward the office.

"Dane? Dane!" When he didn't respond, she returned her gaze to the empty dining area in front of her. Ariel waited and fumed, but she didn't try to work her way off the table. Let him have his little lesson. It was no skin off her nose.

The sound of footsteps had her twisting her head to peer toward the hall and see him amble toward her, a worn leather bag the size of a weekender suitcase gripped in his left hand. There was no way in hell, no matter what he did, that Ariel intended to admit Dane was right. Even if he was.

And she'd be ice-skating with the devil before she'd acknowledge Dane's ability to master her desires. *So what if he turns me on and is the only lover who's been able to give me multiple orgasms. No reason to make his ego any bigger than it already is.*

The leather case was set on the table beside her ribs. Her cheek rested on her upper arm as she watched him unzip it and reach inside. A bottle of lube as well as the vibrant blue butt plug he'd used on her yesterday was placed on the table near her elbow. The thumping of her heart increased, and her bottom twitched at the remembered sting of the device.

A silent curse whispered in her mind as she felt the response of her body dribble along the insides of her thighs. Sharp blue eyes detected the flex and squeeze of her legs as she pressed them together.

"Have you ever played with pain, Tink?" he asked. His hands rested on the open lip of the bag.

"Played with pain?" she croaked. Her mind conjured visions of iron maidens, stretching racks, and other implements of torture from the Middle Ages. "Do I look crazy? Who the fuck would enjoy pain?" She tried to inject a note of heavy disdain in her voice, but judging by the way one side of his mouth kicked up in a grin, Ariel was sure he saw her protests for the empty complaints they were.

"Are you telling me none of your boyfriends tried to talk you into other toys besides a butt plug?" He reached into the bag and pulled out a length of silver chain with clamps at each end.

Ariel recognized the nipple chain from her trip through the adult store. A zing of sensation tingled through her breasts. Her nipples grew rigid and ready as they pressed against the table. Her mouth was unable to form the words to respond. Instead she shook her head.

Holding her gaze, Dane placed the chain on the table between her bound arms. “What about paddles, floggers, maybe a whip?” he asked. From the bag he pulled out a brown leather paddle and a small flogger with flat red leather thongs and a braided handle of red and black leather.

Ariel knew her eyes grew wide with each item he set on the table. Her pussy ached, desperate to be filled. Stretched across the table, she squirmed, pressing her thighs together to dull the urges building inside her.

A small coiled whip was the last item removed, but Dane didn't set it down. He watched her face, summed up something in his head before he spoke again. “Hmm, I don't think you're quite to this level yet.” Dane returned it to the bag and dropped the leather carryall off the table.

Ariel felt her bottom flex, stimulated muscles still sore from the last time she'd taken the plug up her ass. In her mind, based on the fire blazing over her skin at the thoughts, she could almost feel the sting from the strap of leather as it connected with her posterior. Anticipation spiked through her, twisting her core into knots. Her fingers gripped the silk tie binding her wrists. *I will not give in. I will not give in.* The words became her mantra as she watched Dane tuck the flogger into the back of his slacks.

"Is spanking the only form of punishment for a submissive?" She croaked out her question, her voice thick with arousal and curiosity.

He nodded. "It varies from person to person." He returned to the front of the table and crouched down to stay face-to-face with her.

"And you think getting my ass tanned will keep me from breaking your rules?" The excitement built inside. She was on the brink of climax at the thought of his applying the flogger or the paddle to her backside. She hoped her expression didn't betray her excitement. When she glimpsed the flicker of amusement in his blue eyes, Ariel began mentally reviewing the litany of curses she knew.

"You like it, don't you, Tink?" He tugged the flogger from his waistband and dangled it over her hands; the knotted ends barely brushed the backs of her fingers. "When I took you over my knee on the third day, I could see it."

"See what?"

"How it turned you on. How the slap of my hand against your bottom made you wet."

Ariel spluttered and stammered. "I did not! That's a damned lie."

"No, sprite, your act of outraged denial is a lie." He stood up and caressed first her left arm, then her right with the leather thongs of the flogger. "I can smell how hot you are. I'll bet your pussy would soak my hand if I put it between your legs right now."

Ariel stayed mute, determined not to admit how right he was.

He didn't balk at her tight-lipped silence. The leather smoothed over her shoulder and along her back; it raised chill bumps wherever it touched. Every muscle in her body tensed to keep from arching into each stroke as he worked the strands down her back and over her bottom.

"You want this, don't you?" Dane taunted. He flicked the handle, snapping the thongs over her ass.

She bowed upward; a moan slipped free.

"So responsive." His breath warmed her cheek and stirred the soft tendrils of her hair beside her ear. "And such a shame."

"Wh-what?"

He gathered the paddle from the table and knelt to return it and the flogger to the bag.

"You're not—Are you finished?" Ariel stammered out her question. Desire twisted tight inside her belly. Disappointment arrowed through her when she considered the possibility that Dane might not use the paddle or flogger on her.

"Oh not yet." Dane rose and picked up the nipple clamps.

Ariel propped herself on her elbows. Her gaze followed him as he dangled the chain from his fingertips.

"But you must remember, punishment is not about giving you pleasure, Tink. And you would enjoy a sound flogging or a good paddling far too much." He gathered the clamps into his palm and tucked them into his pocket before stepping away.

"So what, then? If it's not going to be a spanking?" She watched him cross the café to the front windows, his every step measured with a deep breath as she tried to calm her hammering pulse. The want stayed stubborn, refusing to subside. "What are you doing?" Unease rose to fight for supremacy within her chest.

"Setting the stage." He wandered from one window to the next, twisting the rods and adjusting the closed shades to allow a bit more light into the café.

From her position draped over the table, Ariel trembled at the thought of someone looking through the windows to see her. "Stop, Dane."

He ignored her and went to the last set of blinds.

"You can't seriously expect me to allow you—"

Dane walked from the front of the café to the hallway. Lights were extinguished, leaving the dining area lit only by the emergency lights from the kitchen and the late-afternoon sunshine filtering through the windows. "You seem to dislike public displays of affection, Ariel."

He returned to the table and stood in front of her; his gaze held hers as she shifted on the table in an attempt to get free. She glared up at him. "They're not bad. As long as I keep my clothes on."

"Or when it's not you you're bringing attention to, but someone else." Dane's hands slid the buttons on his shirt free, and then he shrugged out of it. He draped it over the legs of an overturned chair close by. He took his time as he stripped out of his shoes, socks, trousers, and underwear. The tip of his aroused cock glistened with moisture.

A tiny voice in her mind cheered at the evidence of his interest. But her mouth went dry at the concept of a stranger peeking through the blinds to see them.

"How can you think embarrassing me like this can be beneficial? It's humiliating. Not to mention dangerous. If anyone passed by and decided to look through the shades, there could be problems for the café," Ariel argued. She watched him pass her. Twisting her head, she lost sight of him as he repositioned himself behind her. The feel of coarse hair on the insides of her legs sent a warm tickle of sensation through her lower body.

"Punishment is finding a consequence that acts as a deterrent to a sub's behavior." The *rip* of cellophane was followed by the distinct sound of a condom being rolled over flesh. Soon after, his hands smoothed over her back, caressed her hips, lifted her as his cockhead rubbed between the plump, wet lips of her pussy.

Ariel was torn. Her body screamed for satisfaction, but her mind was focused on the shadowy figures passing on the sidewalk on the other side of the glass and fabric barrier. "Dane, please. Close the shades."

The first inch pressed forward, nudged past the entrance of her body. "No."

"Please," she begged, even as her body rocked backward, deepening his penetration.

The heat of his chest covered her back, the warm, muscled contours of his arms bracketed her, his hands cupped hers. "Watch the windows, Tink." He pushed harder, completing his possession and absorbing the shudder of acceptance pulsing through her body.

"I can't. Not with the shades open." She gasped, and she rocked back into his rhythm, matched each thrust with her own, absorbing the shock of advance and withdrawal. Hoped he'd increase the tempo.

"You will, or I'll open them more." Dane's threat wasn't empty. She could hear the determination in his voice through the sensations that swamped her common sense.

Ariel moaned. Her body spiraled closer to climax as he altered his pace. "Couldn't you have done something else?" The protest was instinctive. Her mind was separate from the warmth and heat engulfing her body.

"Only other option would have been more satisfying to you than a true sub," he responded reasonably.

Ariel was baffled at how he could sound so rational and calm while his hips increased their tempo and began pounding into her. The wood of the table beneath her grew slick with the perspiration peppering her skin. Near her hips, the fluid of her arousal dampened the surface and smeared her body from pussy to belly button.

"What option—*oh God, don't stop*—what option was that?" Ariel gasped and moaned, her mind caught between giving in to the flood of sexual need inflaming her and understanding Dane's reasoning. She choked off a cry when she saw a shadow hesitate near the front door.

If he looked in, he would see her. Her cheeks were on fire; her breasts were sharp-tipped mounds stroking the polished wood. What exactly would he see if he did manage to look past the shades to the inside? After a long pause, the figure walked on, and Ariel breathed again.

"Keeping me from you."

Dane's matter-of-fact tone froze the breath in her lungs. Had she really come this close to meeting a man who knew how to stand up to her? *Or is this another instance of his teasing me until I change my mind about him?*

A firm thrust from behind sent Ariel's thoughts scattering to the winds. The underlying comment from his words echoed in her mind. When he mentioned separation from her, at the same time her climax broke loose, radiating from her core to her extremities, she couldn't smother the cold dread that struck her. The thought, the first inkling of such an offense, sent her heart slamming against her ribs in an attempt to escape. The idea of not being around Dane—of not having him to harass and torment—left her with a hollow sensation. *But isn't that what I've worked toward? It's a contest to him. Keep it that way. Let him think it's just sex. I'll be safer that way.*

His lips nipped her left earlobe as eddies of satisfaction washed through her in the aftermath of her orgasm. "Hopefully you'll remember this situation before you decide to forget who's the boss here again."

She schooled her tone to stay calm. The words slipped free. "Only in the office," she reminded him.

"For the time being." Dane chuckled as he resumed his pace. He ignored her protests of being incapable of another fiery climax.

Passion spiraled upward, swept Ariel into the vortex, a cry on her lips, and another figure paused near the doorway.

She held her breath and waited, gnawing her bottom lip raw in an attempt to subdue her vocalizations of pleasure.

Another laugh rumbled in Dane's chest and vibrated against her cheek. He never broke stride.

Chapter Twelve

Day 25

Over a week later Ariel winced and shifted her stance at the twinge between her legs. Leaning over the marble-topped counter, she smoothed the melted couverture into a thin layer, then scraped it back into a lump in the center of the stone. Each action was routine and familiar, unlike the thoughts zipping through her mind.

What the fuck had she been thinking ten days ago when she'd answered the door, knowing it was Dane on the other side? She shook her head, spread the chocolate out thin again, before repeating the process of corralling it into a pile in the middle of the stone. “I wasn't thinking,” she replied softly. *And were you thinking when he came home with you the next night? And the next? And the next? And what about when he tied you to the table? Or when he used a magic wand in your ass?*

The muscles in her backside, hips, and legs trembled at the memory of the previous night's play and the activities Dane had subjected her to over the last week. “Enough already,” she snapped. The silicone paddle skittered across the marble, leaving uneven lumps of chocolate on the surface. Ariel tried to concentrate on gathering the mass into a pile again, even as she continued to argue with herself. "It's only sex. It's not like I'm hooked on the guy."

So why were you biting off DeeDee's and Sadie's heads when they asked where Dane was? And if he was coming back?

"I was not biting off their heads—"

"If you're talking about little chocolate bunnies, I might not be too concerned, especially if the poor buggers are part of that goo you're playing in." Ariel turned from the counter at Dane's teasing comment.

Damn, he looked yummy in his faded jeans and navy blue T-shirt. So tempting, in fact, that to keep from jumping on him, Ariel gripped the paddle in her hand hard enough her knuckles turned white. In an effort to deny her interest in him, she turned back to the chocolate and scooped it into the bowl with the rest of the melted couverture. "Where've you been? I thought you had some billing to double-check?"

His warm hands coasted over her shoulders, tugging the collar of her shirt down to expose the base of her throat. The soft stroke of his lips preceded the nip of his teeth and the rub of his tongue over the offended spot. "Miss me?"

Ariel fought the urge to relax back into his chest. Lifting one shoulder in an attempt to look unconcerned, she sniffed. "Not hardly." She turned away, carried the stainless steel bowl to the other side of the counter, and stirred the contents, carefully blending the chocolate together.

"So what were you doing with that?" Dane nodded to the bowl.

"Tempering the couverture."

"Tempering?"

Ariel nodded. "It's a process that better incorporates the oils and cocoa so it keeps longer when I have to store it."

Dane picked up the red silicone paddle and rubbed his finger along the edge. A wicked gleam lit his baby blue eyes as he leaned forward and smiled. "Hmm, I have to say, the thought of using this"—he held up the five-inch-wide utensil—"to spread some of that chocolate over your body certainly would have me wanting to keep something longer. Not to mention harder."

Ariel rolled her eyes at the lame joke, but her body reacted. First her nipples went hard. Then her pussy heated and grew moist, reaffirming her attraction to the dratted man. "Down, boy." She kept her tone stern. "Remember where you are and who's in charge here."

He set the tool down and crossed his arms over his chest. "Bad day?"

The bowl was left on the counter. Ariel forced herself not to shuffle when she crossed to one of the racks that held the various pots, pans, baking sheets, and tins. Twinges and protesting muscles made themselves known, but she worked to hide the evidence from Dane's keen gaze. "It might have gone easier if I could have gotten some of my work done instead of answering the phone to find purchase orders." She prepared the pan and poured the chocolate into it. "I had that damned cordless phone attached to my ear for so long today, it's a miracle I don't look like some hunchback."

The scrape of the spatula against the bowl filled the silence as Ariel scooped the last of the chocolate into the pan to form. She carried the bowl to the sink and dropped it and the spatula into the hot, soapy water. "I mean, hell, you're the one who's supposed to be handling the office while my sister's away. I have enough to manage without your job on top of mine."

"You're probably looking forward to next Tuesday."

"That's five days away. If you mean I'll be happy when Alayna gets back, you're damned straight."

"Come on"—Dane leaned against the wall next to the sink—"you can't tell me I've been that impossible to deal with."

No way would she admit anything to him, good or bad. "No, but with Alayna around I can concentrate on my cooking and not—"

"Not what? Not having to stay in control all the time? Not going home by yourself?" He followed her back to the counter as she covered the setting chocolate with cheesecloth and slid it onto one of the wire cooling racks.

"Not having some bossy bastard make decisions for me," she snapped, getting in his face as he leaned against the wall between the walk-in refrigerator and the ovens.

"And you've loved every second of those decisions, Ariel. Admit it."

"That's sex, Dane. I'm talking about—"

He shook his head and crowded close, backed her up against the refrigerator, and braced his hands on the brushed chrome, blocking her in. "It isn't only sex, Tink. I've done a hell of a lot to give you time to focus on your food. You just don't like admitting that it's nice not to have to be in the driver's seat for once."

"Not true." She ducked under his arm and squeezed past him. "I like to be in charge because I'm good at it."

"In the kitchen maybe, but not in the bedroom. Or the office." Dane grabbed her arm and swung her around to face him. "As many times as you've found excuses to come into the office, and as quickly as you take to my direction, it's obvious you'd rather submit than dominate."

"Are you back to that?" There was no way Ariel was going *there*. The fact that part of her knew he was right only made her more determined to deny it.

"It isn't like you can refute it." Dane let her go and crossed his arms over his chest as he gave her an assessing look. "It isn't as if you've made any effort to change my mind."

Hackles up, she planted her hands on her hips and glared up at him. "Really? And who is it who's been avoiding the kitchen? Hmmm? I don't see you coming in here to get the supply orders or to help me check stock."

"I've been here nearly fifteen minutes, Ariel, and you've made no effort to direct me," he pointed out.

"I've work to get done. I don't have time for screwing around." She turned her back on him. Ignoring the shiver of awareness that skated up her spine from his attention, she gathered the red paddle from the marble along with the other tools she'd used to work on different preparations for the next day's sweets.

"Then put me to work," he suggested. "Commands don't have to be centered on sex. Rituals are often involved in D/s relationships."

"Rituals?" Ariel's steps slowed as she crossed to the sink and set the tools in the wash water.

"Everyday, mundane tasks can be incorporated into the routines preceding or following play." Her confusion must have been apparent when she turned to face him. After a significant pause, but before she could ask exactly what he meant, he elaborated. "Preparing the clothing to be used in a scene that will be acted out. Taking a shower either alone or together, or a bath. Those can all be considered rituals."

Ariel could feel her cheeks heat as she recalled the directions he'd given a few days before when they'd stepped into a shower together. Having already climaxed several times, she'd considered their bathing together a preparation for sleep.

She'd been wrong.

Now, based on the connection he made to routines, she could see how the careful cleansing of a partner's body could factor into both play and everyday behavior.

"So if I told you to clean the dishes in the sink and get them into the dishwasher, you'd do it?"

Dane didn't bother to respond. He crossed to the sink, grabbed the scrub brush from the ledge, and set to work removing the larger food particles stuck to the pans before he loaded them into the industrial dishwasher.

When he finished, he drained the sink, wiped his hands, and carried the towel to the bin for laundry before turning to face her.

Ariel hesitated, then ordered, “Wipe down the counters.” She would have told him the steps to take, but again he surprised her by going immediately to the cabinet containing the cleaning supplies. He was methodical and careful as he rubbed the cloth over the top at least four times before getting a new cloth and striding to the next counter.

A flicker of satisfaction tingled in her belly. Every time she'd entered the office over the last ten days, his directions to her had been more sexual than focused on completing work. Ariel's mind conjured pictures of the less wholesome and more erotic tasks she could direct him in.

When he finished and put away the supplies in their respective places, he leaned against the supply-closet door and waited. She could see his thoughts taking on the same sexual nature they'd followed in the office. And the temptation was there. The urge to order him to bare his cock to her, to direct him again, to show him the power she could wield over his body's needs.

But now wasn't the time. Later. She'd planned everything so carefully for tonight. If she allowed herself to give in now, her plans for the evening would be anticlimactic.

“Wash your hands.” She nodded toward the sink.

Dane held her gaze as he soaped his hands, then rinsed them. After drying them on a fresh towel, he crossed the room to stand in front of her, an arm's length away.

"We both have some work to do," she said. She ached to ignore her brain, but she couldn't. At least not yet.

"Am I excused to return to the office?" Dane asked. There was no tone of curiosity or confusion in his voice, but she could see it reflected in his blue eyes.

Why don't I feel satisfied at keeping him off balance? Ariel nodded. "Some of the paperwork is done. I was able to total up today's sales and get the deposit slip filled out before placing it in the safe. I left the other reports for you to finish." She glanced at the huge white analog clock on the wall above the sink. "I don't think it should take you more than an hour."

"I'll see what's left to be done." He stopped at the kitchen door leading to the hall outside the office and told her, "I'll have to go back to my office for an hour or so. The emergency this morning not only delayed my coming here, but also interfered with me getting reports finished for a new client."

Ariel tried to still the twist of her stomach. Was he making an excuse to avoid her? Was this his way to place distance between them in preparation for Alayna's return?

"I probably won't get through until well after six, perhaps seven, tonight. If you'd rather postpone dinner to a different night…?"

His question only intensified her disquiet. *And why does the thought of him avoiding me hurt? Wasn't that the purpose of all this*? Ariel swallowed but stayed calm. "No, I was planning on a little after seven for dinner."

"Okay. Let me know when you're ready to leave, and we'll make the deposit. Then I'll escort you home."

Ariel nodded, not trusting her voice. It wasn't supposed to happen this way. She had a plan, and nowhere in that design was there room for falling in love. Not with a man who refused to let her control him. Or who could make her enjoy being controlled and commanded by him.

* * *

Dane had finally finished putting the papers away in the file cabinet and turned to shut down his computer when the buzz from the outer office indicated a visitor. Jordan hadn't mentioned any appointments for this evening when Dane sent him home a few minutes after five. Clicking through the shutdown procedure, he called out, “I'm closed.” Dane's head came up when a shadow blocked the light at the door.

“I'll only be a minute, Mr. Reese.” Grimm's quiet voice practically had the windows vibrating.

“How can I help you, Mr. Dawson?”

“Just Grimm, sir.” He stepped into the room, turning sideways to allow his massive shoulders to fit through the door.

Dane stepped around the desk when he saw the cool look from Grimm's dark eyes. Dane tucked his hands into the hip pockets of his jeans. “All right, Grimm. And please, call me Dane.”

Grimm nodded and drew a deep breath; his thick arms were crossed over his chest. “I want to know what you mean to do with Miss Ariel.”

“I'm not sure what you mean by 'do with her'?” But he had a damned good idea, Dane admitted to himself, trying not to feel provoked by the man's intrusion into his relationship with Ariel.

"She might not admit it or look like it, but Ari is a good girl." He stepped closer. "Her daddy and mama were nice people, and they would turn over in their graves if I let someone hurt her." His gaze grew fierce. "Or her sister."

"You knew Ariel's parents?" Dane tried to deflect the tense atmosphere in the room. "I wasn't aware—"

Grimm shifted, his hands dropped to his hips, and he looked uncomfortable. "I'm sure you know I did some time."

Dane nodded.

"Well, Ari and Al's folks were good to my mama while I was…away. They even paid for her funeral when I couldn't." He ran his hand over his bald head, then continued. "After I got out, they helped me get started again."

"That was nice of them." Dane waited; he sensed there was more.

"After their parents passed, I kept an eye on 'em." Grimm's lips thinned. "I don't want them to get their hearts broke over some fancy man who's only lookin' for a piece o' tail."

Dane crossed his arms over his chest and met Grimm's gaze head-on. "I appreciate your concern, and I think Ariel and Alayna are very lucky women to have you watching out for them."

For the first time, a grin flickered across the ebony face. "But I should mind my own damned business, right?"

"It would be appreciated." Dane offered a half smile. "Getting Ariel to admit to anything more than what she wants is hard enough without you mucking up the waters and making her dig her feet in deeper to keep from doing what others think she should."

The laughter rumbled through the room like the rattle of a freight train's wheels. "Yup, that's Ari. Stubborn little brat."

"Sprite," he corrected and then added, "And independent."

"To a fault." Grimm shook his head. "That girl would drown before she'd admit it was rainin'."

Dane motioned him out of his office and into the open reception area. Locking his door, he glanced at the clock and cursed. "Damn."

"You late to get to her house?" Grimm pulled open the door to the sidewalk.

"How—"

"The men I have in my house, they like the food. If I can't be around to make sure the girls are safe, I usually set one of them to keep an eye on the café when they're closing up." Grimm smirked. "They've all had a hell of a chuckle over how quick the two of you have been to get to her place the last week."

At thirty-nine and with his background in D/s, Dane hadn't thought anything could embarrass him anymore. But heat filled his face knowing that this behemoth and his ex-con friends had been keeping tabs on Ariel's and his activities.

"As long as they stay on the other side of the street and don't try to get too close, I'll concede the point," Dane grumbled. After he set the alarm and stepped outside, he locked the door and held his hand out to Grimm.

"Thank you for letting me know you're concerned." He was surprised when the big man didn't try to intimidate him by crushing Dane's hand in his huge fist. "I can't promise I won't break her heart, but I can swear that I don't intend to hurt her in any way. Hell"—Dane chuckled—"most of the time I can barely get her to admit how much she likes me being with her."

"Well, I have to say, Ariel did pick a man this time and not some boy." After Grimm released his hand, the smile he flashed Dane showed off the brilliant whiteness of his teeth. "If I thought you'd swing the other way, I'd give my girl a run for her money."

Dane couldn't help but laugh. "Thank you. I think."

Grimm glanced at his watch. "You better get going before she starts thinking you've stood her up."

Dane watched Grimm climb into his big red truck and fire it up before he slid into his own car and drove the few blocks over to Ariel's house. He wondered what her response would be if he repeated what Grimm had said.

Chapter Thirteen

Ariel took a deep breath through her nose and let it out noisily from her mouth in an effort to still the butterflies ricocheting off the walls of her stomach. She didn't want the dinner to be a romantic one, not with the plans she had in mind. After having gone online to research some of the practices between Dommes and subs, Ariel figured this was safe enough for her first real foray.

The last scene she'd instigated in the dining area of the café had been more about one-upmanship than domination. “The whole purpose of this is to show him that I'm as capable as he is of directing someone to satisfy my needs.” Her voice didn't sound as convinced as she'd hoped it would. Her fingers slid over the black leather bustier she'd purchased the day before and had just put on minutes earlier.

“He's never going to take me seriously. I'm an overgrown cartoon character to him.” She groaned, shook her head, and reached for the first hook. The ring of the doorbell stilled her fingers before she grabbed for the comfortable blue and black plaid flannel shirt she usually wore to bed.

It would cover her up, at least from the neck to the knees. The black leather chaps would be able to pass for pants as long as she kept the shirt on.

She gave the stilettos a mournful look but padded barefoot into the hall when the bell sounded a second time. "I'd probably break my damned ankle with them anyway," she grumbled.

"I rang—" Dane's gaze drifted from her face down, then paused when he spotted the black leather on her legs and her bare feet.

"Yeah, sorry." Ariel dropped a quick look down to make sure she'd fastened all the buttons. "I wanted to change into something a bit more comfortable." She motioned him inside.

After she shut the door, Dane stopped in the entry and cupped her chin. Holding her still, he pressed a soft kiss to her lips and then stepped away.

Ariel's head spun, and her heart stopped at the sweetness of the gesture. Did this mean something significant? Were his feelings starting to deepen to match the ones she had for him?

Whoa! Hold on! What feelings? Ariel gasped at the thought of developing more than a simple attraction for Dane. Something deeper, more significant—that wasn't supposed to happen, was it? Hadn't she already had this discussion with herself at the café? Hoping to dispel her unease, she coughed, then asked, "Uh, what was that for?"

"Because I forgot to do it when I came into the café tonight. And I missed you today." His gaze was direct, a clear indicator that he wasn't giving her a line.

"Umm, thank you." She hurried past him and darted into the kitchen to make sure everything was as she'd left it.

A wine red tablecloth covered the small round kitchen table, and a single red pillar candle sat in the center. There were no plates or silverware, only the three covered dishes placed around table, with napkins beside each of them. The edges and corners of several foil packets were discreetly tucked beneath the dishes and near the base of the candle stand.

"Hmm, looks like you did have something planned." Dane leaned in the doorway. His gaze roved from the table with the single chair pulled up to it to Ariel.

The heat in his eyes stirred the craving in her belly. The confidence that had wavered, leading her to don the oversize sleep shirt, resurfaced. Keeping him off-kilter was the key to maintaining power. A gleam in his eye kept her from shedding her cover. *Better to have him wonder what I've got on underneath.* She could tell his curiosity had been piqued.

Her bare feet quiet against the tile, she padded to the counter, then asked, "Would you like something to drink?"

She poured chilled fruit juice into one of the wineglasses she'd set out earlier. "I have some fruit juice, or wine if you'd prefer."

"Fruit juice, please." He crossed the kitchen and stood beside her. His fingers caressed hers as she passed him his glass. "Were you planning on something in particular, Tink?"

"Well, we are in my kitchen." She smiled, then sipped her juice.

Dane chuckled. "Ah, quite the nice trap there."

"And I've been reading about rituals." Ariel stepped to the table and pulled the chair out. She made sure to tuck the shirt under as she sat down, to keep her bare ass from meeting the chilly seat. "You said Dommes and subs practice all kinds of rituals." She rolled the stem of her wineglass between her fingers, spinning the crystal slowly on the red cloth.

"And you wanted to experiment?" Dane carried his glass to the table and stood over her. He set his drink beside hers and cupped her chin in his hand. At the slow caress of his thumb along her jaw, over her chin, and onto her bottom lip, Ariel's nipples pressed against the black silk lining her leather bustier.

Ariel shrugged and fought the urge to shift as arousal wet the triangle of silk covering her pussy. "If you're brave enough to try it."

Dane held her gaze as he leaned down until he was so close, his face blurred. His lips settled on hers. The damp tip of his tongue caressed her bottom lip before his teeth nipped it. "I'm all yours, Ariel. Direct away."

The kiss was short, an exchange of pressure. It offered the temptation of his taste before he stepped away from the chair and awaited her command. Ariel ordered her fluttering heart to slow. She had thought this evening's events out very carefully.

Rising, she smoothed her hands over his T-shirt. "I want to make sure I truly understand the role a dominatrix would play, Dane. I don't want to mess this up."

He kept his hands by his sides as she caressed the stretch of cotton over his pectorals and ribs. “I'll answer any questions you have. All you have to do is ask.”

“I understand a sub's primary concern is his mistress's pleasure. So does that mean the mistress's primary interest is in showing the sub when he is and isn't performing well?”

Dane stood still under her exploration. The firming of his nipples was visible under the smooth cotton, and she took the time to fondle the covered peaks with her fingers.

“In some cases, yes, but as with a male Dom and female sub, making sure to reinforce a sub's understanding that their duty is to satisfy their Dom or Domme's wishes is paramount.”

“You explained to me that making the sub kneel, lower their eyes, and refer to the dominatrix as 'Mistress' or 'My Lady' are ways of reinforcing their position in the relationship.”

Dane nodded. “Yes.” His wry grin and direct gaze forestalled her next question. “But I won't do those things for you, Ariel, since I'm not a submissive. I have no inclination to submit or to be reminded of such a position.”

“So how can I prove I can be a Domme?” Ariel stepped back and set her hands on her hips; one of her bare feet tapped the tiled floor. “If you won't take on the role of submissive—”

“Outlast me.”

“Excuse me?” Ariel knew her expression was one of confusion.

"Show me you can control your body better than I can." Dane grinned. "A Domme often masturbates her sub to orgasm without allowing him the privilege of actual intercourse. She controls whether his climax is swift or long and drawn-out."

"Or denied altogether?" Memories of his denying her orgasm when he used the vibrator on her flashed through Ariel's mind, quickly followed by the lesson in chocolate she had conducted and his exercise in showing her different methods of punishment for a sub.

"If his behavior warrants it." He hooked his finger into the top of her shirt and tugged her close. "Now, sprite, what did you have planned tonight, because I'm starving."

Ariel fought the urge to ask *what for*? Based on the glint in his eye and the grin on his lips, she was sure he wouldn't list food.

"Nuh-uh." She shook her head and stepped to the table to light the candle. "We're standing in a kitchen, Dane, so I get to be the boss." Ariel wondered if Dane would recognize her challenge as she intended it. Simply an extension to the game they played in the café.

Dane conceded with a nod. "As you wish. What's your first directive?"

Ariel smiled. "Take off your clothes."

To be honest, she had only intended to have him remove his T-shirt, but his comment about a Domme's right to masturbate her sub brought to mind the first time she'd directed him to pleasure himself. The original intent of that scene took on new meaning. Did she dare repeat it? Could she reenact it without losing sight of the purpose of the exercise?

Dane complied. He shed each item, then carefully folded it and set it aside. His T-shirt came off first, then his shoes and socks before he added his jeans and boxer-briefs to the stack.

Ariel's mouth went dry. In the time he'd been sharing her bed, she'd got to know various details about Dane's erection. She knew he'd been circumcised as a child, that it would take more than one of her hands to encircle it, and that his balls were the most sensitive spot she'd found on his body. She also ached from the magic wand and butt plugs he'd introduced her to, the latter of which she'd taken to using under her clothes for a few hours while she worked during the afternoons at the café. Anticipation filled her every night he came over. Each time, she wondered if Dane would finally take her ass, but each night he left without doing so.

Maybe tonight?

"Sit—" She coughed and cleared her throat. "Sit in the chair and face the table."

Ariel pushed back her sleeves, then thought better of wearing the shirt with the dishes she'd prepared. Turning away, she undid the first few buttons, pulled the shirt over her head, and dropped it onto his neatly folded pile of clothes.

"I do love your tat." Dane chuckled. He traced his fingers over the capital *H* and *K* and the pitchfork crossing them horizontally. "You never explained why you chose to put it there."

Ariel glanced over shoulder and peeked at the inked design gracing her right butt cheek. Looking up, she grinned as she met Dane's gaze. "Hey, Gordon Ramsay gets me hot, but every episode of *Hell's Kitchen* has me wanting to tell him to kiss my ass at least once."

The smirk on Dane's face diminished as she faced him and let him get a good look at her outfit. The black leather bustier nipped in her waist and pushed her already ample assets into pillowy mounds with the nipples carefully concealed. The matching leather chaps hugged her hips and fastened at her waist and around the tops of her thighs, but they left her ass and pussy exposed. The only thing covering her was a small triangle of black silk. The V-string design of the thong left her ass revealed, but Ariel cared little about that.

Returning to the table, she picked up the smallest serving dish and removed the cover. "I hope you like sweet food." She grinned.

Ariel stepped up next to him, then swung her leg over his lap so she straddled him in the chair.

Dane was sure this would be a true test of his ability to control his body. The scent of her arousal drifted up from her mound, and his cock jerked with interest. He'd been semihard all day, and her greeting at the door hadn't helped. His erection twitched as if it had sniffed out a prime piece of real estate and was ready to buy. Dane forced himself to remain calm as she lifted the bowl to his chin.

She took her time swirling her finger through the contents before she plucked out three or four coated almonds and held them to his lips. The bite of spicy chili mixed with the mellow flavor of honey. He sat straighter on the chair even as his lips closed over her fingers, and his tongue curled over the pads to suck off the warm, sticky coating.

Once he'd licked away every bit of the honey, his hands rose to settle on her hips, but she shook her head at him.

"No, no." She waggled her finger. "Hands by your sides. No touching without permission."

Dane slid his hands along the outsides of her thighs, teasing her before he settled them on the edge of the chair near his hips.

Five more times she served the deliciously spicy almonds. Each time her fingers set the nuts on his tongue, he took his time cleaning any residual honey from her fingertips.

Ariel leaned down and pressed her lips against Dane's, lapping up the little bit of flavor and stickiness clinging to his lips. Before he could deepen the caress, she eased away, set the almonds down, and covered them before selecting the next dish.

He watched her uncover it and pick up a small white roll similar to an unfried egg roll. She then dipped it into a tiny dish in the middle of the platter. Holding his gaze, she lifted it to her lips and bit down. His mouth watered at the crunch of fresh vegetables and the pungent scent of shrimp. If there was one thing he enjoyed, it was fresh spring rolls. It didn't matter if they had shrimp in them. The ache of his cock surpassed his growling stomach with every second he watched her eat the savory treat.

She dipped the roll again, then lifted it to her lips, but this time she took too long to reach her mouth and some of the sauce dripped onto her chin and breasts.

Still astride his lap, she leaned close. Her expression was innocent, but her breasts were a sinful temptation. He sniffed as he dropped his chin and lapped the golden fluid from her cleavage; the spicy sauce only made the enticement that much harder to pass up.

"Open," she whispered in his ear.

Lifting his head, he did as instructed, opened his mouth, and bit through the rice-paper wrapping. The blend of noodles and shrimp, crunch of bell pepper, and spice of the sauce were familiar, but he was curious about the scent and taste of mint, along with the unique peppery flavor he couldn't quite place. "What did you use in these?"

She smiled as she dipped the end of the roll and popped it into his mouth. "You like?"

He nodded, savoring the taste as he chewed.

"Most of it you probably know." She dipped a second roll and took a bite.

"I recognize the shrimp, bell peppers, noodles, carrots, and celery, but I've never had mint or pepper in a spring roll." Watching her dip the roll and carry it toward his mouth, Dane noticed the heavy coating of sauce. The way it dribbled over her fingers and splashed onto his abdomen. He took the rest of the roll and chewed, but his interest in the ingredients waned as her fingers wiped at the golden liquid, smearing the sauce more than cleaning it up.

“Hmm, I seem to have made a mess. Stay still.” Her gaze held his as she eased one leg between his and lowered her bottom onto his right thigh.

When she broke eye contact, Dane suspected what she would do next and made an effort to chew and swallow his food before her mouth opened over his belly. He barely made it. Hard as his cock was, his hips jerked upward at the brush of her cheek against his shaft. Her tongue swirled through the dusting of hair below his navel before it dipped into the depression and lapped up the bit of sauce that had spilled inside. Making her way upward, she sucked and licked at the seasoned oils coating his skin. Her wet pussy rocked over the tensed muscles in his thigh.

His fingers gripped the seat to keep from directing her mouth south to the leaking tip of his dick. The thick piece of meat in question had ideas of its own; it grew harder and arched closer to his abdomen, bumping against Ariel's chin as she did one last swipe of her tongue from his sternum to his navel. A whisper of a kiss brushed its sensitive crown as Ariel stood up and reached for one of the napkins on the table.

She held his gaze and licked the sauce from her fingers, her mouth lingering to suck on the very tips before she wiped her hands off on the napkin. Ariel reached for the dish of sauce and cradled it in her left palm before she selected another roll from the plate.

After straddling his lap, Ariel dipped the roll into the sauce, then used it like a paintbrush to coat the firm muscles of his chest. He gritted his teeth at the sting of the chili seasoning in the sauce and the cool slide of the rice paper over his skin.

When she raised the morsel to his lips, he held her gaze and devoured nearly half of it in a single bite. Pieces of noodle, shrimp, and vegetable escaped the leftover half and dropped into the sweet and spicy mixture glistening on his flesh.

Her tongue slid between her lips and stroked over and around his pectorals. Her teeth nipped at the solid muscle beneath his skin every time it twitched or flexed. His nipples ached, their firm crowns tight and begging for attention. Dane panted and tried to maintain control following the scrape of her teeth across each firm peak. She opened her mouth over first one, then the other.

Finally she lifted her head; her lips were wet and swollen, but the fire in her eyes was growing. Determined to turn the tables on her, he lifted his hand to cradle the one she cupped the dipping sauce in. "May I feed you?"

Caution dimmed the heat in her gaze, but she nodded. Dane lifted the sauce from her hand and the remaining bit of roll from her other, then leaned forward to place both on the table behind her. He made sure the heated length of his cock pressed firmly against the wet panel of her panties. Shifting his hands to her waist, he pulled her closer and stroked along the side and back of her garment before he raised his fingers to the first hook.

"My skill won't be as good as yours. And I wouldn't want to ruin your clothes. Perhaps we should take them off?" He kept his voice low and his gaze on hers as he caressed the warm curves of her breasts with his middle, ring, and pinkie fingers, while his index fingers and thumbs played with the fasteners.

He was sure Ariel could read the intent in his deep blue eyes, but he could see her determination not to back away from his challenge.

Propping her elbows on the table behind her, she grinned. "Wise idea. You may remove my top." She waited a heartbeat, long enough for him to slip the first hook free before she added, "We wouldn't want you to earn a punishment for soiling my new leathers."

Dane met her gaze with a brow arched over his left eye. His silent admonition only egged her on. He wanted to see how far she'd go. A second hook was released. Ariel's gaze drifted down. With each loosened hook, she rocked forward and back, rubbing against the base of his cock. Her gaze tracked the spill of his semen as it slid over the reddened, plum-shaped head, then coasted over the throbbing veins and the thick ridge of tissue along the underside of his penis.

He watched her shiver in response to the wash of cool air over her sweat-dampened breasts and belly. Ariel's attention returned to Dane's progress as he slid the bustier from around her and dropped it to the floor beside the table. Holding her gaze, Dane reached past her shoulders to collect the bowl and spring roll, then waited, measuring her level of control.

It was there, held tight and close. The knowledge that she worked to rein in her desire to match his reinforced his intent to show her how his mastery would complete her. She'd sworn never to submit to him, but her body told him otherwise.

The problem he could see forming was her unreasoning intent to best him at his challenge. She seemed to worry about being under his command, despite what her betraying body might suggest. It was his responsibility to show her she had nothing to fear.

With that in mind, he cupped the bowl in his palm. "Dip it like this, right?" he asked, the roll poised over the sauce for the briefest of moments

Ariel nodded. She scrutinized his every move. Her expression revealed her suspicions that she might end up wearing part of the chili-ginger sauce.

And Dane didn't disappoint her. A sharp shift of his hand sent a tiny wave over the lip of the bowl. Golden fluid splashed onto the side of one breast and her belly. More dribbled over his fingertips and down onto her navel and lower abdomen. A soft gasp slipped from her lips.

"Oh, I am sorry." Dane's apology carried all the sincerity of a Ponzi schemer promising to pay back his investors.

"Lick it up," she ordered. Leaning forward, she ate half the roll he held between his fingers. Her gaze held his as she slowly chewed.

Dane set the bowl back on the table. "As you wish." He smiled. Lowering the last bit of roll to her belly, he used it to wipe up some of the spilled sauce. His tongue followed the slow slide of rice paper along her skin; it lapped up anything left behind. The stroke of it over her skin made Ariel gasp, and Dane grinned at the flex of her muscles under his lips. When he lifted his head, he popped the roll into his mouth and chewed quickly.

She wouldn't be outdone. “Give me your hand.” Ariel tapped the back of his right hand, the fingers still slick with sauce.

Dane held it up to her.

Her gaze locked with his, Ariel wiped the backs of his fingers over her breasts, smearing the sauce onto her nipples, then took each of his fingers, one at a time, into her mouth and sucked off the lingering moisture. Once finished, she released his hand, rested her elbows on the table behind her, and smiled up at him. “First clean my breasts.”

“And then?” Dane waited. He stroked his hands over her belly before he rubbed his fingers along her wet panties.

“You must have spilled some on my pussy, so you'll have to lick it up as well,” Ariel advised him.

Dane was sure her amusement was in response to the humor that flashed in his eyes. “Hmm, I don't recall—”

“Are you questioning me? Refusing to follow an order in my kitchen?” She tilted her head to the side and lifted her eyebrows.

“No, merely stating a recollection.” Dane smirked as he lowered his head to slide his tongue over her peaked nipples.

“Mmm.” Ariel's eyes closed. She tipped her head back; the look on her face reflected a sensual enjoyment of the swipe of his tongue along her skin, the tug of his teeth, and the suction of his mouth as he suckled first one breast, then the other. “You have a very talented mouth, Dane. I'll have to make sure to put it to good use.”

The nip of his teeth on the slope of her breast startled a cry from her lips. She sat up to stare down at him.

"Did that hurt?" He tried to look guileless, but he sensed Ariel's inner rebel stirring at the warning in his gaze.

"No, merely surprised me." She shrugged.

As his mouth finished cleaning the last of the sauce from one breast and traveled to the other, Ariel dropped one hand from the table to grip the thick length of his cock. Precum glistened on the bulbous tip with a few dribbles trailing down to his balls. Squeezing tight, she dragged her fist from base to tip and back down in several quick jerks, drawing a hiss from Dane's lips.

"Too tight?" she cooed, assuming a wide-eyed, innocent look.

Dane shook his head and leaned back in the chair. Settling his hand over hers, he halted the motion and drew a deep breath. His other hand plucked at the wet silk covering her mound. "What shall I do with these?"

Ariel grinned. "Anything you'd like." She slipped her hand from beneath his and returned her elbow to the table behind her.

The thin elastic snapped easily in his fists. He discarded the thong on the floor beside his chair. The black leather chaps framed her naked mound. The evidence of her arousal shimmered on her skin.

"Have you forgotten what I told you to do?" Ariel asked with a teasing smile.

"No, merely evaluating the best method." Dane stroked his fingers over the plump folds and dipped between them to trace the wet entrance to her body.

"Method?"

Dane nodded. "Yes. You'll notice the distance between your pussy and my mouth. In order to reach it, I would have to bend down, which limits the area I can reach." He leaned over; his hands gripped her hips and angled them upward, allowing him only enough room to lap and nuzzle the upper slope of her mound.

Ariel groaned and shifted, drawing his attention to the swollen nubbin.

Dane sat up, lowered her bottom back to his lap, and made sure to brush the damp curves with the tip of his cock. "See, not enough contact. A second way would require removing the plates from the table and blowing out the candle." He glanced past her shoulder at the objects in question and then shook his head. "Too much work, I think."

Ariel nodded in agreement.

"There is another way," he offered. Sliding his arms beneath her thighs, Dane raised her pussy to his mouth. Her legs dangled over his arms, and her shoulders rested flat on the table.

He watched her as his tongue stroked over the soft flesh of her mound. He hummed in appreciation at the taste of her cream. The slide of his lips eliminated the moist evidence along one thigh before he transferred his attentions to the other.

His gaze challenged Ariel to try to look away. She stared right back. Her eyes followed the path of his lips and tongue. Her intent to win their battle of wills was clear in her gaze. Ariel smiled and smoothed her right hand over her belly and up to her breast. In the same slow, stroking rhythm he used to tease her sex, Ariel squeezed the pale globe and tugged at the rosy crest. The flare of arousal darkening his eyes was reflected in hers, but when he nuzzled between the folds and began to circle her clit, Ariel shook her head.

"Uh-uh, Dane. No touching inside." As precarious as her position was, he could see she acknowledged his control over her, but instinctively she seemed to know she could trust him to stop when she told him to.

Slowly, reluctantly, Dane lowered her ass back to his lap. His breath the slightest bit accelerated, he waited, his hands on her hips.

Sitting up, Ariel slid her hand from her breast to her pussy. "Very good job, Dane." She stood up, stepped back from the chair, returned the bowl of sauce to the platter, and set the cover over the leftover spring rolls. "You've earned your dessert."

Dane leaned back in the chair and grinned. "And that would be?"

She uncovered the last plate and held it up for him. "These."

Dane groaned and shook his head. A layer of thick, creamy filling rested between two chocolate cookies. Ariel set the plate down on the table in front of the chair and picked up one of the cookies. Resuming her seat on his lap, she held one to his lips, and he bit down on it.

Sweet cream and chocolate filled his mouth. It was delicious, but it was not what he wanted. What he craved. The desire was hot in her eyes, but she was as determined as he was to keep from succumbing. After swallowing the first bite, he held her gaze and leaned forward to take a second, slid his lips over her fingers, and nipped the very tips with his teeth. As he bit into the treat, Dane pressed hard enough to force some of the creamy center to overflow the edge of the sandwich and spill into Ariel's hand. Several thick drops splashed onto his lower abdomen and cock.

"Such a messy man." Ariel moaned. She looked down at the sticky filling between his legs.

He watched as she popped the last bit of sandwich cookie into her mouth and licked the smear of filling from her palm. Dane waited, watching her expression as she focused on the thick jut of his erection; he hoped she'd do what he wanted, but he wondered if she'd devise some other means of pushing his control.

With a shake of her head, she gave him a scolding look. Both humor and yearning gleamed in her eyes. She slipped off his lap and ordered, "Lift yourself up so I can clean you off."

Dane cursed silently as she reached for a napkin from the table. He braced his hands on either side of his seat, lifted his ass off the chair, and kept his feet planted on the floor.

He nearly lost his grip when Ariel bent at the waist and licked the icing from his stomach. Her attention shifted to the base of his cock as she licked away the other smear of gooey sweetness and glanced up at him. "Seems you have another mess that requires cleaning, hmm?"

He swallowed, his focus centered on her as she smoothed her tongue up the length of his penis. Base to tip, she stroked up the solid column of flesh like a child licking an ice-cream cone on a hot summer's day. Each time she reached the tip, she swirled over the crown, dipped the tip of her tongue into the tiny slit, and then started all over again.

Once she'd made her way all the way around, she stood up and dabbed at her lips with the napkin. "Mmm, delish." Waiting until he'd settled back onto the chair, she asked, "Would you like another cookie?"

Dane shook his head. Turnabout was definitely fair play, he determined. He eyed the cookie she'd set aside and asked, "Would you like me to feed you one?"

The flutter of the pulse at her throat betrayed her excitement. Her dark red nipples were crinkled crests on her full breasts, and her cunt had grown wet again. He wondered if she'd deny him his opportunity to tease. She was close. But so was he. Despite his years of experience, he was learning she was more than a challenge. Ariel was his match, his complement, both sexually and intellectually.

Her slight nod was the first indicator followed by her soft "yes." She retrieved a cookie from the plate and held it out to him.

Dane took the treat with one hand, and with the other at her waist, he drew Ariel back down onto his lap, her hips tight to his, the plump folds of her sex pressed over his cock. She squirmed once, then stilled as the motion parted her flesh and settled his hot length against the firm jut of her clit.

"Have you tried eating these from the inside out?" Dane asked, then eased the cookies apart to reveal the soft, creamy center.

With one half up to his lips, he licked at the creamy filling. "Mmm, sweet." He held it to her lips and waited for her tongue to peek out. It slipped along the same path his tongue had taken. "It's not as sweet as your cream, but it's good," he whispered.

Before she could pull away, he set the cookie against her lips and waited for her to take a bite. While she chewed, her gaze never left his. Dane took a bite as well and then offered the last morsel to her.

His other hand still held the second half of the cookie, the layer of cream thicker on this part than the previous. Taking care not to make it appear too obvious, Dane let the cookie slip and—*plop*—land on the slope of her breast.

Ariel gasped and jerked upward. Her eyes went wide at the rub of his erection along her clit and the slide of the cookie along her breast. Dane smeared the cream over her nipple before withdrawing the cookie and tossing it toward the table.

"Terribly clumsy of me," he admitted, the lie falling easily from his lips. He pulled her tighter to him so he could snag one of the foil packets she'd tucked near the base of the candle. Tearing it open, he shifted her away long enough to roll the protection on with one hand before he pulled her close again.

"I-I can't be—" Ariel panted. Her hips rocked over his. One of her hands gripped his shoulder as she stammered.

"Can't be what?" Dane gave her no ease. He tilted her hips, opened her up so his latex-covered shaft once again rode between the wet, pouty lips.

"Cleaning up this m-mess." Ariel swallowed, wiggled her ass on his lap, and ground her clit against him. "Take care of it."

"As you wish."

The slide of his mouth over her breast brought a groan to her lips. The friction of his cock over her sensitive nubbin sent tremors through her thighs. Her breath hitched and then increased; against his lips he could feel her heart double its rhythm.

When his teeth pulled at her nipple, scraping at the creamy covering he'd smeared there, Ariel groaned. The flex of her abdomen hinted at a first pulse of climax snaking through her center. He could see the will she used to stop it. She arched closer with the second tug of his teeth against her peaked nipple.

Damn it, she was fighting, but Dane could see it was a losing battle. Ariel hadn't attained enough skill in controlling her body yet. A third, long-drawn-out pressure snapped her tenuous hold.

Rising onto her toes, hands gripping his shoulders, Ariel slid up so the crest of his cock was snug against her pussy. Their gazes locked, and she slammed down, thrusting him deep inside, filling her body with his heated shaft. Arousal and passion flushed her cheeks and burned in her eyes. Ariel pumped up and down, riding him in a furious rhythm.

Dane grasped her bottom. He tried not to hurt her with his grip, but the press and release as he tried to guide her motion only made her fight against his direction. Her internal muscles gripped and relaxed. His restraint grew tenuous as she worked herself over him.

His mouth left her breast and captured hers. Their tongues thrust in tandem with the ride of her body over his. Dane kept pace with her easily. He sensed the moment her spiraling need broke free. It washed through her and vibrated along her nerve endings and tissues, exploding her senses as climax shattered every cell.

When her pace faltered, Dane took over. He rocked her up and down, pulled her close, pressed her so tightly to him that not even air could fit between them. Dane felt a second orgasm spasm along her limbs and up her spine as his climax crested. Their hips slammed together, parted, then reunited. Cries commingled. Fingers clutched at shoulders and buttocks. Stars exploded in front of his eyes as he held her gaze and watched her surrender to pleasure.

The soft commands he whispered in her ear and the stroke of his hands along her back as he held her close eased the intensity of sensation, keeping her safe as the world spun around them.

He cuddled her as the candle burned down. Their breathing slowed, and the sweat on their skin dried, but still Dane held her, savoring the smell of her arousal and satisfaction. The slide of her fingers across his back and down his spine once again stirred interest in the flesh still semihard and snug inside her.

With his legs stretched out beneath the table, Dane nuzzled his nose against the shell of her ear. “Shall we adjourn to the bedroom, Tink?”

Ariel's arms tightened around his back. “Mmmm, don' wanna get up,” she muttered. Her body flexed around his as she tucked her head beneath his chin.

“Then I'll do all the work.” He chuckled and rose easily from the chair, one arm around his woman's back, the other keeping her body joined to his. Careful to keep his balance, he leaned forward to blow out the candle before he exited the kitchen and headed down the hall to Ariel's bedroom.

Ariel clamped her legs around his waist. Her hands hooked over his shoulders, and she hummed in appreciation at the advance and retreat of his cock inside her with each step he took. Dane had to admit the feel of her riding him was returning life to his body faster than he'd anticipated. When she used her internal muscles to squeeze and release pressure on him, Dane lifted his hand from her back to land a firm swat on her bottom. "Enough, woman. Wait until we get you naked."

Ariel eased back and pouted up at him. "Don't you like my chaps?"

Dane pulled her close to press a hard kiss to her lips. "I prefer what's between them." Stepping toward the bed, he reached around with one hand to release the hold of her legs and lifted her free of his body.

Their combined groans echoed in the quiet room as Dane settled her onto the bed. Ariel propped herself on her elbows and watched him walk to the door and switch the overhead light off, then cross to the nightstand and turn the bedside lamp on. Neither of them averted their eyes as he stood beside the bed, watching her watch him deal with the used rubber and dispose of it in the trash bin beside the nightstand.

Amusement and intent glimmered in her eyes as she smiled up at him. "You like what's between them, huh?"

Dane nodded and eased onto the mattress near her feet. "Oh yes, sprite. I find what's between your leather leggings particularly appealing."

When he reached to undo the snaps along the outside of one of the legs, Ariel pulled her foot away. "Do you like what's in front"—one hand traveled downward to stroke over her bare pussy—"or what's in back?" Rolling onto her hip, she held his gaze over her shoulder as she smoothed her fingers across the tattoo on her bottom, then slid her fingers into the crease.

"Ariel?" Dane held himself still, not wanting to make a move should Ariel change her mind.

He'd taken his time over the last week preparing her body to accept his, but he'd waited for her to make the final request.

"Please, Dane. I've been so good." Ariel rolled onto her belly, tucked her knees under her, and lifted her butt in the air—a clear sign she offered her body to him.

The black leather created the perfect frame for her bottom. The full, round curves edged in black leather, the colorful tattoo decorating one cheek.

He wouldn't deny her request. "Yes, you have been very good." When he leaned over to pull the nightstand drawer open, Dane examined the contents for what he required. The last plug he'd used on her lay next to the blue vibrator, a depleted box of condoms, and a bottle of lube. Taking the lube and several condoms out, he shut the drawer and took a seat on the bed behind her.

The *rip* of cellophane and the sound of latex over flesh were loud in the room. The rasp of Ariel's breath increased in concert with Dane's as he coated his cock and the rosy hole of her anus with lube. The *snap* of the bottle's lid closing mingled with Ariel's cries for more. Dane tossed the bottle aside and used his fingers to tease her pucker into relaxing. "You know how to do this, baby," he assured her as he eased the first finger inside.

When she moaned and pushed back, opening herself to his probing, Dane smiled. "So good, Ariel. That's it. Take it in." He worked the lube along the interior wall, making sure the channel was well prepared. "Okay, let's do two." He pulled the first digit free before he started to press a second one in beside it.

Beneath him, Ariel moaned. Her body trembled, and the plump lips of her pussy swelled with arousal. When she would have arched her bottom higher, as if reaching for a faster, deeper penetration, Dane settled his free hand on her lower back and pushed down. "You're not ready yet, love."

"Please." Ariel gasped; her head turned to the side, and her eyes focused on him and the motions of his hands as he worked a third finger inside, stretching her.

He still had doubts about her decision as he flexed and spread his fingers in her ass. Her body trembled at the sting of sensation as it shivered through her and sparked a slow burn.

"God, please, Dane," she begged again.

The tone of her voice and the flush on her cheeks told him more than words. He could see the evidence accumulating that nothing mattered to Ariel as long as he commanded her body. Over the last week he'd watched how turned on she became when he pushed the plugs or wand inside her butt. Anticipation rather than antipathy glowed in her eyes when he touched her, coached her to accept his orders. Her body yearned for the thick length of his cock as much as his body craved sheathing itself in her. "Are you sure you want this?" Dane asked.

Ariel writhed in front of him, her ass tilted up, glistening with lube. "Please, Dane, now."

"Okay, baby."

He pressed the tip of his cock against the puckered entrance, squeezed past the first ring of tight muscles. The shaking in her limbs increased. Ariel's respiration grew broken, labored.

"Take a deep breath," he reminded her as he pushed. One hand on her lower back held her still; the other hand slid beneath the leather on her hip. His fingers flexed in time with the slow advance of his body into hers.

Ariel tensed on the bed; pain battled arousal. Her fingers fisted the sheets and pulled them free of the mattress as he worked his way deeper. "Oh God, more, please." She sobbed. She tried to push back, to take more of his hot, thick member as he advanced past the second ring.

"Christ, Ariel, slow down." Dane shifted his hand to grip her other hip to halt her movements, drawing a cry from her lips.

"*No.*"

Dane froze. Sweat trickled down his face and stung his eyes. "Am I hurting you?" He wasn't sure how he'd do it, but one word from Ariel and he'd pull free. Leave his fantasy of fucking her ass unfulfilled until she was ready to try again.

"Yes." She sobbed. Her eyes were squeezed shut as she quivered under his hold. "Don't…"

He could barely hear her. Trying to keep his cock as still as possible, he eased down, rearranging her position to get as close as he dared to her. "Don't what, Tink? Do you want me to stop?"

Releasing her stranglehold on the bedding, Ariel reached back and gripped his wrist. Her breathing ragged, she looked up at him with tears in her eyes. "Don't stop. Please. I need…I need more."

Dane didn't realize he'd held his breath until it bled slowly out of him. The coil of heat in his balls began to spread. His ass tingled with sensation as he pressed forward, his gaze focused on the myriad expressions suffusing Ariel's face. "I won't stop, Ariel. I promise."

The last few inches that sank inside brought his balls snug against her most sensitive flesh. Ariel squirmed beneath the rub of his lightly furred sac. Her shifting and gasps increased as Dane pulled out and then pressed back inside. He took his time, his pace slow, rhythmic until the rock of Ariel's hips beneath his became more forceful.

"Shhh, slow down," he cautioned.

But Ariel would have none of it. "More," she growled. Her hand left his to grip the edge of the mattress above her head.

"No." Dane tried to make her see reason.

Again she wouldn't listen. Pressing back harder, faster, Ariel fought the hold he had on her hips. She snarled in anger as he stilled her motions again and again. "Fuck me. I want it harder, Dane."

Dane relented, coveting the same increased pace. “Hard and fast, Ariel?”

Ariel's head bobbed up and down rapidly. “Yes. Hard. Fast.” She gazed over her shoulder at him, the passion hot in her gaze, the flush of climax in her face, the pulse of it through her body. “Please.”

“As you wish, love.” Dane smiled and leaned forward to press a kiss to the corner of her lips. He allowed his desire to rule. He pulled back, then thrust hard and deep as he relinquished control, grunting with the force of each advance and retreat until he pushed Ariel flat to the mattress, his body pressed along her back. Dane interlaced his fingers with Ariel's as they gripped the edge of the bed.

Their mingled cries and groans filled the bedroom; the scent of sweat and sex permeated the air. He held off long enough to see Ariel tumble over the edge into climax before his orgasm exploded through him. Breath ragged and senses drained, Dane had barely enough strength to roll onto his side, taking Ariel with him, his body still firmly connected to hers.

* * *

Her body ached in all the right places as Ariel lay curled in bed, with Dane tucked up against her back. At some point, he must have switched off the lamp, but the exact moment when he did so was lost in the fog of postcoital bliss. The drift of his hand along her arm and onto her waist and hip confirmed he was as awake as she was. She doubted the worries going through his head were the same ones bouncing through hers. She doubted he was bedeviled by the way her body had submitted so easily to his command. Or that her arousal only seemed heightened with every order he'd whispered in her ear. That it had only taken twelve days of hot, wicked sex to coax her into doing things she'd never let another man attempt. And she craved more. The tantalizing images played in her mind as her eyes stared at the bedroom wall. Floggers, paddles, nipple clamps, and thick, sturdy leather cuffs.

No, Ariel told herself, if he were worried about anything, it was probably how long he'd have to continue buttering up the little sister by fucking her. Or perhaps it was whether she'd quit snipping at him now that she'd let him—

"I'm curious." His whisper and warm lips along her nape stilled the whirlwind of thoughts in her head.

Ariel shifted and rolled onto her back to stare up at him. The glow from the outside streetlights filtered through the curtains. The dim light kept the room from complete darkness, but the way he leaned over her placed his face in shadow. There was no way to know what he was thinking except to ask. "Curious about what?"

"How quiet we'll have to be once your sister gets back." He leaned down to kiss her. The curve of his lips matched the amusement in his voice.

It was time to stop. She was becoming way too comfortable with him around. The fact that he felt at ease enough to intimate they would be together after her sister came home was too much. Too close to the fantasies she'd been building in her mind. She needed to end it. Now. Before he did the walking away.

Ariel turned her head to break the kiss. It was easy to understand why Dane would ponder the logistics related to their being together, but not for the same reasons as she. Rolling away from his touch, she didn't think before responding. “Why would we have to be quiet? You won't be here.”

It was obvious from the way he'd phrased his question that Dane's interest remained purely sexual, nothing more. Not like her. In her head, she cursed the tears burning the backs of her eyes as she fought to keep him from knowing how his words hurt. She'd give up her kitchen before she'd admit how much she'd come to care for the bastard, when he obviously couldn't be bothered.

Dane must have sensed something was wrong, because he reached across her to turn on the lamp. “I'm not sure I follow your logic here.” His voice took on the clipped, businesslike tone he used with obnoxious suppliers and rude customers.

Refusing to look at him, Ariel shrugged; she could feel his gaze on her. The bed shifted behind her. She guessed he had sat up, but she wasn't about to confirm her suspicions. “What's there to explain? In five days Alayna will be back, and you won't be here except when you and Logan come in for lunch.”

“That doesn't mean I'll be leaving you, Ariel. What we have—”

That brought Ariel up, the sheet pulled close to cover her nudity. “What we *had* was sex, Dane. Plain and simple. A little something extra to spice up the challenge you threw out.”

"That's not true."

Ariel leaned against the headboard and shook her head. "It is. We're consenting adults who scratched an itch. That's all. And now it's time to stop."

Dane's expression grew dark. "And if I don't want to? Stop, that is."

"This isn't all about you. If I want it to stop, it stops. Ask any of my boyfriends."

"I'm not one of those kids you can push around, Ariel," Dane warned, but he made no attempt to try to intimidate her.

Why couldn't he stay on his side of the counter? I was a helluva lot better off when all I could do was fantasize about what he'd be like in bed. Pushing past the pain, Ariel ignored her wounded heart and finished what she'd started—cutting him out of her life. "Did you ever think I might get bored?" A blow to his pride would surely send him packing and make him determined never to see her again.

"Bored? Turned on, jacked up, or excited would be a better description of what you are, Tink." The sarcasm was heavy in Dane's voice.

Ariel gave it back. "Oh please. Those were just games," she lied. "If you're that upset about it, we can call it a draw."

Dane's expression didn't give much away, other than his disbelief. "You don't have to lie to me, Ariel. I know admitting to enjoying submission can be frightening. Especially when your independent nature makes you believe otherwise." He cupped her face in his hands and held her gaze.

"You don't know anything," she denied. She prayed the sorrow, confusion, even the fear of caring too much weren't visible to his intent gaze. Let him think this was all about her not wanting to be mastered.

"I've been doing this a long time, sprite. If there's one thing I know, it's how to recognize a submissive."

"I'm not."

He leaned close and pressed his lips to hers. "You are. You ought to think through what would be best for you. My interest won't go away, but a woman who isn't willing to face what is essential to her and take the risk of going after it isn't a woman strong enough to be a dominatrix, let alone my submissive."

She jerked free of his hold and spat out, "Who says I want you to be in charge all the time?"

"You did." He forestalled her response by adding, "Not in words, but in actions, Ariel. Your body recognizes what you are by your very nature. Now you have to acknowledge it." Leaning down, he cupped her face again and pressed his lips to hers.

Something in his face told Ariel he wouldn't argue the finer points with her. He would accept her rejection. He would let her push him away. Damn it, he was going to leave. There were still five days before Alayna returned. *If she returned.* Ariel ignored the voice warning her that her sister could choose not to come home. The same internal voice that knew when the right ingredients had been mixed together for a fabulous new sauce or marinade.

That would leave Ariel alone. Not just temporarily. Permanently. She clenched her fists in the bedding to keep from reaching out to Dane. To stop herself from latching on to him and begging him to stay. To not leave her.

Pulling back, he shook his head. "You'll never be happy until you unleash the woman you are, Tink. Whether with me or another Dom later in your life, it's important to let that part of yourself free."

She stayed silent as he climbed from the bed, dressed, and walked out. The soft *snick* of the latch on the front door released her paralysis. Ariel slid down the bed and rolled into the warm spot Dane had occupied. *I knew he'd go. It was only a matter of time. I don't need him. I don't need anyone. I'm safer this way.*

Ariel stared at the wall, tried to believe what she told herself, and ignore the tears wetting her cheeks.

Chapter Fourteen

Day 30

If Ariel had known how hard it would be to pull herself out of bed for the last five days, she doubted she would have. Knowing how much her sister was counting on her to keep the café going, Ariel had shown up each morning, but the fun wasn't there. Dane's parting words resounded in her head so many times, she wondered if she would ever be able to turn them off.

What was worse was how right he was.

Damn him.

And she missed him.

Damn him again.

Ariel dragged her stainless steel bowl from the rack, ignoring the fact that she'd been in the process of cleaning up after a busy lunch rush. DeeDee and Sadie had seen the last customers out an hour earlier, and the rattle of salt and pepper shakers confirmed they were tidying up the dining area. She set the temp on the lower oven, twisted the switch to Bake, and started to gather the components for Alayna's favorite double-fudge brownies.

"We need to talk."

At Sadie's no-nonsense tone, Ariel turned from the pile of ingredients on the central island. "What's wrong?"

"You are." DeeDee huffed, pulled one of the stools to the station, and settled onto it.

Sadie collected the other stool and sat beside her coworker. "Yes, you."

"What did I do?" By memory, Ariel measured and poured the ingredients into the bowl.

"You've been moping around here for the last couple of days. Even the customers have commented on it," DeeDee explained.

"I have not—"

Sadie shook her head. "You have. And Dane hasn't been any better."

Ariel cursed the way her body reacted to the sound of his name. "What has he been doing?"

"Nothing." DeeDee frowned.

"Nothing?"

Sadie nodded. "He hasn't stopped to chat or talk to anyone. He comes in, goes to the office for a few hours, and leaves."

"I haven't seen him—"

DeeDee threw up her hands. "That's the problem, Ariel. You haven't seen him, and he hasn't seen you. What the hell did you do?"

"Me? Why is this my fault?" Ariel demanded.

"Well, you were the one always pushing him and making comments to get under his skin," Sadie started.

"Then last week it was like, *whoa*, you two couldn't stay away from each other." DeeDee giggled.

Ariel shuffled her feet and fiddled with the measuring spoons beside the bowl, embarrassed that her attraction to Dane had been so obvious.

Sadie leaned an elbow on the counter and propped her chin in her hand. "Yeah, I was afraid I'd walk in on the two of you doing the wild thing on the desk in the office."

"Or against the walk-in refrigerator," DeeDee added.

Ariel could feel her face flush. If they suspected what Dane and she had done in the dining area, they'd never let her hear the end of it.

"I don't know what happened between you two, Ari, but you better fix this," Sadie ordered.

"There's nothing to fix." Ariel denied.

DeeDee moved to the food-recycling bin and tipped it toward her. "Liar. If there weren't something to fix, why did you ruin six dozen oatmeal-raisin cookies and two dozen double-chocolate cupcakes?"

"So I overcooked a few things." She shrugged, refusing to admit how distracted she'd been.

"You never overcook things, Ariel," Sadie pointed out.

"I have—"

"When?" DeeDee and Sadie asked in unison as they looked at her.

DeeDee added, "In the six years I've been working here, I haven't once seen you burn toast, let alone the number of cookies and cupcakes you have today."

"If it had been Alayna, I would have expected it, but not you," Sadie agreed.

"I'm making up for lost time," Ariel sniped back.

"You're frustrated as hell and refuse to fix your screwup with the man in the office." DeeDee snorted.

"He's here?" Ariel didn't doubt the other woman. Her body had been tingling for nearly an hour. The sensation was similar to the sting of shock when she was little and would drag her feet across carpet and then touch something made of metal.

Both nodded as they turned to collect their coats and purses from the tiny lockers near the back door. "He came in about an hour ago," DeeDee told her.

"And he looks as miserable as you," Sadie added as she flipped her ponytail over her shoulder after she shrugged into her coat.

"If he's so miserable, why can't he be the one to talk to me?" Ariel asked as she followed the waitresses to the front door.

Sadie smiled and patted Ariel's shoulder as if calming a mentally confused person. "Because you've had your panties in a twist about the man since he walked in the door."

"I have not," Ariel lied.

"You have. And you've done everything but put a gun to his head to drive him away," DeeDee pointed out.

Ariel couldn't deny that. She had made every effort to push Dane out the door. To keep him from replacing her sister in the office. To keep from letting him have a piece of her heart.

"If you won't do it for yourself, Ariel. Do it for us," Sadie suggested.

"For you two?"

DeeDee nodded. "Yeah. Since the two of you have stopped sniping at each other, business has dropped off, and the tips aren't as good."

Stunned at the remark, Ariel didn't have a chance to respond as both girls slipped out the door and walked away. Their laughter carried back to her as she closed and locked the café's front door.

Had she and Dane really been putting on a performance for the customers, Ariel wondered as she headed back into the kitchen. She didn't allow herself to glance down the hall toward the office, where a light shone under the closed door.

She stared at the ingredients for her sister's favorite treat on the counter. Needing the routine of cooking to help her process, Ariel mixed up the batch of brownies, spread the batter in a baking pan, and put it in the oven.

As she cleaned up the station and gathered the fixings for the fudgy frosting, Ariel took the time to seriously contemplate the past few days.

"I'm not that miserable," she muttered as she mixed the icing, covered it, and set it aside.

At the sink, she rinsed, then stacked the dishes and tools into the dishwasher. "So what if I spend all my free time sleeping? And I'm tired of having to be here at the crack of dawn every day." *But you used to like that.*

"I just have to take some time to get past this. I've dumped other boyfriends before," she grumbled as she wiped down the counters and tidied the different stations. *You've never acted like this with any of those guys. You can't even sit down at the kitchen table to eat.*

"I like eating while I watch TV," Ariel retorted, although she knew it wasn't true. "And so what if I've been sleeping on the sofa? Nothing says I have to sleep in my room. I'm a grown-up."

Who won't admit the man she loves makes her want to give in to his every command.

"That is not true." Ariel argued with herself. "I never said I didn't like letting him be in charge. I only said—Oh never mind." She pushed the thoughts away and checked on the brownies. She switched off the oven, pulled the pan out, and set the finished dessert on a cooling rack. "It takes strength to admit when you're wrong," she muttered to herself. *It's not that I was wrong, so much as*—Ariel didn't try to finish the thought. "I was afraid of what he makes me feel." The stool Sadie had used was next to Ariel, so she settled onto it. "I'm still afraid."

* * *

Dane didn't turn from the spreadsheet on the screen when he heard the muted voices in the front of the eatery. He glanced at the clock on the computer and confirmed the noise came from the departure of the two waitresses. Which meant Ariel had locked the door and was ready to shut down the kitchen.

The smell of chocolate drifted into the room. It stirred memories of the first lesson he'd received about the stuff. It also drew to mind the last night he'd spent with Ariel and the rich flavor of the cookies she'd fed him for dessert. His cock twitched and began to ache as his thoughts conjured images of Ariel as they made love—her face flushed, lips swollen from his kisses, her body tight around his, drawing him deeper, milking every drop of life from him.

Dane pulled his glasses off, rubbed at his eyes, and cursed softly. He'd known she'd be a pain in the ass. Her sister had warned him to watch out for her. But damn it, Ariel Valerian wasn't supposed to worm her way into his soul. He was nearly forty. He had been happily single and enjoying his life until that blue-haired sprite had come along.

And that argument. Where the hell had all that crap come from about calling a draw on the challenge they had? He hadn't made any comments even remotely associated with ending the challenge or leaving. He knew Logan would bring Alayna back today, not for another hour or so, but he knew Ariel's big sister was on her way home. He had wondered how they could continue to see each other, and Ariel had blown it all out of proportion. As if she was scared and determined to be the first one to walk away.

That thought gave Dane pause. He'd been aware how reluctant Ariel was to face the submissive side of her nature. Yes, there were dominant elements to her personal makeup, but the overriding one was sub. He'd seen and developed it in too many other people to not see it in the woman he loved.

Ah shit! He winced. *I used* that *word about a woman*. Not that he wasn't willing to admit how he felt about Ariel. He just worried she would refuse to reciprocate on pure mulish, stubborn principle.

"Sitting around here won't get her to admit to anything except she likes to cook and thinks the only good man is a silent one," Dane groused as he made a final glance at the chart in front of him.

The heady smell of chocolate again reached the office. Shaking his head, he debated the rationale behind confronting Ariel about the decision she'd made and how it would affect the rest of her life. The other, more emotional part of him sneered at the idea of meeting with her after the way she had dismissed the idea of being submissive to him. Dane was sure as he pushed to his feet that his weren't the only feelings to have been sacrificed to Ariel's desperation to keep anyone else from taking over.

Perhaps it was time they cleared the air. He didn't want her sister to come home to hostile living quarters. And he sure as hell wanted to know if he waited in vain for a woman who wasn't willing to bend. After saving the document and shutting down the computer, Dane stood up, crossed the hall, and stepped into the kitchen.

The second the door swung open, Ariel knew Dane had more on his mind than the evening deposit. She rose to her feet and pushed the stool beneath the counter.

"Can we talk?" he asked, crossing to stand on the other side of the workstation.

She shrugged. "Sure." *If he goes first, I'll know where I stand. Maybe I won't have to tell him anything.*

"About the other night. I don't want you to think that I wanted to end what we have together."

Ariel crossed to the rack and pulled off the pan of brownies. The metal was cool to the touch, but the bottom was still warm. "I kinda figured that out."

Dane continued talking. "I know you have a very strong personality, Ariel. One that has cowed a few men, but my observations about your nature—they weren't from a selfish standpoint. I didn't say it because I'd prefer you assumed a submissive role with me."

"Then why? None of the other guys I've dated have ever raised such an uproar when I told them I didn't want to see them anymore." Ariel smoothed the icing over the brownies, not wanting to meet his gaze in case there wasn't anything more there than casual interest. Or a wish to win the bet they'd had.

"I would think by now you'd realize I'm not like the boys you've been involved with, Tink."

She shivered at the nickname. "Oh, I figured that one out too."

"And?"

Her head came up. Their gazes connected. His expression challenged her. As if he believed she'd never admit she was wrong. *Ha. Try again, surfer boy.*

After swirling the chocolate icing into place, she dropped the spatula into the extra frosting at the bottom of the bowl and then faced Dane. “I'm about to get to the point where I admit that you could be right in your estimation.”

Dane eased around the counter and stood beside her. “Which estimation is that?”

“The one where you said I gain more satisfaction from taking directions than giving them.” She watched as he lifted her hand from the counter and found the smear of fudge frosting along the base of her thumb.

Dane raised it to his lips, his gaze holding hers, and licked the chocolaty, sweet goo away. “And where would you say you can take the best orders?”

Ariel let her lips curve in a lopsided grin. “Anywhere.”

“And who would be giving these orders?” Dane queried; he wrapped one arm around her waist and pulled her snug against his frame. The other hand still held hers; his lips explored the sensitive lines in her palm.

Her other hand came up to thread her fingers through his curly blond hair. “Well, considering the only dominant I could possibly tolerate bossing me around is you, I think the prospect pool is awful shallow.”

Dane chuckled. “Good thing I'm more than willing to spend all the time necessary to teach you how to enjoy submitting to me.”

Her fingers tightened in his hair and gave a slight tug. “Eh, watch it, Mister. Don't think I'm some kinda pushover just because I love—”

Dane's grin deepened. “What was that, Ariel? Because you love? What? Taking orders from me? The multiple orgasms I can give you?” He teased her even as he pressed close, letting her feel how his body responded to hers.

Ariel knew she might as well confess everything. He'd get it out of her eventually, and maybe, considering the satisfied gleam in his eye, it was possible he reciprocated her feelings. “Oh, I love all of that, but unbearably arrogant as you are, I have to admit I lean toward loving you sometimes too.”

“Good answer,” Dane praised before his mouth covered hers, coaxed her lips open, and teased her tongue into play.

Four days of denial had the heat burning in both of them. Ariel could feel the hammering of his heart in time with hers. The grip of his fingers tightened as he held her to him. Though she was sure he felt the same for her, Ariel wanted the words. Leaning back, she pressed her hands over his chest and smiled up at him. “Aren't you forgetting something?”

“What's that?”

Ariel tugged the hem of his T-shirt free of his jeans. “Oh, maybe a few words?” she suggested as she pushed the shirt up his chest and over his head.

“Oh yeah.” Dane nodded. “Take off your clothes, Tink.”

Ariel laughed as she toed off her sneakers and stripped out of her black slacks and panties in one pull. “Here? Now?”

Dane's fingers started at the bottom of her chef's coat and Ariel's at the top, pushing buttons through buttonholes.

"Definitely right here"—he canted his head toward the workstation beside them—"and right now."

Coat undone, she shrugged it off, then stripped out of her tank top and bra before balancing on one foot and then the other to tug off her socks. "Those are some pretty good words, Master Reese, but I was thinking of three other ones." She motioned to the pan of brownies. "Better get those out of the way. They're for Al when she gets home."

Dane obliged and carried the pan to a different counter. As he returned, his fingers flicked open the buttons on his jeans, but he didn't push them off. His warm hands hoisted her onto the stainless steel surface, drawing a hiss of surprise from her lips at the chill beneath her bottom. Stepping into the cradle of her thighs, he pushed and opened her to his touch. Two fingers parted her plump lips, which were wet with anticipation and arousal. Ariel groaned at the rasp of his rough fingertips along her delicate flesh, but she didn't try to pull away. He stroked over her clit, sending a shiver through her body before the two fingers dipped lower and pushed inside.

The movements were too shallow to be painful, but too slow to satisfy. As she reached for purchase on the smooth surface behind her, Ariel bumped the bowl, scraping it along the counter as she gripped the edge. Dane's attention shifted from her to the bowl.

"Three words?" he asked. His free hand slid through the icing on the bottom of the container. Dane lifted a thick glob, nipped off some, and hummed in appreciation. "Could the three words be *love your chocolate*?"

Ariel watched as he coated her crinkled nipples in the icing before drawing a trail from between her breasts to her navel with the confection. Swallowing heavily, she shook her head. "Not quite those three words." Her breath froze in her lungs as his mouth covered the crest of her breast.

His tongue lapped at the crown. He sucked away the icing on one nipple, then traveled to the other breast and cleaned it too. "Mmm. Better than lemon." He lifted his gaze to hers and grinned. "Well, were those the three words?"

Before she could reply, he started at her sternum and began drifting downward, eating the smears of chocolate from her skin. Shaking her head, she told him, "Not those three words either."

Her palm, slick with sweat, slipped out from under her. Ariel reached for something and upended the bowl of frosting. The glossy brown topping, having grown warm, spilled over the counter and onto the floor.

Ariel arched toward the heated slide of his cock against her. Her hand, coated in chocolate, gripped his hip. He thrust home, burying himself to the hilt inside her. His breath whispered over her lips. "How about I love you? Would those be the three words?"

Ariel moaned. "Oh God, yes. Those are the words. Now fuck me please, Master Reese."

"As you wish, my sweet little pixie," Dane assured her, and he picked up the pace.

Dane urged her to hold off climax, while Ariel begged to let go. A sheen of sweat coated their skin and mingled with the spilled icing as their bodies rocked together. She could feel the sticky topping in her hair, on her hands, and along her back. In the kaleidoscope swirl of sensations, her hands slipped and scrambled for purchase along Dane's back, leaving her mark on him in sweet, chocolaty smears and transferring the icing to the insides of her thighs as she wrapped them around his hips.

Ariel's first climax slammed through her, making her cry out, head thrown back as she pumped against Dane. Her second orgasm rolled over her as the swinging doors of the kitchen opened. Over Dane's shoulder, through the haze of sexual gratification, Ariel vaguely registered her sister's shocked face. The stunned but amused features of Logan Abram came into focus behind Alayna as Dane's climax set off a third, more powerful explosion inside Ariel.

Ariel buried her head against his shoulder as she cried out. "Oh God. Fuck! Yes!"

"Christ!" A woman's gasp was audible over Dane's gruff exclamation.

"I guess that's one way to kill a guy." Logan's amused chuckle covered the ragged breaths Dane and Ariel struggled to control.

Logan's presence in the kitchen meant that the woman with him could only be Alayna. Dane could imagine how surprised Ariel's sister was. It wasn't every day a woman walked into her restaurant to find her sister naked on the counter with her legs wrapped around the waist of a seminude male and both of them smeared head to waist in chocolate icing.

Alayna commanded, "You are so cleaning that up!"

Rich male laughter spilled through the room.

Dane pretended to be oblivious to their audience. They'd leave eventually. He could count on Logan to take care of any residual anger Alayna might harbor. His hands smoothed over Ariel's back, his lips caressed her neck, and his cock started to regain its rigidity. The smile Ariel aimed at her big sister was sated and happy, even as heat flushed her cheeks and she attempted to hide her body behind his larger frame.

"Hey, Al. Made your favorite brownies." She waved in the general direction of where Dane had placed the pan. "Why don't you take them on home and share them with Logan." Ariel's breath hitched when Dane gave a particularly deep stroke of his cock inside her. "We've got…three more days to make up fo…to make up for."

"Three?" Dane grunted. Lifting his head, he smiled over his shoulder at his business partner and Alayna and then turned back to grin down at Ariel. "Tink, we haven't even finished day one yet."

Alayna spluttered, and Logan laughed as he grabbed the pan and steered his woman out of the kitchen.

"Looks like you're in trouble, sprite," Dane quipped. His body stroked slowly in and out of her sheath.

"You're right there with me, captain. Now make it worth my while." She tugged him closer.

"Is that an invitation?" Dane asked.

Ariel traced his lips, her fingertips smearing chocolate from there then along his chin. "Depends on how long you're able to last."

"How's forever sound, Tink?" Dane used his tone, the look in his eyes, the very stillness of his body to signal the seriousness of his words to her.

She didn't miss a beat in responding. Arching close, Ariel nipped the confection from his skin. "Only if you promise we can play with your flogger and paddle."

Dane arched a brow and studied her face. "Hmmm, does my sprite feel like the necessity to be disciplined?"

Ariel tightened her legs around his hips and adopted a pouty look. "I have been very naughty. Perhaps I could do with another lesson."

"I know exactly which room."

"Really?"

Dane smiled at the gleam of excitement in her bright green eyes. "Oh yes, Tink. Just the room. It has floggers, handcuffs, paddles, nipple clamps, butt plugs, and all the other delights I want to introduce you to."

"Will I get to use them on you?" Mischief flashed in her gaze, matching the sly grin painting her lips.

Dane laughed. She'd look beautiful strapped to the St. Andrew's cross and facing the two-way mirror in Room Seven. Her body would dance under the sting of the paddle or flogger, but the blush heating her cheeks and drenching her inner thighs would come from the words he'd whisper in her ear. *Smile for your audience, Tink. Show them how well my sprite takes her punishment.*

Her body pulsed around him, and the heat intensified as he increased his pace. The gasps slipping from her lips could have been a reaction to his lovemaking, or they could have come from the promises he whispered in her ear.

Keeping his pixie on her toes would be a challenge well worth his devoted attentions. And the judicious and repeated application of leather to her sexy, heart-shaped ass.

Qwillia Rain

Qwillia Rain grew up loving books. From an early age she was creating stories to go with the pictures. By high school she was penning romances for her friends and shocking them with the graphic nature of the love scenes. After leaving her home in Las Vegas, Nevada for Anchorage, Alaska, Qwillia discovered there were other authors who enjoyed throwing open the bedroom doors and exploring the darker side of human nature. She left Alaska for Billings, Montana, but the travel bug struck again. Currently, Qwillia resides in Raleigh, North Carolina, drawing inspiration from the history, scenery, and rich diversity of the South.